To Dance until Dawn

Girls Who Dare, Book 12

By Emma V. Leech

Published by Emma V. Leech.

Copyright (c) Emma V. Leech 2020

Cover Art: Victoria Cooper

ASIN No.: B088PXM796

ISBN No: 978-2-492133-13-8

Table of Contents

Members of the Peculiar Ladies' Book Club

Prunella Adolphus, Duchess of Bedwin – first peculiar lady and secretly Miss Terry, author of *The Dark History of a Damned Duke.*

Mrs Alice Hunt (née Dowding)–not as shy as she once was. Recently married to Matilda's brother, the notorious Nathanial Hunt, owner of *Hunter's*, the exclusive gambling club.

Lady Aashini Cavendish (Lucia de Feria) – a beauty. A foreigner. Recently happily, and scandalously, married to Silas Anson, Viscount Cavendish.

Mrs Kitty Baxter (née Connolly) – quiet and watchful, until she isn't. Recently eloped to marry childhood sweetheart, Mr Luke Baxter.

Lady Harriet St Clair (née Stanhope) Countess of St Clair – serious, studious, intelligent. Prim. Wearer of spectacles. Finally married to the Earl of St Clair.

Bonnie Cadogan – (née Campbell) still too outspoken and forever in a scrape alongside her husband, Jerome Cadogan.

Ruth Anderson– (née Stone) heiress and daughter of a wealthy merchant living peacefully in Scotland after having tamed a wild Highlander.

Minerva de Beauvoir (née Butler) - Prue's cousin. Clever and resourceful, madly in love with her brilliant husband.

Lady Jemima Rothborn (née Fernside)– happily installed at The Priory, skilfully managing staff and villagers and desperately proud of her heroic husband.

Lady Helena Knight (née Adolphus) – vivacious, managing, unexpected and adventurous, having finally caught her Knight in shining armour.

Lady Matilda Montagu (née Hunt) – no longer ruined but blissfully married to the Marquess of Montagu. At last! Adoptive mama to Miss Phoebe Barrington.

Prologue

Ten years later…

Dear Jasper,

Thank you for the invitation to Holbrook and the trouble I know you have put yourself to on my behalf. My efforts to reintroduce myself to society have met with mixed results. I regret to discover I have become so anxious at the thought of making another disastrous marriage that I find fault with most every young lady I meet. It's monstrously unfair when I am far from perfect, but I have become gun shy and can find nothing to tempt me into risking such a dreadful mistake again. Yet I must marry. You know as well as I that I must sire an heir and, in truth, I am lonely. I am sick of my own company and I long for a companion. I can only envy you and Harriet, and thank you for your help in aiding me to meet a suitable young woman.

I think my demands are not unreasonable. I do not seek a great beauty or a vast fortune, only good humour, good sense, and someone who would be a friend to me.

Keep your fingers crossed that I may discover such a treasure under your roof.

—*Excerpt of a letter to The Right Hon'ble Jasper Cadogan, The Earl of St Clair, from The Right Hon'ble Maximillian Carmichael, The Earl of Ellisborough.*

8th March 1826, Holbrooke House. Sussex.

"I take it this week has so far not produced the results we had hoped for?" Jasper asked as they walked back from his workshop.

Jasper was a craftsman of considerable skill, though few but his closest friends knew it.

Max shrugged and gave a rueful smile. "What's wrong with me, Jasper? I know all the young women here are amiable and kind, or you'd not have invited them for me. I thought all I wanted was that: someone to be a friend to me."

Jasper laughed and shook his head. "Good God, man! You might be a widower, but you're not in your dotage yet. Do you really not think to fall in love?"

"I am not averse to the idea," Max replied, frowning. "I'm just a realist. It's never happened to me before, so why should it now? Perhaps I am not suited to such emotions?"

"What rot," Jasper said in disgust. "You were trapped in a miserable marriage at far too young an age, then you were in mourning. When exactly have you given yourself the chance for such a thing?"

Max snorted. "I've been back in society for some time now, Jasper, and I've not been shy about my intentions."

"No, there's a veritable hornet's nest of interest buzzing about who will be the next Lady Ellisborough and, from what I hear, there's plenty of offers for the position of mistress, too. You're a popular chap."

"Hmmm," Max replied, deciding not to answer that.

"Father!"

Jasper looked up as his son, Cassius, ran pell mell towards them.

"Phoebe is here!" the boy exclaimed, his excitement palpable.

"Oh, she made it. Your mama will be pleased."

"And you should see her, Papa," Cassius added, his eyes wide and grave. "She's in prime twig."

Jasper cleared his throat as his son ran off again.

"A chip off the old block, eh?" Max murmured, laughing.

"My son has an eye for beautiful things," Jasper replied with a quirk of his lips.

"It will be good to see Lucian again. It's been an age since I was last at Dern."

"Indeed," Jasper said with a nod, a slight smile flickering at his lips. "You've not seen Phoebe for a while, then?"

"No, it must be over a year. Longer, even. Not that I saw much of her when I visited. I never knew girl less able to sit still for five minutes together," Max said with a laugh, remembering the vivacious young woman. She must be nineteen by now.

"Well, come along, then. If Phoebe is here, the house is bound to be in chaos."

Jasper's words were well-founded. By the time they had returned to the house, Lady Helena was playing the piano and an impromptu dance had begun. A few of the ladies invited to meet Max were exchanging rather scandalised glances at such an event in the middle of the afternoon, but the children were delighted and crowing with laughter as Phoebe took her turn dancing with them. Apparently, she was teaching them a new dance that was all the rage this year, and she was laughing as uproariously as the children while she did so.

Max smiled to see it, even though it did all seem rather outrageous for a grey Monday afternoon.

"Phoebe, dear," Jasper's wife, Harriet, called. "Do be careful! The floor is awfully slip—"

Before she had finished the sentence, Phoebe gave a shriek and landed hard on her bottom with a flurry of skirts and petticoats, giving the room a good look at her ankles. There was a stunned silence before the dreadful girl burst out laughing.

Max hurried towards her, only too aware of the outraged expressions from some of the ladies turning to disapproving ones, though Lady Helena was spluttering with laughter too.

"Are you hurt?" he asked in concern.

He did his best not to notice her pretty ankles as he reached down to help her to her feet. Goodness, when had she turned into such a beautiful young woman? Surely it hadn't been *that* long since he'd seen her last?

"No, only my pride," she said, her eyes alight with merriment as she looked up and realised who her rescuer was. "Oh, Max. How lovely to see you."

She beamed at him, such a joyous, carefree smile that Max's breath caught, an odd sensation lancing through him and making his chest feel tight. How bright she was, how very alive. Had he ever been alive like she was? Had he ever been that free?

She hesitated, and Max realised he was staring at her. He cleared his throat and forced a smile, though his nerves were all standing on end with alarm.

"Would you like to dance, Max?" she asked, perhaps just out of politeness as there was a doubtful glint in her eyes.

"No," he said, faintly, shaking his head.

Dancing with Phoebe seemed a dreadfully dangerous idea, and one he would do well to avoid.

She gave him a faintly pitying look and patted his arm. "No, of course not."

With that she turned and ran back to find another dance partner—Cassius, this time—who was staring at her with an expression of rapt fascination.

Max watched as she instructed all the children, showing them the steps and laughing wildly with them. She lavished praise of them when they got it right, and was patient and kind when they made a mistake. Max could not take his eyes from her, could not stop this strange and daunting feeling from taking a hold. Something had bloomed in his chest, taken root in his heart, and he did not know if he wanted to allow it to grow. Phoebe was not the kind of woman he was looking for. She was too young, too outrageous, too… *everything*. Except he knew, *knew* as he watched her, watched her bring life and vibrancy and laughter to all of those around her… he didn't have a choice.

Chapter 1

Lucian,

We should be delighted to come and celebrate Phoebe's twentieth birthday. Ellisborough is with us. I will assume you're happy to include him in the invitation as I hear he practically lives at Dern of late anyway. I have the unsettling suspicion Cassius is plotting something diabolical with Philip and Thomas, so heaven help us. No doubt Phoebe will adore it, whatever it is.

—Excerpt of a letter to The Most Honourable Lucian Barrington, Marquess of Montagu, from The Right Hon'ble Jasper Cadogan, Earl of St Clair.

7th February 1827. Dern, Sevenoaks, Kent.

"Well?" Phoebe asked as she turned this way and that, a critical pucker of concentration between her blonde brows.

"You look breathtaking, darling," Matilda said, smiling at her adopted daughter. "Papa will be so proud of you."

Phoebe span around with a rustle of skirts and closed the gap between them, hugging Matilda tightly.

"Thank you, Mama, and not just for the gown or for today, though today has been marvellous. *Everything* has been splendid."

"You have had quite a successful start to the season," Matilda agreed dryly. "Six proposals of marriage *and* a duel. In your first season you only had three by now. Oh, and a bout of fisticuffs."

Phoebe snorted and pulled a face, such unladylike gestures that did not seem to harm her popularity a whit. She was outspoken, reckless, defied every convention wherever possible, and would give her poor Papa a nervous collapse in the very near future. Unlike the rest of the world, who found the marquess' icy gaze a terrifying prospect, she could wrap her papa about her pretty thumb, and did. In reality, Lucian was her uncle, not her father, but Phoebe had longed for the parents she'd lost as a small child, and so they had adopted her. Phoebe was as much Matilda and Lucian's child as their two rambunctious boys, Philip and Thomas, though Phoebe enjoyed to rough and tumble just as much as their sons did... possibly more.

No amount of scolding by her governess had ever stopped her climbing trees or hiking her skirts up to paddle in a stream. Matilda knew what protected her from much of the criticism for her often appalling behaviour. Even though the world now knew her to be the illegitimate daughter of Montagu's younger brother—despite some gossipy souls still insisting she was truly Lucian's daughter—there were few who could resist her particular brand of vivacious charm. The fact she was a wealthy heiress did not much damage her marriage prospects, either, and her behaviour only deterred those of the highest birth... and not all of them at that. Yet few dared incur the wrath of her powerful papa. Where other girls would have been censured, Phoebe was called *an original*, and deemed *full of life*. Mostly. Lucian could not protect her from everything. There were those who were cruel about her origins, not that Phoebe seemed to take the slights to heart, retribution being far more her style. It was becoming apparent she had inherited not only her looks from the Montagu line. She had given them both some heart-stopping moments over her first season and the beginnings of this, her second.

"Did none of the young men who offered appeal to you at all, darling?" Matilda asked, a little curious. "Not that there is any rush, of course, but Lord Grant seems a charming fellow."

Phoebe laughed as she tugged on her gloves, shaking her head. "Oh, he is. Charlie is a lamb, and a particularly good friend, but I could never *marry* him. What a ghastly idea. He should drive me to distraction. Do you know, I don't believe he's ever read a book in his life?"

Matilda nodded, amused, and a little regretful for poor Lord Grant, who was doomed to failure. He wasn't the only one.

"Ellisborough is here," she said lightly.

"Is he?" Phoebe said, frowning as she searched for her other glove. "That's good. At least Papa won't be bored. Oh, drat the thing, where has it gone?"

"Here, love." Matilda retrieved the glove from the floor where it had been dropped and handed it to her. "He's not come to entertain Papa, Phoebe."

"Hmmm?" Phoebe yanked up her full skirts so she could see to wriggle her feet into her slippers. "Why else, then? He's Papa's friend."

Matilda sighed. It was true, Maximillian Carmichael, Earl of Ellisborough was Lucian's friend, introduced to him by St Clair. He was not of their generation, however. It was likely the scattering of grey in his dark hair that gave him the impression of sophisticated elegance, added to the somewhat world weary air about him. An exceedingly handsome and eligible fellow, with broad shoulders and deep brown eyes, Max had seen life and it had not always been kind to him, yet in reality he was only eight and twenty. Phoebe, however, had given the poor fellow something close to benevolent uncle status, and refused to regard him any other way.

"Ready!" she exclaimed with a squeal and then rushed from the room before Matilda could say another word.

"You might be," Matilda said, laughing in the silence her vivacious daughter had left behind. "Somehow, I doubt the rest of us are."

***

Phoebe bit her lip and stared down at her empty bowl. The chocolate roulade had been delicious, and she very much wanted another serving. Her stays were already pinching, though. She frowned at her bowl a bit longer, considering, when a discreet cough made her look up. Denton was at her elbow. He gave her a surreptitious wink, slid another helping into her bowl, and retreated. Phoebe smothered her grin of appreciation and tucked in.

The table was alive with animated conversation and many of her favourite people were here. The Earl of St Clair and his wife, Harriet, and the earl's brother Jerome, with Bonnie. Phoebe adored Bonnie, who was terribly droll and almost as good at getting into scrapes as Phoebe was herself. Helena and Gabe were here, too. Helena looked ravishing in a stunning gown of deep emerald silk, studded with black jet beads that twinkled when she moved. There were also a selection of eligible bachelors, and some of Phoebe's friends. The children had all gone to bed now, which was rather a shame as Phoebe adored them. She hoped to have a big family when she finally married… if ever she could discover a man in whose company she could imagine being for a lifetime. She wanted a grand passion, the kind of love affair that her parents had experienced, though she knew it was unrealistic. Love stories of the kind they had lived did not come along very often, but Phoebe still longed for it. She wanted desire and excitement, a man who would make her breath come fast and her skin ache with longing. The only kisses she had been given so far had been horribly disappointing. Oh, they'd been pleasant enough, but there had been no intensity of feeling, no thundering of her heart, no sense that she would die if she could not be in that man's arms again the next day and the next, and every day after that.

Not being a fool, she knew the kind of marriages she saw before her in her parents and their closest friends were not always possible, and were often hard won. So, meeting some nice young man in a ballroom and marrying him and living happily ever after did not seem to be the correct way to go about it. Surely there would be some cataclysmic event, some sign that *he* was the one? She needed someone who would fight dragons, not *for* her, but *with* her. Someone who would not lock her away in a gilded cage to protect her from the world, but face its challenges and dangers at her side. A man like her father was for her mother. What she had learned during her first season, was that such a man seemed to be about as realistic as the dragon itself.

Having scraped her bowl clean for a second time, Phoebe let out a breath and leaned forward, trying to ease the pressure of her corset from squeezing her stomach too fiercely. Perhaps that second helping hadn't been a good idea.

"It was worth it."

Phoebe looked to her left to find Ellisborough's amused gaze upon her.

"What was?"

"The roulade. I believe it was worth the discomfort you're in. I'll bet that corset is laced too tightly to accommodate it, though."

Phoebe blushed.

"Gentlemen do not refer to a lady's undergarments," she said, sounding uncharacteristically prim, but there was something about Max that always made her feel like a naughty child.

He was effortlessly sophisticated, always said the right thing— except to her— and was universally adored. Characteristics guaranteed to make her appear like an absolute hoyden—which she was—but still. Even Papa liked and admired him. It was nauseating, and she acknowledged the sensation of being out of sorts. Max made her cross and jittery and she did not understand why that was.

The earl chuckled beside her. "And ladies don't hike up their skirts and climb into parties via a window, but...."

"That was an accident," she hissed, irritated with him for bringing the subject up again. "I just went out for a breath of fresh air and some fool locked the door behind me."

"You went out with Beecham," he said, a disapproving note slipping into his voice.

"For some air," she insisted, annoyed now. She glanced up at him despite her better judgement and huffed at the pained expression of patent disbelief he returned. "Well, I trusted him, which I agree—with hindsight—was idiotic of me, but I thought he was my friend. I didn't know he would go all love-struck and stupid the moment he got me alone, nor that he would be so ungentlemanly as not to take no for an answer. I had thought better of him than that."

"So had I," Max said darkly. "Though he'll not make such a mistake again, I'll wager."

Phoebe smothered a grin, remembering how Mr Beecham had curled in on himself with a cry of agony as she'd introduced her knee to his soft parts with enthusiasm. Max still did not look happy about it and, at the time, she'd struggled to stop him challenging Beecham to meet him at dawn. His anger had rather shocked her. Max never got angry.

"I *was* foolish," she said, hoping to placate him. "But I dealt with him quite well on my own. I just... I just wasn't expecting it of him."

Max shook his head at her, incredulity shining in his dark eyes. "I do not understand why. All men leave their brains behind and turn into mindless idiots when they get near you. Is it your perfume, I wonder? Do you drug them with Eau de Opium?"

Phoebe batted her eyelashes at him.

"No, it's my winning personality," she said in a breathless singsong voice.

His lips twitched. "Hmmm. Well, whatever it was, you were lucky I noticed and let you in again, or you'd be married to the fool by now."

Phoebe grimaced, still wondering how it was that Max had noticed her predicament. "I would not. I'd rather be ruined."

"Keep on with pranks like those and you will be," he said mildly.

With difficulty, she repressed the urge to stick her tongue out at him. She might not be a well-behaved young lady, but she was not a child. The wretched fellow seemed to insist on rescuing her, even on the occasions when she didn't need it. He always seemed to be witness to her most embarrassing moments, forcing her to take whatever hand he offered to haul her out of difficulty. So, yes, sometimes he rescued her when she *needed* rescuing, too. She looked around as he chuckled.

"What?" she asked. Did she have chocolate on her chin?

"I was just wondering if you wanted to stick your tongue out at me or stab me with your fork. Going on your expression, it could be either."

Phoebe rolled her eyes at him.

"Ah, yes," he murmured. "That was my third option."

***

The next morning, Phoebe led the children on a treasure hunt she had laid out around the garden. The prize was a lovely picture book with dragons and knights and tales of derring-do, and she was looking forward to reading to them later. It was early yet and most of the adults still abed, though Phoebe thought this quite the nicest time of the day. Their breath blew steamy clouds on the frigid air, the sunlight sparkling on a landscape white with hoar frost as the frozen grass crunched under their boots.

"Where's the next clue?" her eight-year-old brother Thomas demanded, tugging at her sleeve. His cheeks were flushed with cold, his blue eyes bright with excitement.

"Pip has it," she said, sending him merrily chasing after his big brother, who was striding ahead with Harriet and Jasper's son, Cassius.

Cassius and Pip were both eleven years old, and the closest of friends. Bonnie's twin girls, Elspeth and Greer, were hurrying behind them, determined the boys should not get to the next clue first. Their little sister, Alana, had missed the fun, as had Helena's youngest daughter, Evie, both having been too sleepy to be roused from bed. The elder girl, Florence, had been striding beside Phoebe, holding her hand, but now ran after the rest of the children, determined not to be left out.

"Good morning."

Phoebe turned, squinting into the sunshine to see Max striding towards her.

"What are you doing up?" she asked, surprised. "I thought fashionable people were always abed until noon."

"I'm relieved to discover you believe me fashionable," he replied. "And whilst I admit I sometimes I allow my indolent nature to get the better of me, I am not blind to the allure of a lovely winter's morning."

"That's nice. Well, if you want someone to talk to, Papa is likely at breakfast now. Oh, Pip, do help Greer, she's slipped on the ice. Greer... Greer, darling, are you hurt?"

***

Lucian sighed as he saw Phoebe rush off to see to Greer, leaving Max alone without a backwards glance. Matilda had hopes of Max and Phoebe making a match, but she was a romantic soul and always wanted everyone to be perfectly happy. She believed Max was just the kind of steadying influence that Phoebe needed, someone who would keep her safe whilst allowing her rather wild spirit to remain free. Lucian agreed and would approve the match happily, only Phoebe simply did not see the man as anything other than a family friend. Lucian had made this point to Matilda, and it was why he now found himself up at some ungodly hour of the morning. He smiled, remembering his wife and the contented tangle of warm limbs he had left sated in his bed. If not for her insistence, he'd still be there, but she had been adamant that he have a word with Max and give him some advice. How the devil he was supposed to do that, he wasn't certain, nor did he have a clue what advice to give.

"Max." Lucian hailed him, but the fellow did not turn, his gaze trained on the children and Phoebe as she led them off into the distance, like some beautiful pied piper. "Max!"

That time he was heard, and Max raised a hand in greeting.

"Have you eaten?" Lucian asked, rubbing his gloved hands together to try to get the circulation back to his fingers.

"Not yet."

"Thank God. Come inside out of this perishing cold."

Max hesitated, watching Phoebe disappear into the woodland.

"I believe that is the last clue they're after," Lucian said, his tone dry. "They'll descend on the breakfast parlour with the appetites of ravening beasts within the half hour, I promise you."

There was a soft huff of laughter as Max turned back to him. "Ah, do you think I'll have more appeal at the breakfast table?"

"Well, if you look like a rasher of bacon, you'll certainly grab her attention."

Max returned a rueful smile. "I'm almost desperate enough to try it."

Lucian laughed as he was supposed to, but heard the bleak edge to the words, light-hearted though they were.

16

"She has turned down ten marriage proposals to date, Max. Believe me, you are not alone." He hesitated as they fell into step, retracing the path back to the house. "Do you still mean to offer for her?"

There was a long, heavy silence before Max answered.

"No."

Lucian looked at him, and Max shrugged.

"She doesn't know I exist, at least not as a suitor. I've no wish to make her uncomfortable and, to be honest, I'm not certain my ego could stand the blow of her astonishment at being asked. No. The truth is, I'm too old for her. We both know it."

"You're eight and twenty," Lucian retorted, laughing. "And believe me, I'm in no hurry to see her married off. If you were to give her time—"

"Of course I would," Max replied at once. "I'd wait as long as she wished. Only I don't think it will make the slightest difference. I'm simply not what she is looking for. Sooner or later she'll fall head over ears for some handsome young poet, or an artist, and that's how it should be. I'm far too sensible a catch to appeal to her adventurous spirit."

Lucian glowered at the idea and Max laughed.

"You only approve of *me* begrudgingly, Lucian. No one will ever be good enough for her."

"Not true. It's not the least bit begrudging. It's only that I don't want to see her go too quickly. You are a good man, a kind one, and one whose values are aligned with my own. You'd move heaven and earth to make her happy and, what's more, you have seen enough of life to understand what is important and what is not, and to recognise when you have something precious in your hands."

"Oh, I recognise it," Max replied, his tone wistful. "But it is far from in my grasp. I may as well be staring at the moon."

Lucian frowned, but could add nothing further. He was not about to push Phoebe into a marriage she did not want. Her happiness was the only thing he had ever desired, but he did fear her reckless nature would lead her down a path there was no coming back from, and the idea made his chest tight with worry. A man like Max would protect her, keep her safe, and Lucian knew that, above all, he'd do anything to make her happy.

It was painful to see the way the fellow's eyes lit up whenever Phoebe came into the room, but there was nothing to be done about it. Ultimately, Phoebe would make her choice, and all they could do was pray she would be happy with it.

***

Max watched as Phoebe organised everyone into playing parlour games. The children were rummaging through drawers, trying to find enough counters to play with. God, but she was lovely. Dressed in a pale blue silk gown that hugged her lithe figure, he was hard pressed to look anywhere else. He wasn't entirely certain what she'd done to her hair tonight. It was some mad complication of braids and ringlets, and part of it had somehow even been wrangled into a bow. It was utterly bizarre, though Max found a great deal about lady's fashion bizarre, and yet somehow she made it appear perfectly charming. To him, she was a breath of fresh air in a life that had been far too stultifying.

Max's father had died when he was a young man, leaving his estate close to ruins and his family in jeopardy. Max had done his duty, he'd worked all hours to save what he could, and he'd married well at the tender age of twenty. The same age that Phoebe was now. It had not been a happy marriage, though he'd tried his best. When his wife had died, three years later, along with the child she'd been trying to bring into the world, he'd been numb with too many emotions, chief among them guilt at having failed on all counts. His wife had been a stranger to him, despite his best efforts, and he'd lost both her and the son he'd hoped for. So, he had buried himself in the business of bringing the estate back to what it had once been. Now everything was flourishing once more and, with good management in place, it needed less of his attention than it had. An estate must have an heir, though, and so he had returned to society, with the notion that he might find a woman he could be friends with, one who would be a companion to him as well as a mother to their children, if they were to be so blessed. He had not been so foolish to consider that he would fall in love.

Though he had become friends with Lucian over five years ago, through St Clair, and often spent time at Dern, he had never considered Phoebe as anything other than Lucian and Matilda's daughter. Then, quite by chance, he had seen her again, only to discover the rather gauche young woman he'd last seen had blossomed into something… quite spectacular.

He'd not been able to keep away since.

She had stolen his breath and his heart, and he could do nothing but curse his own stupidity, for she would never dream of considering him a suitor. As far as Phoebe was concerned, he was old and dull, and she never turned her gaze his way. It did not matter that he was one of the most eligible bachelors on the marriage mart. It did not matter that he was besieged with female admirers, many of whom were her friends, all wishing to capture an earl for a husband. Not to mention those beautiful widows, wanting a sophisticated lover to amuse them, who cast their lures his way. Phoebe simply did not notice. He was her father's friend, and he had unwittingly got himself lumped in with those far older than he. It was the grey hair, he reflected bitterly. Though he'd fared better than his father, who had been completely grey by his mid-twenties, the scattering of that colour at his temples made him look distinguished, and gave him the appearance of more seniority than was his due. He had even considered dyeing it before telling himself not to be such a blasted fool. He'd had one wife who could barely tolerate the sight of him, and he'd not have another. With time, he would get over this ridiculous infatuation and find someone who at least enjoyed his company. It wasn't too much to ask, after all. Many women did. That he felt compelled to remind himself of the fact, despite plenty of evidence, only showed how far he had fallen.

"What's this?" asked a small voice.

"Oh, do be careful, love," Phoebe said, hurrying to the sideboard, where little Evie was flourishing a battered-looking top hat. "That's rather precious."

"Oh, it's our hat!" Bonnie Cadogan cried in delight. "You've still got it."

"Of course," Matilda said, laughing. "It's an heirloom for our children."

All of those gathered knew the story of the Peculiar Ladies, the intrepid band of female friends who had caused such a stir among the *ton,* more than a decade ago now. Phoebe rescued the hat before the children could dive into it and open all the paper slips, each one of which had a dare written upon it. According to the stories, those dares had been instrumental in cementing their friendships, and had played no small part in how they'd met their respective husbands.

"Oh, Max, do hold this for me, please," Phoebe said, holding the hat out to him as she tried to untangle little Alana, who had discovered that one of the boys had tied the ribbons on her shoes together. The poor girl was sitting on the floor with a face like thunder, that promised retribution to whichever boy had been foolish enough to do such a thing.

"Should I take a dare while I'm about it?" he asked, peering down into the hat at the dozens of slips of paper.

Phoebe laughed and looked over her shoulder with a quizzical expression. "Of course not. You'd never do it."

Max winced. Well, there it was. Phoebe had been banned from taking a dare by Matilda, who was adamant that the girl needed no encouragement. Yet she believed him too hen-hearted, too dull to even consider it. He stared down into the hat, a heavy sensation of inevitability in his chest. Phoebe was not meant for him, and it was about time he resigned himself to that fact. A little burst of indignation and anger flared in his heart, even though he knew it was for the best. Whatever it was that possessed him, he did not know, but he looked around to see if he was being watched, and then tugged a slip of paper from the hat and stuffed it in his pocket.

Chapter 2

Dearest Phoebe,

I'm so disappointed your parents cannot attend my ball this year. It seems a pity that you be left out, however. Do come and stay with us. I believe I may be able to persuade your father that I am a suitable chaperone.

Eliza, Lottie, and Jules will be thrilled to see you too.

—Excerpt of a letter to Miss Phoebe Barrington from Her Grace, The Duchess of Bedwin.

5th March 1827. Beverwyck, London.

Phoebe gasped and leaned back against the wall of the ballroom, fanning herself vigorously. Prue's balls were always well attended, but this one was an absolute crush. She had danced every dance, her feet hurt, and she was far too hot. With regret, she looked down at her dance card to see she had given the next one to Mr Jameson. He was a big, jovial man, and she liked him very much, but he was a terrible dancer and would likely stomp all over her toes. She winced at the idea.

"Is it so bad?"

Looking up she discovered a face she'd not seen before. He was handsome—and he knew it—and he was smiling at her. He was tall, blond, and supremely elegant, his blue eyes bright and just a little wicked.

"Is what so bad?" she asked, aware she ought not speak to the fellow. They'd not been introduced. Another of those stupid rules she so despised.

If someone seemed interesting, why not talk to them? But no, you had to find someone else who knew them, and you, and would vouch for you both before they would deign to introduce one to the other. As if they had exchanged an unwritten contract guaranteeing the good behaviour of all parties. Almost as if the giving of your own name had some mystical power. It was ridiculous.

"You looked as if you were considering something unpleasant," he said, tilting his head a little to one side.

"Like eating a slug," she said, the words out before she could consider them. Oh, how terribly gauche. What a nitwit he would think her now, and he the only interesting man she'd met all night. She met lots of nice men, charming men, a good many fools too, but this was the only interesting one so far.

Far from being revolted by her answer, he gave a bark of laughter.

"Exactly like that," he said.

Phoebe returned a sheepish smile. "Actually, it isn't so bad at all. Only my feet hurt, and I'd like to sit down for a while, but I promised the next dance."

Rather shockingly, he reached out and took hold of the dance card dangling from her wrist, his gloved fingers brushing hers as he lifted it.

"Mr Jameson," he said, returning a sympathetic smile. "Oh dear. *Just* like eating a slug."

Phoebe smothered a laugh, a little outraged, but amused too. "Oh, no. Not in the least. You are too harsh, sir."

"Perhaps," he said softly. "But I am a wretched fellow and horribly jealous. How am I to stand watching that big oaf lumber about the floor with you, when I know you would prefer to stay and talk with me?"

She stared at him, eyes wide.

"That's rather unkind," she said, not liking him speaking about Mr Jameson so. "And dreadfully conceited."

"True, though," he said. There was a glint of challenge in his handsome face, his gaze trained intently upon her. Daring her.

"Miss Barrington?"

With a little relief, she looked up to see Mr Jameson had come to collect her.

"My dance, I believe," the fellow said, beaming at her.

Phoebe took his hand.

"Indeed it is," she said, turning to glare at the blond man even as she felt a little pang of regret for leaving his company. She turned her gaze resolutely back to Mr Jameson and smiled. "I have been so looking forward to it."

***

Max winced as he saw Jameson step on Phoebe's toes for a second time. The poor girl. She did not complain, though, only laughed good-naturedly as Jameson coloured and stammered another apology. She was dressed in a pale gold silk this evening, and the candlelight set her aflame, the warm glow shimmering on her hair, her skin, and the gown as she moved about the floor. He was by far from the only poor fool who could not keep his eyes from her. Longing flared to life, a burning desire to be the man who held her in his arms. He stamped on it, trying to snuff it out, even though nothing had worked to date.

He'd kept away for the last month, trying his best to enjoy the endless parties and social whirl, yet finding himself bored to tears.

His fault, of course. If a man could not find satisfaction in the company of others, he must surely look to himself for the problem. Not everyone could be counted upon for scintillating conversation, but there was pleasure to be found in a polite exchange, a well-worn story, if you were willing to be pleased by it. As much as he wanted to be, as much as he remembered how these exchanges were supposed to proceed, he felt always as if he was telling a joke, only to realise he'd forgotten the punchline.

Unwillingly, his eyes were drawn back to the dance floor, and to Phoebe. He slid his hand into his pocket, feeling the rustle of a small piece of paper there. *Fool.* Turning away, he fought his way to the refreshment room, knowing that word fitted him only too perfectly, but unable to do a thing about it.

***

Phoebe thanked Mr Jameson for the dance and gave an inward sigh of relief. Moving quickly, she hurried out of the ballroom, hoping to find a quiet corner to catch her breath and ease her poor toes. She headed for the long gallery, where many people were strolling and enjoying the cooler temperature whilst admiring the paintings. Seeking out one of many deep set alcoves, she spied an ornate padded bench, unoccupied, and sat down with a sigh of relief. It was a shadowy nook, too public to be scandalous but still reasonably private, and so she took a moment to slip off her shoes. Glancing up to be certain she was not observed, she reached down and massaged her toes with a little sigh of pleasure.

"Did you lose any?"

Phoebe started and looked up.

"Oh, it's you," she said, relieved it was no one she need worry about as she saw Max standing over her.

"In the flesh," he agreed, moving forward and holding out a glass to her. "I thought you might need fortification after your ordeal."

"Is it champagne?" she asked, perking up.

25

He hesitated and she sighed, knowing it was only orgeat. Of course Max would not bring her champagne.

"I assumed you'd be thirsty," he said, sounding rather apologetic.

She was, and she supposed it wouldn't do to down a glass of champagne. It would make her burp.

"Thank you," she said, politely, taking the glass from him. "That was thoughtful of you."

"Are they very sore?" he asked, staring down at her toes.

"Just a little bruised. Nothing terminal."

Max sat down beside her and was silent for a moment.

"It was good of you to dance with Jameson," he said at length. "He's a nice chap."

"He is," she agreed, taking a large swallow of her drink. "I just wish he weren't so heavy."

They sat in silence again, watching some of the other guests stroll up and down the gallery. Phoebe sat up a little straighter as the blond man she'd seen earlier passed by. He glanced into the alcove and caught her eye. His lips twitched and he winked at her, before moving on. Phoebe felt a smile tug at her lips.

"Who introduced you to Alvanly?"

Phoebe looked up, a little startled by the sharp edge to Max's voice. "I'm sorry?"

"What blithering idiot introduced you to Baron Alvanly?"

"No one," she said, a little indignant at his tone. No doubt he meant the handsome man who'd winked at her. "I don't know him at all."

"Keep it that way," he said tersely. "He's not the sort of man you should be associating with. Don't speak with him."

She was aware that Max was now thrumming with tension, but was too angry to pay it much mind. "Forgive me, Lord Ellisborough. I was unaware that you had been appointed my guardian. Oh, wait… you haven't, nor have you been asked to act the part of my father."

"I don't want to be your blasted father," he snapped back, and Phoebe was so shocked at the anger in his words—and at being sworn at by him—that she could only stare.

Max was always so polite and charming. No one ever put him out of countenance. Except her, it appeared. He coloured a little and seemed to gather himself.

"Forgive me," he said, his jaw rigid, his usually amiable face a blank. "That is… I humbly beg your pardon, Miss Barrington. That was unforgivably rude. I ought not have spoken so. Only, Baron Alvanly… *please,* stay away from him. If I can say nothing else right this evening, I do know that your father would echo my words."

"Thank you for your warning," she said tightly, pushing her slippers back on and ignoring the pain in her toes as she did so. "I shall tell Papa how well you play your role of guard dog. I'm sure you'll be well rewarded. Would it be all right if I go and speak to the duchess now?"

He said nothing, knowing he was being taunted, he but got to his feet as she stood.

"Good evening," she said, before turning and walking away from him.

Drat the man. How dare he presume to tell her how to behave and who to talk to? Perhaps he was right about Alvanly, but there had been no need to act as though she might be fool enough to elope with the man. What kind of ninny did he think she was? Fuming, Phoebe stalked back to the ballroom, fully determined to dance with Baron Alvanly before the night was out.

***

27

15th March 1827. Drury Lane Theatre, London.

"Goodness," Bonnie said, looking to her husband, Jerome, who pulled a face as they walked out of the St Clair's private theatre box.

"What a load of hysterical drivel," he said, deadpan, at which Bonnie went off in peals of laughter. "Well it was," Jerome insisted, shaking his head. "I'd much rather have seen a comedy than that mawkish display. I felt like opening a vein myself by the end of it."

Phoebe frowned a little, having been rather disturbed by the story of unrequited love. The young hero of the piece had fallen madly in love with a woman who was, in turn, married to an older man. Eventually, aware he could never have her and would bring her nothing but disgrace, he shot himself in the head. It did seem rather overblown and mawkish, and yet, she had heard stories of people dying for love. Was such a fierce emotion attainable? Was *that* the kind of helpless passion she wanted? It certainly did not seem advisable. How uncomfortable to feel such desire for someone you could never have. Phoebe could feel nothing but pity for the poor soul.

Waiting patiently, she tried to keep out of the way of those leaving the theatre as Bonnie and Jasper chatted to some acquaintance of theirs.

"The man was a fool," whispered a voice in her ear, the flutter of warm breath against her neck making her shiver.

"Baron Alvanly," she said, as she turned to discover he was standing rather too close. She attempted a step back, only to discover there was not one to be had. There was a dreadful crush of people milling about still, so she supposed he had little choice but to stand so near. "In what way was he foolish?"

The baron took her hand, eyes twinkling as he held her gaze. "Not to take more decisive action, of course. Surely a woman does not want a man who sits on the sidelines and does nothing but sigh with melancholy that he cannot be with his beloved?"

Phoebe frowned, pondering the question as she removed her hand from his grasp. "No, but he did not wish to bring her disgrace or cause problems in her marriage. He was trying to consider her feelings."

Alvanly snorted. "By blowing his brains out on her account. I'm sure she was touched."

Phoebe bit her lip, trying not to laugh.

"You say the most dreadful things," she said, once she had mastered her voice enough not to snigger.

"If what I hear is true, we are well suited."

There was such a gleam of amusement in his eyes she could not take the comment as a slight. Besides which, it was true.

"What should you have done, then?" she asked, curious now.

"Me? Why, I should have been her lover. Nothing and no one would have kept me from my beloved, but then I'm wicked to the bone, Miss Barrington. Surely you know that. Has no one warned you off yet?"

"Yes," she replied, as delighted by his honesty as she was scandalised by his words. "Of course they have."

"They're right," he said with a sigh. "Which is why you are dying to get to know me better."

"You conceited beast!" Phoebe slapped a hand over her mouth, but she could not take the words back. Far from being annoyed, however, Alvanly's eyes lit with delight.

Slowly, he leaned forward and whispered in her ear again— too close, too intimate.

"Guilty as charged." He straightened, and this time his gaze was more serious. "We're alike, you know. You and I. Both of us are infuriated by rules and the opinions of others. The only difference is, I have ceased to care, or to heed them. I do as I please, and the world can whisper and gossip to its heart's content. I don't care. I'm not sure you're brave enough to break free of your bonds, though, are you?"

Phoebe stared at the baron, uncertain of what to say. She felt just as he'd described, frustrated that society thought women ought to be quiet and well-behaved, and do as they were told. She did not enjoy the idea that he thought her craven, though.

"I don't care for the gossips, which you'll know if you've heard the slightest thing about me."

Alvanly shrugged. "Oh, you say that, but I doubt it's true. It's one thing to be a little outspoken, to play mad games that make the old ladies shriek and dance with too much enthusiasm. It's another to live life freely. What would you do this week, for example? If you did not have to consider your reputation?"

Phoebe did not have to consider that too long.

"There's a boxing match," she said wistfully.

Alvanly grinned.

***

Jack set his battered tricorn hat down on the table. Phoebe was almost certain it was the same one he'd worn when she was a child. He folded his massive arms and glared at her. "You're up to no good, ain't 'cha?"

Jack Green, who once travelled under the notorious sobriquet of 'Flash Jack' had retired from life on the high toby when Phoebe had been a girl. They had met when he'd accepted a job, the object of which had been to put a period to the life of the Marquess of Montagu, Phoebe's father. That her father's uncle had given him the job said all that was needed about the life her poor papa had lived as a boy. That the once notorious highwayman would now lay down his life for said marquess, illustrated anything else that might be necessary. As with any poacher turned gamekeeper, Jack took his job very seriously indeed. He was not adverse, however, to sharing his knowledge, especially if one waited until he was just a little foxed. Which he only ever was on his evening off. Never, *ever*, did he imbibe when he was working, aware that would mean instant dismissal.

They had established an odd friendship over the years, where Jack watched over Phoebe like the little princess he seemed determined to view her as—despite plenty of evidence to the contrary—and Jack seemed to her to be some burly guardian angel. He had taught her to pick a lock, cheat at cards, and do many things that a young lady ought not even to know about, but which might get her out of trouble if she fell into it… or into trouble if she weren't trying hard enough to avoid it. Either was equally likely where Phoebe was concerned, and she did like to be prepared for all eventualities.

"What makes you think I'm up to no good?" Phoebe asked, striving for an air of innocence.

Judging on the snorting noise Jack made, she needed to work on that.

"'Cause you are always up to some mischief or t'other, Princess. You got an itch that seeks trouble and adventure, excitement. I know 'cause I had it too, once upon a time. And if you were goin' somewhere what your Pa knew about, you'd not be out here asking like it were some great secret."

Phoebe sighed and mirrored Jack's stance, folding her arms. "I just want to go to a boxing match, Jack."

Jack's eyes grew round. "I gave up risking getting my neck stretched some years ago. I ain't about to get meself all cut up into little bitty pieces by your papa for doing something as addlebrained as that. A boxing match, indeed. Reckon ye need Pippin to lay some of her magicking on me afore ye'd get me to dance to that tune."

Phoebe huffed with impatience. "Oh, it's not fair. Why do men get to do all the interesting things, and I'm supposed to sit at home and look ornamental?"

"Ah, come now," Jack wheedled. "T'ain't like you don't get to do all sorts as other young ladies don't. Lord is a fair man. Taught ye to fence and to shoot and do all manner o' things you ain't supposed to."

Phoebe made a disgruntled sound. "That's true, I know it is, but I'm not allowed to *tell* anyone I can do those things, Jack, let alone show them, so what's the point?"

Jack nodded his understanding and stepped forward, chucking her gently under the chin with a hand like a ham hock. "Reckon we all chafe against what we oughta be and want to be at times, Princess. It's what we do with what we can that sets us apart, I reckon."

Phoebe sighed gloomily. "I suppose so."

"Cheer up. Come on, I'll let you cheat me at cards."

"I don't cheat *you*, Jack," she retorted.

"Then you're a little fool," he said amiably, winking at her as he went to fetch his cards.

Chapter 3

Jasper,

Much as I appreciate the thought, do keep your nose out of my romantic affairs. I agree Miss Rochester is lovely and amiable, but I do not need you to arrange a dozen events to throw us together at every opportunity. And no, I am not still mooning about like a lovesick schoolboy. I am quite cured of my ailment, I assure you. The lady has made her position plain and I have no desire to shoot myself or throw myself in the Thames, so there is no need to trouble yourself.

That being said, I should be delighted to attend your blasted dinner party.

—Excerpt of a letter to The Right Hon'ble Jasper Cadogan, The Earl of St Clair, from The Right Hon'ble Maximillian Carmichael, The Earl of Ellisborough.

18th March 1827.

Phoebe tugged the hood of her cloak forward so she was better hidden beneath the voluminous fabric. In one pocket she held a small pearl-handled pistol—a present from her father—and there was a knife in her boot. She might have been idiot enough to risk her reputation for the thrill of doing something forbidden, but risk her neck she would not.

Why was she here?

She asked herself the question but could not deny the shiver of excitement that rippled down her spine. There was a large gathering at Moulsey Hurst now, as the hour for the boxing match drew near. All around there were the shouts of hawkers and costermongers who gathered wherever there was the chance of a good turnout. The scent of food, mingled with the jostling enthusiasm of a crowd out for fun, was ripe on the air. The rich perfume filled her nose, alongside the less enjoyable tang of those who still had not taken Brummel's counsel to wash daily to heart.

Scanning her surroundings, Phoebe grinned as she saw Baron Alvanly standing in the spot they had arranged to meet. His gaze fell upon her, and his eyes grew wide. That would show him not to underestimate her, even if she was not fool enough to believe his taunt had no other side to it. Alvanly was in the market for a rich heiress, having pockets to let, and Phoebe did not doubt he'd manoeuvre her into ruination if he could. It was all a part of the game, though, besting these men who thought her a sweet little mouse with whom they could toy like some big, lazy cat. He would not be the first to discover that Phoebe had been taught to use her own claws, and that she would, if provoked.

Why she could not be content to be a well-behaved young lady and go to balls and parties, and just enjoy the social whirl, she did not know. Perhaps it was the edge of danger that had haunted her younger years, the constant presence of her great-uncle and his determination to steal the title from her father. Though she had always believed her father would keep her safe, she had known there was real danger there. She had revelled in the trust Lucian had placed in her, trust enough to teach her how to shoot and to explain to her the reality of a world that could be treacherous. He had lived with the constant threat of his own murder, and perhaps something of that had rubbed off on her. Perhaps she even missed the camaraderie they'd shared then, when it had been the two of them against the world.

Whatever it was, it made her an enigma. As much as she was popular and sought out for her company, she was never quite at ease. Always, she was aware of the difference between her and those other young ladies, aware that they did not know what to make of her. She liked and admired many of them, and had nothing against marrying and having a family. She looked forward to it, but... but surely there was more. Could she not have an adventure or two before she did as the world expected of her? No, was the simple answer. Adventures equalled ruination. Or, at least, they did if you were found out.

"Well, I'm blowed," Alvanly said, his expression one of delight. "I admit it, I did not believe you daring enough to come. I apologise."

Phoebe shrugged. "That's all right. Why would you? But do hurry, or we'll be too far back to see anything."

She kept close to him, her hand on his arm, for no other reason than that it was safer to do so. Her free hand remained in her pocket, and she had stuffed a small bag of coins under the neck of her dress. Cutpurses in places like these would lift it from anywhere else in a second, without her knowing a thing about it.

There was quite a crowd gathered now, carriages lining the field with people crammed on the tops of them to get a better view over those that circled the ring. At the very front, the men sat cross-legged on the floor with everyone beyond the first few lines standing. The air of anticipation rose steadily with the noise as the combatants took to the field.

The fight, between a huge Irish man by the name of O'Sullivan, and a wicked looking devil called Evans, was quite a spectacle. Phoebe was torn between horror and admiration for the two men. Her admiration was all for their physiques, as they were stripped to the waist and the sight not one she'd ever had the chance to enjoy before. It was strangely... *energising*, the sight of two large, muscular men stripped to do battle. Their courage too was impressive. Good heavens, but she could hear, almost feel the

35

echo of each hit as fists hit flesh with cruel force. As the fight went on, however, she was forced to admit it was not to her taste. The roar of the crowd was deafening, baying for victory, full of bloodlust as O'Sullivan put Evans in the dirt for a third time. Evans' eye was swelling, blood dripping steadily from a cut on his eyebrow, and both men were filthy and bruised. He'd not last much longer.

Well, she had come, and she had seen a boxing match, which had been the object of the exercise, alongside proving to Alvanly that he ought not underestimate her. Now, though, excitement turned to distaste for the brutality of it, and it seemed a good moment to make her escape. If she waited until the end, there would be more likelihood of trouble, with those victorious too over-excited and those who'd lost too angry to tolerate it. Alvanly was totally riveted on the fight and not paying her the least attention, and so she slipped away, easing back through the crowd.

***

Max groaned as Evans hit the dirt for a third time. The end was pretty much a foregone conclusion now. He smacked Jasper on the shoulder and shook his head.

"I'll see you later and pay up," he promised as Jasper grinned at him, turning his attention back to the fight and his brother, who was still yelling encouragement to Evans.

Jerome would not like losing to his older brother.

Pushing back through the spectators, Max kept a sharp eye out. There were always villains a-plenty, ready to snatch a watch or a purse, or anything else they could get their hands on, and turn a profit. Once at the edge of the crowd he strode out, relieved to be away from the raucous atmosphere.

What the devil was wrong with him?

Perhaps Phoebe was right. Even though she'd never actually said as much, it was obvious she thought him old and dull, and certainly he felt bored to death. The only time his blood ever surged in his veins was when she was near, and it usually led to him putting his foot in his mouth. He never meant to, but she was so damn reckless and the idea that she might come to harm made his heart stutter in his chest. He kept an eye on her as discreetly as he could, stepping in when he feared she may come a cropper. That Alvanly might draw her into his debauched set gave Max nightmares. Worse than that, contemplating that the fellow's handsome face might find favour with Phoebe brought a fierce surge of jealousy that left him feeling shaken and wretchedly unhappy.

As if the mere thought of her had conjured a vision, his gaze was drawn to a slight figure walking quickly, quite some distance ahead. There was something about the woman, the way she moved, that made his breath catch, but… no. It couldn't be. Not here. Even Phoebe wouldn't….

Good God, what was he saying? Of course she would!

He quickened his step, but saw to his dismay that he was not the only one to have noticed a lone female as she turned into an alley, heading back to the main road where she might hail a hackney carriage. The man hurried after her, following her into the alley.

Max ran.

It was likely no more than seconds, though it felt a lifetime before he raced around the corner at breakneck speed, his hat flying to the ground as he skidded in the filth that carpeted the alley. He ignored it, too intent on getting to Phoebe, until he stopped short, riveted by the sight before him.

"I di'n't mean no 'arm, now, miss," the fellow was pleading, backing away from Phoebe, who had levelled a pistol at the fellow, her hands perfectly steady.

"Oh, you just meant to lift my purse and help yourself to whatever else took your fancy, no?" she retorted, anger flashing in her blue eyes.

"I just wanted your purse and those pretty earbobs, nowt else. I'd not have hurt ye. A fellow has to eat, lady," the devil pleaded, his eyes never leaving the barrel of the gun pointing at his face.

"A fellow need not accost lone females in the street and try to frighten them to death, though."

Max could hear the anger in her words, and a brittle edge that made his heart clench and want to rip the fellow limb from limb. She had been afraid, not that she showed it.

He approached softly, not wanting to startle her.

"Miss Barrington, may I be of assistance?" he asked, knowing he was likely to be told that no assistance was necessary, thank you very much.

Likely it was true. She had the situation well in hand and needed no rescue from him. Any vague notion of being her knight in shining armour withered and died. Phoebe could rescue herself and needed no hero to do it for her. Not him, at any rate.

"Lord Ellisborough," she said, her voice steady. "You have an uncanny knack of turning up at such moments." Her blonde brows drew together with suspicion. "Are you following me?"

"No!" Max said at once, almost drawn to admit he'd been avoiding her. "No, I was at the match with St Clair. Strangely, I did not think to look for you."

"Strange indeed," she remarked, her lips twitching just a little. "I'm glad you're here, actually...."

Well, that was a first.

She hesitated, looking just a little uncertain. "Er... what do I do with him now?"

Max bit back a smile. "Are you going to shoot him?"

The fellow facing the business end of the pistol made a choked sound.

"I would have, if I'd not seen him ahead of time, but he has all the grace of an elephant. Really, sir, you are ill-suited to a life of crime. You'll be dancing with Jack Ketch in no time if you keep up such a line of work."

"Ah, miss, just let me go, eh? I ain't done ye no harm."

Phoebe snorted. "You make it sound like you meant none, either, which we both know is a rotten lie."

Max moved closer to her and put his hand over hers, both slender and gloved, and holding the pistol firmly.

"Get," he said to the man, his voice brooking no argument.

The villain did not need telling twice. He legged it out of the alley and was gone in seconds. Max gently pushed her hands down.

"Well done," he said softly.

Only then did she look up at him and let out a breath of relief. She returned a smile he suspected was more bravado than pride, but she'd never let him know she'd been rattled, and he'd not press her to admit it.

Phoebe un-cocked the pistol, her hands trembling, and tucked it into the pocket of her cloak. She looked back at him, putting her chin up.

"Well, go on then," she said with a sigh, resigned to her fate.

Oh, no. Not this time.

"Go on what?"

"Aren't you going to scold me? Tell me what a dreadful girl I am and demand what I was doing?"

The desire to do all those things, plus giving her a good hard shake for terrifying him so, was a living thing beneath his skin. He ignored it.

"I assumed you were watching the match," he said lightly, taking his time going to retrieve his hat.

He took a deal longer inspecting it for dirt, relieved it had not fared too badly, and giving himself time for his heart to slow to something less likely to kill him.

"That's it?" she demanded, narrowing her eyes at him.

God, she was lovely. Now he knew she was safe, he could recollect the sight of her, pistol in hand, sure and determined, and felt a swell of pride. An equally fierce protective instinct rose too, the kind that wanted to take her home and keep her safe, to shelter her from the world, then search out that villain again and break his bloody neck. He ought to have beaten the bastard bloody before he let him go. The desire to seek retribution for her had been tangible, but he'd not wanted her to see that. He looked back at her, knowing he could tell her none of this.

"What else do you want? You made your feelings perfectly clear, Miss Barrington. You do not need or want my opinions nor my protection."

She looked a little uncertain now, big blue eyes regarding him doubtfully.

"Yet you came running anyway."

"As I would to any woman I thought might be in danger," he said tersely.

"Of course," she said at once, an apology in her eyes. "I know that. I know you would. Thank you."

He nodded, not trusting himself to say any more. Now he was wondering who she'd been at the bloody match with, for surely she'd not have been so reckless as to go entirely alone. And, if she had met someone, where was the bastard now? What manner of man would not have seen her safely home again? What kind of fool had taken his eyes off her for a moment among such a crowd?

"Do you have a carriage waiting?"

Phoebe shook her head. "No. I... I was going to hire a hackney."

Max once again restrained the urge to demand what the devil she'd been playing at, wandering about this part of London alone—hiring carriages alone. His heart seemed to perform a strange acrobatic flip as he considered everything that might have happened to her. He clenched his jaw against the rebuke building in his chest. If he scolded her, she would only grow angry and run away again, and she was right, he had no say in her life.

"My carriage is a short walk from here. Would you allow me to see you home?"

He prayed she would agree, for he could not allow her to continue alone, and yet he desperately did not want to fight with her again.

"Yes. Thank you."

Thank God.

As she laid her gloved hand upon his arm, a little of the violent anxiety, the desperate need to protect her that had been singing through his muscles, seemed to ease away, and was replaced by an altogether different kind of tension. He tried his best to look at ease, to keep his voice placid, and attempted a conversation with her.

"What did you think of the fight, then?"

Max looked down, wondering at what he saw. Her features were extraordinarily fine, her skin almost translucent, her eyes the colour of cornflowers in some lights, and in others that of a sky before a storm broke. How could something so fragile and lovely encase such a formidable will? The combination of delicacy and determination, beauty and recklessness, drew him in as if he'd been caught like a fish, the hook dug in deep and sure.

"I don't exactly know," she said, glancing up at him.

Max looked away, afraid of what she might see in his eyes. She didn't want him, he knew that, and he'd not make things worse by allowing her to see how much he wanted her. It would make things uncomfortable for them both.

"At first it was rather thrilling," she admitted. "They looked quite heroic and brave, and the excitement of the crowd was intoxicating, but as it went on, as Evans was hurt and yet still kept getting up…."

She shivered, and his body was so acutely aware of hers that the slight tremor seemed to vibrate through him too.

"Then it seemed ugly, barbaric, and I wanted to stop it."

"Why did you come?"

To his relief, she did not take the question as a criticism.

He felt her gaze on him though and could not help but meet it, discovering a wary quality to her expression, wondering whether to give him the truth.

"Because I've never been, because I'm not supposed to, because… I wanted to do it anyway, for the thrill of it."

Max nodded, having known as much. She was like some wild thing behind a fence: she might have the entire world at her back, but the notion that there was a fence at all made her wilder still, and determined to escape. Whoever married her would not have a comfortable life, and that was what he wanted, was it not? He'd wanted a friend and companion, comfort and security, and some measure of happiness. Phoebe would bring chaos and adventure, and no little trouble to whatever man dared to take her on.

"I suppose I disgust you."

He looked around in alarm, aware of the defiance of the words, and aware of something else too, something a touch vulnerable, which he could not put a name to, but would have given anything to have identified.

"Why would you suppose that?"

They had reached his carriage and he handed her up into it, waiting until she sat down. He watched as she shrugged, her eyes downcast.

"You're always disgusted by me," she said softly.

Max laughed then, incredulous that she could so misconstrue his feelings for her. He stared at her for a long moment before he replied. He reached out a hand and took hers, giving her fingers a brief squeeze.

"Disgust is the very last thing I feel for you, Miss Barrington."

Before she could reply, he closed the carriage door and barked instructions to the driver to return her to St James's. He did not trust himself to be alone in a carriage with her, and it would do her reputation no good if anyone discovered he had been. Retracing his steps, he returned to Moulsey Hurst and hoped he could track down St Clair. With luck, his brother Jerome would be in the mood to drown his sorrows.

***

Phoebe stared as Max slammed the carriage door closed. Well. She did not know what to make of him. He'd seemed… different today. And whatever had he meant by that?

Disgust is the very last thing I feel for you, Miss Barrington.

She pondered this, frowning, and uncertain of the strange fluttering sensation in her chest. The events of the day had been unnerving, though, and Phoebe found herself too overwhelmed with exhaustion to think clearly. The fear and excitement of what had happened seemed to drain from her, taking all her energy with them. All she wanted to do was have a lie down in a quiet room and try to regain her composure. If she were perfectly honest, she'd never been happier to see Max in her life. She knew she could handle the situation, and *had* handled it, but nonetheless it had been frightening. To see him striding down the alley towards her had been such a relief, she'd not even cared that he would scold her soundly for being such a little fool. It had been foolish to go alone, she'd known that, but… but oh, she'd *done* it. She had done it, and she had managed, and she was still alive, and….

And why hadn't he scolded her?

She felt almost disgruntled, which was ridiculous. Except that Max always scolded her when he discovered her up to no good, and that was normal. She'd come to expect it of him. That was who he was and how he acted and today… today he hadn't seemed like he usually did, and that was… disturbing.

Odd.

What was he playing at?

Perhaps he'd given up on her and couldn't be bothered with scolding her any more. That thought rankled and made her stomach feel odd and squirmy. Perhaps he'd just decided not to, as it always ended in a row, and instead he'd go straight to her father and….

Oh!

Phoebe quailed at the idea. Papa was the dearest, most indulgent father a girl could possibly have, and she adored him, but… but if he thought she'd put herself in danger….

Oh dear.

Sinking back into the squabs, Phoebe felt each mile that passed in the same manner as a villain approaching Tyburn. Well, she had to face her fate. There was no avoiding it. She drew in a shaky breath. Avoiding it might not be possible, but that did not mean she had to look forward to it.

Lud. Now she was in the basket.

Chapter 4

Dearest Matilda,

I was so glad to hear of all the dreadful things your boys have been up to this past week. Frogs in boots seem to be a favourite here too. I wonder if they are born with such thoughts in mind, the diabolical creatures. Honestly, Lyall and Muir are set on giving me a nervous collapse. I wouldn't mind but Gordy is worse than the two of them put together. I daren't let the three of them out of my sight for a moment. They're both going to be as big as their father, which naturally brings every lad from miles around in to scrap with them. I seem to spend my days tending bruises from fights, scrapes from climbing trees, and wringing them out after they've fallen in the loch... again! Not that they complain, they're always laughing and seem utterly bewildered by my fretting over them.

I sympathise with every broken window, vase, and shredded nerve, I assure you. Have you found slugs in your slippers yet? That one will stay with me till the day I die.

—Excerpt of a letter to The Most Honourable Matilda Barrington, Marchioness of Montagu, from Mrs Ruth Anderson.

21st March 1827, Montagu House, St James's, London.

Phoebe concentrated on piling cherry jam onto a scone. Mama had not yet come down for breakfast, but her father was here, and his piercing gaze had settled on her. She could feel it boring into her brain, and did not dare look up and meet it.

"Bee," he said, his tone soft and enquiring. "You'd really do better to confess. You've been sat upon thorns these past few days. Who exactly is it you keep expecting to arrive?"

Phoebe swallowed, knowing she was doomed.

"No one," she said, striving for innocence.

Her papa sighed, quite obviously disbelieving her. Her stomach squirmed and she put the scone down with regret, knowing it would stick in her throat.

"Bee," he said again, a little sterner now. "I can't abide lies, you know that."

Guilt made her stomach squirm harder and she knew she couldn't evade him now he was on the scent. He need only ask her outright what she'd done, and she would be forced to tell him. An evasion was one thing, but she'd not lie, and he knew it. Better to confess all, as he'd suggested, than make him ask her. She had jumped every time someone had knocked at the door, expecting Max to come and reveal all, but the days had passed and Max had not come.

Why?

Phoebe took a deep breath, her heart thudding in her chest, as she forced herself to meet her father's eyes.

"You'll be cross," she said wretchedly.

"How cross?"

Phoebe swallowed.

A muscle in his jaw ticked.

"I see."

"I'm fine." Phoebe forced a bright smile, hoping that fact would ease the tension in the room. "There was no harm done, and no one saw me. Well, no one who would say anything." She considered Baron Alvanly for a moment. "I think."

Her father waited, staring at her, his silver eyes unnerving as she felt he could see just what she was thinking. Phoebe clutched the chair, willing herself to be brave and not run from the room.

"Perhaps we should wait for Mama—"

"Phoebe!"

Oh. Her full name. That wasn't good.

"I w-went to see O'Sullivan fight Evans at Moulsey Hurst."

There. She'd confessed.

Phoebe watched him, but his face was a blank. No reaction.

Oh, dear.

"And?" he asked, his voice dangerously calm.

Drat it. How did he always know there was an *and*?

"And… it was all fine. I saw the fight, but… but I didn't much like it, so I left before the end. It was obvious Evans would lose, you see. So I was on my way back to hire a hackney, and a man tried to rob me, but I had my pistol and stopped him, and then Max came, and he told the man to go before I shot him, and then he saw me to his carriage and… and that's all."

There was the kind of silence that made all the hairs on the back of her neck stand on end. Her father said nothing. He was still for a long moment, during which Phoebe held her breath.

Very carefully, with precise movements, he refolded his napkin and set it back on the table, then he got to his feet.

"Tell your mother I am going to Angelo's. I will speak to you this evening about... about your latest adventure. Good day, Bee. Do try not to shoot anyone whilst I am gone." He walked out, closing the door quietly behind him.

Lud.

Phoebe let out a breath and spared a thought for whatever poor devil volunteered to fight her papa at Angelo's this morning. He'd likely be dissected into tiny pieces as her father vented his feelings. Now she knew how Damocles had felt, with that wretched sword suspended overhead by a horsehair. Only, she knew the hair would break this evening when she had to face him again. Gloomily, she decided there was only one thing to do. She would go to Hatchard's and see if she could find a book to take her mind off her fate. With a despondent sigh, she pushed her unfinished breakfast aside and went in search of her maid.

***

Max watched, uncertain whether to be amused or alarmed as the marquess dispatched his fifth opponent in as many minutes. The man's foil skittered across the floor, sliding to a halt on the other side of the large room, where Lucian had sent it sailing. Although he'd finished for the morning, Max had heard the murmurs of appreciation from the audience that had gathered, and joined them to watch. Lucian hadn't even broken a sweat. He seemed irritated that no one had skill enough to give him the bout for which he was so clearly desperate.

"Next," he called, stalking to the end of the room and turning to see who dared try their luck. No one volunteered.

Lucian huffed with annoyance, and then his gaze settled on Max. Max had been friends with Lucian for some time, but it did not mean he could be on the receiving end of that icy glare and not quail a little. Something told him that Phoebe's recent adventure was no longer a secret.

"Max," Lucian said, a tight smile at his lips. "Do you have something you wish to tell me?"

Max pondered this. "I have nothing I *wish* to tell you, Lucian, but I suspect you already know that I could give you information you might want."

Lucian jerked his head, indicating that they go outside to the courtyard. Max followed him, relieved when Lucian set the foil aside before leaving the room.

"Why the devil didn't you tell me?" he demanded, the moment the doors closed.

Max hesitated. "There was no harm done, and... and I did not want her to see me as a man who would run and tell tales to her father. I hoped she might tell you herself."

Lucian snorted. "She did, but only after I pressed her. So, that's why she's been leaping from her skin every time the front door opened. She's been expecting you to come and tell all."

"I imagine so," Max agreed, rather aggrieved that Phoebe should see him in such a light.

He watched the marquess pace, his fists clenching and unclenching before he turned back to Max.

"Was it you she was meeting there?"

"*No!* God, no," Max replied at once, alarmed. "Christ, you know me better than that, I hope."

Lucian let out a breath and pinched the bridge of his nose.

"Forgive me," he said. "I do, of course, only... only that wretched girl will kill me. My heart cannot stand the kind of explosions she sets off wherever her feet touch the ground. It's my own fault. I know it is. I've given her too much freedom, made her too brave, too bloody fearless...."

Max reached out and laid a hand on Lucian's arm.

"She's marvellous," he said softly. "Good lord, if only you could have seen her. There I was running hell for leather, expecting to rescue a damsel in distress, and the poor blighter who'd tried to rob her was stammering his apologies and looking down the barrel of a pistol."

Lucian groaned. "Dear God."

"She's not some foolish green girl who went wandering about London like it was her own back garden. She knew it was dangerous, and she was prepared for it, and yes, of course she ought not have been there. Believe me, I was hard pressed not to shake her for giving me such a fright, but it would have done no good. She'll not change, and it would have only made her dislike me even more."

"I thank God you were there."

"So do I," Max replied. His heart still trembled whenever he thought about it. "Though she would have managed if I had not been, I'm sure. Though I think she was a little pleased to see me for once," he added ruefully.

"So she ought to have been." Lucian's voice was angry now. "And if she was not meeting you, who the devil was it? Who encouraged her? For reckless she may be, but she'd not have gone to such a place entirely alone."

Max hesitated. "I don't know."

Lucian narrowed his eyes at him. "But you suspect."

"No, truly. I have no proof, no reason to suppose," Max protested.

"But you *do* suspect," Lucian repeated, his tone brooking no argument.

Max sighed, knowing he would not escape an interrogation.

"Baron Alvanly."

He was unsurprised at the litany of curses that fell from the marquess' lips.

"I'm afraid I was idiotic enough to warn her off the fellow," he admitted, wincing as Lucian glared at him in outrage. He held out his hands in a sign of defeat. "I know. I know it was beyond foolish, but… but it was a reaction and I didn't think."

"Alvanly," Lucian replied, his tone enough to make Max's hair stand on end. "I see."

There was a tense silence and then Lucian let out a breath, returning his attention to Max.

"If I were foolish enough to warn her off as you have done, the results would be inevitable. I do not think her a fool, after all. She must know the man is in the market for a rich wife and that he would be a disastrous husband. I have taught her well enough to be aware of the tricks men use to snare themselves a wife through scandal, so I must trust she can see past his pretty face and beneath the veneer of charm he wears so well. We both must."

Max nodded, not liking it, but aware that Lucian knew Phoebe better than anyone. If he trusted her judgement, then Max must too.

"But that does not mean that we do not watch her, and Alvanly. Can I rely on you to keep an eye on her?"

Max opened his mouth to protest. He had decided to leave London, to leave behind his foolish desire for Phoebe and go home, where he need not bump into her at every other social event. He was tired of longing for what he could not have, tired of being the man she believed would always put an end to whatever fun she was having.

"I know what I ask," Lucian said, and Max hated the sympathy in his eyes. "But I do ask it. My wife…."

He hesitated, and for a moment Max saw fear in the man's eyes.

"She's rather tired of late. I don't wish for her to overtax herself. If she is no better in a few days, we will return to Dern. I would have her see a physician in London, but she won't hear of it. The stubborn creature. She's certain she is just a little overtired. The season—not to mention Phoebe—has been rather energetic."

Max's heart sank, yet at the same time he was a hopeless enough case to be relieved, relieved to have a reason to stay close to her. God, he was pathetic.

"I do hope Lady Montagu recovers soon, and yes, of course I shall look out for Phoebe."

Lucian let out a breath. "I confess that is a weight off my mind."

Max believed him. Now he saw the strain around Lucian's eyes and realised how desperately worried he was about his wife. It was no secret the man was still head over ears in love with her. Despite women setting their caps at him at every turn, angling to be the marquess' mistress, no one had ever drawn his eye from his wife. Those who did not take a gentle hint risked one of his infamous set downs, yet some still dared it.

Noting Max's scrutiny, Lucian frowned. "Please, say nothing to Phoebe. Matilda does not wish to spoil her season by worrying her unduly when there is likely no need."

"Not a word, I promise you."

Lucian nodded before returning a considering glance. "I don't suppose you'd be interested—"

"Oh no." Max shook his head and backed off. "I watched you pick those last two poor devils to pieces. I've had my exercise for the morning, and have no desire for an exercise in humiliation as well, I thank you."

There was a frustrated sigh. "You'll be at the Countess March's ball tomorrow night?"

"I will."

"Very well. I believe Lady Helena and Gabriel are escorting Phoebe."

"I'll look out for her. You've my word."

Lucian nodded and patted Max's shoulder, a rare gesture of friendship that spoke of his gratitude, before heading back inside.

***

Phoebe dawdled on the way back home. She'd whiled away two hours at Hatchard's, but she could not live in the shop the entire day, certainly not all night. No matter how tempting avoiding her father's inevitable scolding was.

"Oh, do come along, miss," her maid, Rachel, urged her. "It's like walking with a snail on a lead."

Rachel was a no-nonsense, sensible girl, one who was unimpressed with intrigues and could not be bribed to send notes to lovers and the like. Not that Phoebe had ever wanted her to, but she might one day, and Rachel was not the girl to do it. Her mother had been canny in selecting her. She was kind and efficient, but could not be wheedled into mischief. Sadly.

"I'm coming," Phoebe replied, not moving any faster as Rachel huffed and carried on. The maid hurried across Ryder Street, moving quickly to dodge a smart curricle. Phoebe let her go, in no way eager to be home. Glancing down Ryder Street, her attention was taken by the sight of a man hammering on the door of the first of a length of narrow town houses. Elegant, but a touch shabby, it rose three storeys high and the black paint on the front door was peeling. Clearly frustrated, the man yelled up at the window above, apparently to no avail as no one answered him. With a final bellow of frustration, the fellow hit the door and turned, revealing that it was Baron Alvanly who was in such a fit of passion. Intrigued, Phoebe glanced ahead to see Rachel already disappearing into the crowd. Too curious to let the thing pass as she ought, Phoebe lifted her skirts free of the muck littering the road and crossed, just meeting with Baron Alvanly as he walked away from the door.

"Is something the matter?"

"Miss Barrington," the fellow said, his mouth creasing into a wide smile. "The matter? Oh, yes. Fool that I am, I have locked myself out and my idiot friend can apparently sleep through Armageddon, for I cannot wake him. I fear I must resign myself to a day of traipsing the streets until he is free of Morpheus' embrace. Still," he added, brightening considerably. "It seems I might have a companion for my lonely hours."

"Oh, no," Phoebe said at once, aware that she was in enough trouble already. "I was on my way home. My maid is just ahead of me, she'll notice I'm gone in a moment."

"Well, at least let me escort you. St James's, isn't it? Then I might enjoy your company for a few moments."

Oh, drat it. Would she ever learn not to stick her nose in where she shouldn't? Curiosity really was best left to cats. Her father was bound to be home by now and if he saw her with Alvanly... *oh, no.*

"I can get you inside," she said, suddenly eager to be free of him.

Alvanly laughed. "How? It's locked. Are you a magician?"

Phoebe returned an uncertain smile, wishing she had a better idea. "Something of the sort. Turn your back, please, so no one can see me."

Alvanly gave her a curious glance but did as she asked. Phoebe moved to the door, extricated a set of special picks that Jack had given her to practise with as a girl and crouched down. It was a simple lock and well-oiled, and it was child's play as she kept the tension on the barrel and flicked each pin in turn. There was a decisive click, and Phoebe stood, tucking the tools back in her reticule. She glanced up then, meeting Alvanly's eyes. He was staring at her with astonishment.

"I think I'm in love," he murmured.

"Don't be so silly," she said, annoyed with him. He'd not once asked how she had managed to get home from the fight, or asked if she was all right. Max would have…. Phoebe frowned, returning her attention to the baron. "Anyway, you can go inside now. Good day to you."

"No, wait. Miss Barrington."

He reached out, taking hold of her arm as she tried to move past him. She had little choice as his hand was firm about her forearm.

"You are the most astonishing creature I've ever met. Will you be at the March's ball tomorrow?"

"I will. *If* you will be so good as to let go of my arm, that is," she added tartly.

He did, though the look in his eyes remained a little daunting. "Then you must save me a dance. Good day, Miss Barrington."

Phoebe nodded and hurried away.

Chapter 5

Dearest Harriet,

Larkin has bid me ask if Cassius would like to come and stay for the weekend. His sister is driving him to distraction, and he feels the need for reinforcements, the poor dear. It's true that dear Grace is a bit of a handful already. She will insist on being Napoleon whenever they play at war, and she refuses to lose as she ought. Solo has suggested she play Wellington instead, but she's a contrary little madam. It puts poor Larkin in such a temper and then they really do fight. I can't think where she gets it from. I was never so bold.

—Excerpt of a letter to The Right Hon'ble Harriet Cadogan, Countess of St Clair, from The Right Hon'ble Lady Jemima Rothborn.

21st March 1827.

Lucian sighed at the sight of Phoebe sitting in the chair by the fire, hands clasped demurely in her lap. She looked incredibly young and quite wretched after his scolding. He'd hated doing it, and had never been terribly good at reprimanding her for her dreadful behaviour. This latest jaunt was enough to make his heart turn over in his chest as he considered all that might have happened to her, though, and he could not let it go. The poor girl had tried her best to make the evening last as long as possible, playing games with Philip and Thomas well past their bedtime in order to avoid the inevitable.

She had borne it though, and he knew she truly was sorry. He also knew it would not stop her from doing it again. Phoebe had a reckless streak a mile wide, a desire for adventure and excitement, and she did not always stop and think twice before she went off in pursuit of it. At least she had taken precautions. That was reassuring and showed him she was not blind to the dangers of the world. But then she never had been.

"I am sorry, Papa."

Her voice was quiet, her big eyes more grey than blue in this light, and Lucian's heart clenched as he saw the echo of his little brother in her expression.

"I know you are, Bee."

Unable to keep up such an atmosphere of disapprobation, Lucian held out his arms to her. Phoebe leapt to her feet and ran into them.

"Are you still cross?" she asked, her voice muffled against his shoulder.

Lucian snorted. "You know perfectly well I can't stay cross with you above five minutes, Bee. I just worry for you. Surely you know how devastated we would all be if you were hurt or unhappy."

"Yes. I do, and I *am* sorry. I don't mean to be a trial to you, truly, but I get so dreadfully bored. I can't sit still and do needlework for hours, and I hate talking about fashion and everyone is so dull, Papa, it makes me want to scream."

Despite himself, Lucian laughed.

"I know," he said sympathetically.

He could only thank God he'd been born male, for he well understood how she chafed at the rules. Phoebe would have done better to have been born in the previous century, where her antics would have made her wildly popular. Whilst she was certainly that now, larks like this one would damage her if they became public knowledge.

Lucian held her by the shoulders and looked down at her. "I will not demand you be good, Phoebe. I know it's impossible. Only, please darling, be safe. I couldn't bear it if anything happened to you."

Phoebe returned a rueful grin. "I'll do my best, Papa."

Lucian nodded. "Away with you, then. Goodnight, sweetheart."

"Goodnight." She kissed him on the cheek and hurried away to bed.

***

22nd March 1827. The Countess of March's Spring Ball, Mayfair, London.

"Oh, Phoebe, what a beautiful gown."

Phoebe grinned at Helena as a footman took her cloak away and did a little twirl for her. It was a pale pink satin with little puff sleeves that sat low on her shoulders. Tightly fitted at the waist, it then flared out and the bottom of the heavy skirts were embroidered with tiny rosebuds in a darker shade of pink.

"Gorgeous!" Helena said, taking her arm. "The poor men will throw themselves at your feet."

Phoebe pulled a face at the idea and Helena laughed, nodding. "Yes, I know. A challenge is far more enticing. You know, Gabe wouldn't even look at me the first few times we met, which naturally made me even more determined to have him. I was quite shocking, I assure you."

"I believe you," Phoebe replied gravely, sending Helena off into peals again.

"So you should, and I pray you do not follow her example," Gabriel replied, shaking his head. "Heaven alone knows what manner of scoundrel you'll find yourself entangled with."

"One like you?" Helena suggested.

Phoebe almost blushed at the look that passed between the two of them, such obvious adoration, and such heat in their eyes that she felt like an intruder. *Heavens.* If only she could meet a man who made her as wild and desperate as Gabe had made Helena. She'd heard the story many times, of course, of their mad race from London to Brighton, and then a different kind of race, one that had been hushed up. Only their dearest friends knew of their desperate flight to Gretna Green with Helena's brother, the duke, in hot pursuit. She could not imagine wanting a man so much as to cast everything aside for him, risk everything for him. She'd do something mad for the adventure of it, for the thrill of it, but she'd felt nothing close to the depth of feeling that she saw between these two, or between her parents.

"Oh, Lord," Phoebe muttered.

Helena followed her gaze across the packed ballroom to where people were gathered at the edges of the dance floor, talking. There was Max, deep in conversation with Lord St Clair.

"What is it?" Helena asked.

"I must speak to Lord Ellisborough," Phoebe said, with the same tone she might remark, *I must have a tooth pulled.*

"And is that such a terrible fate?" Helena asked, her green eyes alight with curiosity.

Phoebe shrugged. "No. Only, I... I owe him an apology, or thanks, or something, and I'm not particularly good at things like that. He always makes me feel like such a ninny."

Helena frowned at her, the curiosity in her eyes deepening. "Why do you think that is?"

"I don't know," Phoebe said, huffing. "He just… he makes me want to be even more dreadful than usual, because I know how much he disapproves of me. Though he says he doesn't, but I don't believe him." She looked up as Helena laughed, the sound soft and knowing. "What?"

"Oh, no," Helena replied. "You shan't hear it from me. You're a bright girl. You'll figure it out… eventually."

"Are you causing mischief, wife?"

Helena looked up, her eyes sparkling. "Possibly," she replied.

Gabe chuckled. "There's no *possibly* about it. Come along and dance with me before you start a riot, you wicked creature."

Phoebe watched, rather envious as Gabe guided Helena onto the dance floor and held her shockingly close, making all the old biddies gasp and mutter. Sighing, she decided she'd best get the onerous part of the evening over with and headed towards Max.

Her stomach fluttered as she drew closer and she told herself it was just because he would likely say something to make her cross. He turned, seeing her before she reached him and finished his conversation with the earl, moving towards her.

"Miss Barrington," he said, politely. "May I say how lovely you look this evening?"

Phoebe smiled and thanked him, not taking much notice of his words. He was unfailingly polite to everyone, and would have said the exact same thing if she'd worn a puce gown with an orange flounce and green lace. She rather wished she had now, just to see if he flinched at all whilst he said it.

"I came to say thank you," she said, wishing she could avoid his gaze, those dark eyes she felt certain could see into her brain and read whatever nonsense she was thinking, and always seemed to find her wanting. "For not telling Papa what I did."

Max smiled at her. It was a good smile, warm and honest, and Phoebe noticed now that it made his eyes crinkle a little at the corners, which she liked.

"I did not want to tell tales on you, and I knew you would tell him yourself, in any case."

Phoebe snorted and then wished she hadn't, remembering too late that it was unladylike. "Well, you had more faith in me than I did. I fully believed I would take it to my grave if I could. Sadly, my nerves are not strong enough to withstand my father's scrutiny."

"I'm not certain anyone's nerves are strong enough for that," Max replied with a wry smile.

"No." Phoebe sighed, relaxing a little in the light of his good humour. "I don't suppose they are."

Max cleared his throat. If Phoebe hadn't known better, she might have thought him nervous.

"Miss Barrington—"

"There you are!"

Phoebe turned and felt a surge of dismay to see it was Baron Alvanly who'd found her.

"You owe me a dance," he said, a wicked glint sparkling in his eyes. He was dressed in immaculate evening attire, tall and lithe and rather splendid, with his blond hair gleaming gold. Well, the devil was handsome, she'd give him that.

"Good evening, and yes, I know I do," she said, daring a glance up at Max to discover his face was rigid, his dark eyes frosty with disapproval.

Well, honestly. She knew Alvanly was a rake and a scoundrel, but they were in a packed ballroom. Dancing with him held no perils. Surely, Max could not object to that. She waited, hoping he would continue whatever it was he'd been about to say.

"Was there something you wished to ask?" she said when he remained silent, ignoring Alvanly's outstretched hand for a moment, for she'd been certain Max would ask her to dance.

"No," he said, returning a tight smile that did not reach his eyes. "Enjoy your dance."

Well, really!

Phoebe seethed with irritation. Alvanly was always popular at events like these. He was funny and charming and a wonderful dancer. She'd look terribly high in the instep if she refused him, rake or no. It wasn't as if she had agreed to go into the gardens alone with him. Max was just a boring old stick in the mud who thought young ladies ought to be quiet and well-behaved, and never stir from home without a man by their side.

Grrrr.

By the time she'd reached the dance floor, Phoebe had worked herself up into quite a ferment of indignation. The unsettling idea that she was horribly disappointed Max had not asked her to dance did not help matters.

"What wickedness is brewing inside that lovely head of yours?" Alvanly asked as he guided her through a complicated turn. "You look ready to strike someone dead."

Phoebe let out a breath, aware that her expression bore no relation to the inscrutable mask her father had perfected, drat it.

"Oh, nothing," she said, knowing the lie was easily discernible.

"Ellisborough is a dry old stick. No doubt he disapproves of both of us. You, the bastard daughter, and me, the loose screw. He can't bear to see people having fun."

Phoebe frowned a little at that, unnerved that he'd read her with such ease. It had never occurred to her that her parentage might disgust Max. The thought made her chest feel tight with anxiety. If that was true, he hid it well, but then Papa was his friend and he was so well mannered with everyone, no matter their birth. Could he really think ill of her for her illegitimacy? How could she tell if he did, or if he just always behaved impeccably? She was uncertain that Max disliked people having fun, though. Oh, how she wished he were easier to read, but though she considered herself a good judge of character—or of bad character, at least—Max always made her feel uncertain of everything, especially her own judgement.

"I believe he fancies you for himself and doesn't wish to see you tainted by association with the likes of me."

These words so discomposed Phoebe that she stumbled, only saved by the tightening of Alvanly's arms about her. He drew her close, too close, their bodies touching for a moment.

"Alvanly," she said, shocked. He released her at once, but she felt hot and muddled and she didn't know why. Surely the baron hadn't caused such sensations?

"I want you too. You do know that, don't you?"

His voice was low and liquid, shivering over her back, and Phoebe was compelled by some force she did not understand to look up into his eyes. They were darker than before, the pupils wide, and she was not so innocent that she did not know desire when she saw it. He stared down at her, his gaze falling to her lips, and she knew he wanted to kiss her. What would that be like with a man like him, she wondered. A small tendril of excitement unfurled deep in her belly. She knew from Mama and her friends— who had all advised her at one time or another—that there was temptation in such men, that desire could lead one into all sorts of trouble. Alvanly was a wicked man, a rake, and so he would know what he was doing. How interesting it would be to let him, just to see what it was like, to see if it were different from anything she'd experienced before. She wondered then how Max would kiss, the thought so startling her that she remembered just what had tangled her emotions in a knot in the first place.

"What did you mean?"

"Surely I don't need to explain what it means when a man wants a woman?" Alvanly murmured, a thread of amusement in his voice.

"No, no, not that," Phoebe said impatiently, noting a flash of irritation in the baron's eyes. "What did you mean about Ellisborough, that he fancies me for himself?"

"Any man here with a pulse fancies you for himself, Miss Barrington. Surely you know that?"

Phoebe laughed and shook her head. "Any man with an empty bank account, certainly, and perhaps some of the others, but not Ellisborough."

She felt the baron stiffen and was a little sorry for having spoken so glibly. She knew he needed to marry money, and did not blame him for pursuing her. He was lazy and over-bred, and had no idea of how to work for a living. What else could he do? Despite not trusting him an inch, she did rather like him, and he was amusing company, even if he would be a disastrous husband.

"You're wrong," he said angrily. "It's not just the money, though God knows I'd be struck by lightning if I said it meant nothing to me, and there's a dozen or more like me, watching as I speak. But I'd want you even if you were penniless, and that's the truth too. Ellisborough is no different. He might act like he wishes you to behave as a nice young lady ought, but he'll be eager to discover more of your tempestuous spirit. He likes it well enough when he's imagining you in his bed, I don't doubt, just like the rest of us poor devils."

"My lord!" Phoebe glared at him, tugging out of his arms.

Thankfully, the dance had ended at that moment, and she thought perhaps no one noticed.

Alvanly looked unrepentant. "I'm sorry, Miss Barrington, to be so crude, but I think you wanted to know. I believe you like a little danger, don't you?"

"I don't think you ought to speak of him so," she said, far more indignant on Max's behalf than her own.

She knew men of his nature said such things to make her blush and to make her curious. Well, her cheeks were burning, and her insides were all in a quake, though she could not understand why, for she'd dealt with men like Alvanly before with no trouble.

"Forgive me," the baron said, smiling gently now. "You have such spirit, such a wild nature that echoes my own so closely, I sometimes forget we tread different paths. I forget just how innocent you are, sweet child. I ought not have spoken so."

Phoebe nodded, accepting his apology, though she did not like being called a child by him. Not that he meant it, the devil. She could still see the dark glitter in his eyes. Well, he was a rake. What did she expect, dancing with such a man? Alvanly sighed, a rueful glint apparent as he watched her.

"Am I forgiven?"

"Yes," Phoebe said, wishing she didn't feel so agitated. She could not decide what it was that made her heart skip about so, but the baron's words had edged under her skin and made her uncomfortable.

"Good. Until next time, Miss Barrington."

Phoebe moved away from the dance floor and headed towards the retiring room, intending to splash some cold water on her face. What was wrong with her? She felt strangely restless and cross, but she did not know why.

"Miss Barrington."

Oh drat. She did not wish to talk to anyone. Hurrying on, she ignored her name, but whoever it was called again.

"Miss Barrington, wait, please."

She turned then, unable to pretend she had not heard a second time when they were so close. It was Max, of course.

"Are you quite well?"

"Quite, thank you," she said, forcing a smile and trying to move away again, but Max caught her wrist. It was only a gentle touch, just enough to stay her movement before he let her go again.

"Did Alvanly…. Did he say something that upset you?"

To her irritation, she could only remember what he'd said about Max, about how Max would be pleased to imagine her tempestuous spirit in his bed. Her cheeks blazed scarlet.

"I'll kill him," Max muttered.

"What? *Oh!* No… No," she said in a rush, realising what he thought.

Indeed, Alvanly ought never to have spoken so, but she wasn't some silly green chit who had no idea what men were like. She knew well enough how to deal with him. It was only when he'd spoken of Max thinking of her in such a way she'd become quite… quite….

"Really, he said nothing you need reprimand him for."

Phoebe crossed her fingers behind her back and hoped her wretched face did not give her away. She did not wish for Max to speak with Alvanly, or for Alvanly to tell him what he'd said.

Max studied her, his jaw tightening. "I see."

What the devil did he mean by that?

Phoebe glared back at him, realising he thought Alvanly had been flirting with her, and that she'd liked it. Indignation swelled in her chest. Max still thought her a fool, he thought her too silly to see the truth of a man like Alvanly. Well, damn him. Let him think it.

"Is that all?" she asked tartly.

Max nodded and let her go, and Phoebe fled.

***

Max watched Phoebe run from him and tried to fight the wave of furious jealousy that rose inside him. No right, he scolded himself. He had no right to such feelings. Lucian had asked him to keep an eye and he would. He would look out for her and pray he could steer her out of trouble. Max could not make her want him or think of him as a man who desired her, as she clearly thought of Alvanly. That she might throw herself away on such a creature, a fellow who would drink and gamble and whore his way through her fortune and make her wretched too…. It made him want to break something. Max clenched his fists and reminded himself that he was a rational human being, and that breaking Alvanly's nose for flirting with her was not a rational reaction. It didn't seem to help.

He took a breath and forced himself to walk the perimeter of the ballroom twice before trusting himself to seek out the baron.

Alvanly looked up as Max approached, a smirk at his lips.

"Well, I wondered how long before you came to speak with me."

"I had to take the time to remind myself I was a gentleman," Max replied, his voice as easy and conversational as the baron's.

Alvanly's eyebrows shot up. "My, my. I admit, that is… unexpected. I had not thought you would take such a direct approach."

"I would. Her father might not."

That gave him pause. There were stories enough about Montagu and the power he wielded for the baron not to take Max's words lightly. The marquess might attack obliquely, and Alvanly would never see it coming. Max could see the glimmer of fear in the man's eyes, there and gone in an instant. Alvanly laughed and shook his head.

"Well, either way. Neither of you has a thing to worry about. I like the girl, but I'd not have Montagu for a father-in-law. No dowry, no matter how large, is worth the terror of enduring that for a lifetime, believe me."

"What are you playing at, then?" Max demanded, sickened that the fellow might be leading Phoebe on, that he might engage her heart and then hurt her with his callous disregard for her feelings.

The baron laughed, shaking his head at Max with a pitying expression. "You poor bastard. She hasn't got a clue, has she? Well, don't fret, Romeo, I won't make her fall in love with me. Not that I think I could, though it is galling to admit as much. She has my measure, I believe."

Max gritted his teeth, not troubling to deny his feelings for Phoebe. Denial would only confirm the man's suspicions.

"Why are you hanging about like a bad smell, then?" he demanded instead, restraining the uncouth longing to shake the truth out of him, or worse.

"Now, there is no need to hurt my feelings, old man. I swear to you, I have no desire or intention to trap the girl into marriage. I just like her. She makes me laugh and she enjoys my company. That's all. I'll not stand in the path of true love, cross my heart and hope to die."

Max felt there was truth in Alvanly's words, but there was something in the man's expression that he could not like.

"Are you going to demand I stay away?" he asked Max, with a considering tilt of his head.

"No," Max replied, though it nearly choked him to do so. "You'll tell her I warned you off, and no doubt that would make her twice as determined to seek you out. No, you do as you please, but you'll have me to answer to if you hurt her, and that's only if Montagu doesn't get to you first."

"Duly noted," Alvanly said, smiling, though the expression did not reach his eyes.

Max nodded and stalked away.

Chapter 6

Dear Phoebe,

*Thank you very much for my birthday presents.
Especially the book by Washington Irving,
which is excellent. I have already much enjoyed
Rip Van Winkle and The story of Sleepy
Hollow. The illustrations are wonderful too,
though the stories never come to life quite as
vividly as when you read them out. I do hope I
may persuade you to read Sleepy Hollow one
day, you will scare everyone witless no doubt,
especially Bella, and I should like to see that.*

**—Excerpt of a letter to Miss Phoebe
Barrington from her cousin, Master Leo
Hunt, aged 12.**

**7th April 1827. Mrs Manning's rout party, Old Burlington
Street, London.**

Phoebe saw Alvanly several times over the next weeks and, as
he was scrupulously polite and as charming as he could possibly
be, little by little she relaxed. It seemed he no longer desired to
make her blush, or to enjoy her discomfort at his lewd talk and
flirtation, and was content to be her friend. Though she knew better
than to trust him, this was such a relief that she forgot the strange
evening and tried to put his words far out of her head. They would
come back to her at times, usually in the quiet moments before she
fell asleep, only to wake the next morning to discover she'd been

dreaming of Max and feeling annoyed and irritable with herself for being such a ninny.

The notion that Max had feelings like that for her was ridiculous, surely. Despite that one time when he'd said the last thing he felt for her was disgust, he treated her as he might an annoying little sister, looking at her with amusement for her entertainment value at best and, the rest of the time, scolding her and wishing she would behave like a young lady ought. Not that she blamed him entirely. Phoebe knew she was spoiled and reckless and ought to be better than she was. Indeed, she did *try*. It was just so... *difficult.* She was too easily bored, and she spoke without thinking, and her temper flared far too quickly. Mama said she was what Papa would have been if life had not taught him to hide his true nature. Happily, it was a lesson Phoebe had never needed to learn, though she rather thought she ought to have done.

Max kept his distance now, though, and rarely looked her way. Phoebe decided that Alvanly really did not have the first idea about the earl if he was so bottle-headed as to believe Max had any feelings at all for her past irritation.

"Do you have any idea what it is Mrs Manning intends to display this evening?"

Phoebe turned to attend the conversation between her Aunt Alice and Aashini.

"I believe it is a picture, but not just any picture," Aashini confided in an undertone which would have been considered shouting in any other circumstance, for the burble of conversation was so loud.

Mrs Manning's parties were always a crush, and it mattered little that every stick of furniture had been removed from her lavish home to make way for her guests. People seemed to enter the house in noisy rivers of rich fabric and wafts of perfume, though Phoebe saw few of them leave. The grand house would soon burst at the seams.

"What kind, then?" Alice demanded, intrigued.

Phoebe floated away from the conversation. So far the evening had been dull indeed, and she was bored to tears. She had already played cards but it was too tempting to cheat simply to amuse herself, and she'd caused enough trouble of late, so she'd decided she'd better stop. At least it was close to midnight, and Mrs Manning always provided a lavish late supper, so there was that. Even the painting that would be shown afterwards was not terribly interesting to Phoebe tonight, such was her mood.

She knew well enough that Mrs Manning was a great art lover and was always on the hunt for some new talent or undiscovered work of genius. There were those that said she was not only an art lover, but a lover of artists, too, for she had taken several as her paramours over the years. Phoebe didn't much care. She was restless and out of sorts after another night where she had slept ill. It made her irritable, and she found she did not much like her own company. Likely no one else did either, she thought with a sigh.

The buffet was opened at last and Phoebe made a beeline for the sweet treats, piling a small plate high with tiny *pains a la duchesse* and other delectable items before finding a quiet corner to munch them in. She had just set her empty plate aside with a sigh of contentment when a familiar voice hailed her.

"Well, and here is a sight for sore eyes."

Her spirits rose a little as Alvanly hailed her.

"Oh, you're here, are you?" she said, smiling at him.

"Indeed I am, you ungrateful creature."

"Ungrateful?" she demanded, her eyebrows going up. "How so?"

"For I only faced this wretched crush to rescue you from boredom and all I get for my pains is an *oh, you're here, are you?*"

Phoebe could only laugh at the reproach in his eyes.

"Oh, you are ridiculous," she said, shaking her head. "But I am glad, all the same."

"I should think so," he scolded gently, taking her arm. "I really don't see why everyone is in such a lather about this stupid picture, though."

"Oh, do you know what it is, then?" Phoebe asked.

"Indeed I do," he whispered, his voice heavy with a conspiratorial undertone. "And I still don't understand the fuss," he added with a laugh.

"Oh, tell me, you wretch."

Alvanly rolled his eyes. "Very well. It's called *Christ Mocked,* and is quite old, and now you know as much as I do."

"Oh." Phoebe was disappointed to hear it was a religious subject, for she did not much care for them. "Well, I'm afraid I am a dreadful philistine, for I cannot find a great deal of excitement in such a subject. I much prefer modern artists, Turner, for example. Though to be sure I can imagine it is of great importance to history."

"No, I know. Think how disappointed everyone will be to discover it is not some shocking new artist's work, like the one she displayed last year."

"Oh, I wasn't here last year," Phoebe said with regret, remembering talk of the scandalous nude that had been displayed. "Papa knew what the painting was and wouldn't let me come."

"Of course he didn't," Alvanly muttered.

Phoebe cast him a sharp glance, but the man just flashed her a grin.

"Come along," he said. "I know exactly how we can enliven this deadly affair."

"Oh?"

Alvanly did not reply. He only tugged her arm, and bore her inexorably up the stairs. Phoebe was not alarmed, for all the rooms, including the bedrooms, had been emptied and were open to the crowds. Up here, as downstairs, the sound of music drifted from a small chamber orchestra and, in some rooms, tables and chairs had been set up for the card players.

She did quail a little as he tugged her past a silken rope, though, tied across a darkened corridor with a *private* sign sewn onto it.

"Alvanly!" she said, resisting him and grinding to a halt. "What are you about? I'll not go trysting with you, if that's your intention."

The baron tutted at her.

"I never expected you to," he retorted, obviously stung by the implication.

"Well, what then?"

Alvanly huffed and looked around to check they were not observed. "This is where the painting is. Mrs Manning will lead her guests up here shortly to view the painting. Just think how shocked she'll be if it isn't there."

Phoebe stared at him open mouthed.

"Oh, don't look like that. Only for a minute," he said, laughing at her horrified reaction. "Just until she gives a little shriek and then I shall go, *ta da*! And present the horrid thing to her again. How funny it will be to see them all squeal in shock and then gasp and wonder how I did it. They shall call me The Magician."

He winked at her and Phoebe frowned, troubled.

"How *will* you do it? The door is bound to be locked."

Alvanly rolled his eyes. "I won't, you pretty gudgeon. *You* must unlock the door for me with your clever fingers, but I'll do the rest. Come along, it will be a lark. I won't tell anyone you helped me, so there's no harm."

Phoebe shook her head. "I... I don't think so...."

Alvanly sighed and returned a mocking expression. "Oh, I see. He's spoken to you at last, I suppose."

"What? Who?" Phoebe asked, wondering at the change of subject.

"No, never mind." The baron waved a dismissive hand and shook his head, turning to go back the way they'd come, but he looked dreadfully hurt.

"No, tell me," Phoebe insisted, making him stop with a hand on his arm. "Do you mean Ellisborough?"

"Of course, Ellisborough, who else?" he retorted with a bitter laugh. "He's always watching us, haven't you noticed? He gives me these dark glares that promise retribution. No doubt he's been dripping poison in your ear and telling you what a loose screw I am, too, and not to trust me an inch."

"No, he hasn't," Phoebe said, frowning. "And I make my own decisions about my friends, Alvanly. You know that."

"You think you do," the baron replied, a tone to his voice she could not like. "Except I wonder how many others have not been as determined to remain your friend, and allowed him to frighten them off."

"What?" Phoebe stared at him in alarm. "Ellisborough would never—"

"Oh, wouldn't he? Then it must have been someone who looked like him that threatened me in that case. He told me to stay away from you, *or else*, my sweet. The *else* was quite clearly finding me in a dark alley and teaching me a lesson. He looked positively murderous, I promise you."

Ellisborough had threatened Alvanly? Phoebe's mind boggled at the idea. *Max?* Max had threatened Alvanly. A strange sensation uncoiled in her belly. It was not entirely comfortable, and she did not like it. She did not like the idea that he was manipulating the people around her, either. How dare he? Even her father would not choose her friends for her. He knew she was friends with Alvanly, and he trusted her to make her own decisions. But Max….

Indignation rose with a wave of heat, and a strong emotion she could not identify, but it had the effect of making her want to grab hold of Max and… and… and strangle him with his cravat. The beast!

At least, she *thought* that was what she wanted.

Her emotions rose in a tangle, hot and uncomfortable, setting her all on edge. Why was Max so often in her thoughts of late, keeping her from sleep, always there with that dark look of disapproval glinting in his eyes?

"Fine," she said, her jaw so tight with agitation she could hardly get the word out.

"What?"

"Fine, I'll do it," she muttered, stalking past Alvanly and down the corridor.

Max had ignored her ever since that scene with the baron, but if he found out about this, he'd be forced to scold her, he wouldn't be able to stop himself, and then… *then*… she'd give him a piece of her mind in return.

It was child's play to get into the room, even without her lock picks. Her hair pins worked well enough, though a few heavy coils of her hair came tumbling down as a result. The lock was simple and sturdy but well-oiled, and it was a matter of moments before she heard that satisfying little *snick*. Alvanly beamed at her, and a tremor of unease rippled through her. She was already regretting her impetuous decision, but there was no going back now.

"You really are marvellous," he said, his admiration apparently genuine. "You know, if not for your terrifying papa, I think I could fall in love with you."

"How gratifying," Phoebe said dryly as she walked into the room.

All she wanted now was for this to be over and done with so she could get out of the baron's company. She wanted to find Max instead and ask why he had threatened Alvanly, and why he wouldn't talk to her anymore. Had she been so awful that he didn't like her at all now? Her heart sank as she realised she could not discount the possibility. Alvanly hurried to light a couple of candles, and they walked to inspect the painting. Phoebe studied it and shook her head, wishing she could see what was remarkable about it.

"It's a dingy little thing."

Alvanly was staring at the painting with awe, which Phoebe thought odd as it was small and unimpressive. It seemed to be grubby, and the paint was all cracked, but the baron was gazing at it in wonder.

"Do you like it?" she asked, surprised to discover it was to his taste.

"Oh, I do," he said, an odd note to his voice. "I like it tremendously."

She stared at the painting again, trying to see what had so captivated him. "How strange, I'd never have thought it was—"

Phoebe turned too late as a large hand covered her mouth, the other holding her arms pinned to her chest. He was far stronger than he appeared.

"Don't make a sound, sweet," Alvanly said. "I should hate to hurt you, but I am quite desperate. That painting is my ticket to freedom, and I must take it. You do see."

Phoebe stamped on his foot and wriggled free enough to thrust her elbow into his stomach. Strongly indicating that she did *not*, in fact, see at all. Alvanly groaned and cursed but did not release her.

"You little hellcat!" he said, though he sounded amused rather than angry with her. "Please, Phoebe, don't make it worse. I *will* hurt you if you make me."

He withdrew the hand from her mouth and Phoebe took a breath to give him a piece of her mind, but swallowed the words as he drew a pistol and levelled it at her.

"There, now. Be a good girl," he said, almost apologetically. "You will be nice and quiet while I tie you up, and no one will be able to blame you for what has happened."

"You'll not get away with this, you blaggard," Phoebe cursed furiously. "*I'll* not let you get away with it."

"Don't be a poor loser, darling. You're up to snuff with most tricks, I'll give you that, but I never thought I'd be reduced to be doing something like this myself. The opportunity was simply too good to miss, though. This ugly little darling is a lost treasure. It's a thirteenth century masterpiece, and worth the best part of ten thousand pounds."

"But I'll be ruined," she said, unable to hide the loathing in her voice.

God, what a little fool she'd been. She'd known he was a wicked fellow, but she'd thought she knew all the tricks he might play on her. Sadly, this one had never occurred. She'd known he was a rake—but a criminal—that she had not counted on.

More fool her.

"Ah, not for long," the baron said, his voice soothing as he stuffed a silk handkerchief in her mouth, almost making her gag as the sweet, floral scent of his cologne filled her nose. "I don't doubt Ellisborough will be swift enough to offer for you. Indeed, he ought to thank me. I've done him a grand favour."

As she could no longer speak, Phoebe had to content herself with glaring at him. Alvanly gave her cheek a gentle pat and moved quickly, tying her arms and legs with a thin rope he withdrew from his pocket. He'd come prepared, then. This had been his plan all along. Fury and regret that she had allowed him to use her this way swamped her. Well, he'd not get away with it. She would have her revenge on him if it was the last thing she did.

Alvanly lifted her, ignoring the way she squirmed, and laid her down on a chaise longue before hurrying back for the painting. It was just small enough to be hidden beneath his waistcoat without being too terribly visible, and she realised now his coat was too big for him, big enough to hide the bulky shape beneath. He turned then, giving her one last smile, and blew her a kiss.

"I *am* sorry," he said, and she heard the regret in his voice before he gave a rueful chuckle. "Just not sorry enough."

And then he was gone.

***

Max frowned. He'd looked everywhere for Phoebe and could find no sign of her. Her aunt, Mrs Hunt, had confirmed she was here and yet… Where the devil was she? He looked up over the crowd to see Alvanly hurrying down the stairs, heading for the front door. What was the blackguard in such a rush for? Alarm bells sounded loudly in his head, and he rushed towards the stairs, ignoring those that tried to catch his eye to greet him. There was an odd tightening in his gut, some sixth sense that told him Phoebe was in trouble. He searched each room, methodically, finding no sign of her, and then saw the roped off area. Casting a glance about to ensure he was not seen, he slipped down the corridor and searched each room in turn. All were dark and empty, except one.

Candlelight illuminated the space enough for him to see the easel that had been set up to display a painting, though no painting sat upon it. A muffled sound of despair caught his attention and

Max's breath snagged in his throat as he saw Phoebe, gagged and bound.

"Phoebe!"

He rushed to her and tugged the handkerchief from her mouth. She sucked in a breath.

"Oh, Max, thank heavens," she said, her voice shaky and uncertain and quite unlike herself.

"Phoebe, love, what happened? Who did this to you?" Because as soon as he knew, he would murder them with his bare hands.

"Alvanly," she spat in disgust as he moved to untie her. "Oh, Max, he's stolen the painting."

"*What?*"

Max tugged the last of her bindings free and stared down at her.

"It's true," she said, her eyes filling with tears. "And it's all my fault. Max, I've been such a stupid fool."

"It's not your fault," he said, desperately wanting to pull her into his arms and hold her tight, but knowing that he could not. "He's a sly, lying bastard. I knew he was up to something. I should have done more... I should have stopped him," he cursed, winding the ropes up in his distraction and stuffing them in his pocket.

Phoebe gave a huff of laughter. "Oh, how angry I was with you when he told me you'd warned him off, but you were right all along. I ought to have listened to you instead of being so pig-headed, and now...well, I suppose I am well served."

Max stilled, a little stunned by her words, but he had no time to enjoy the moment as she continued, her voice despairing.

"Oh, what a wretched mull I've made of everything, and it *is* my fault, Max. I picked the lock. He'd never have got in here without me."

Max stared at her, wondering why he was surprised.

"You... picked the lock," he said faintly.

She nodded, her bottom lip trembling. "That grubby little painting is worth a fortune, and now I'm an accessory to a crime, and there will be such a scandal, and Papa... Papa...."

Her voice quavered.

"No," Max said, shaking his head. "No, there won't be. I'll make it right, I promise."

"Oh, Max," she sobbed, and to his astonishment and delight, threw her arms about his neck.

He couldn't move for a moment, couldn't breathe, and then his brain gave him a swift kick and told him not to be such an idiot and he put her arms about her, holding her tightly, just as he'd wanted to.

"I'll make it right," he said again, the words whispered this time.

She gasped and looked up at him, her eyelashes spangled with tears. Max's breath caught in his throat, his eyes falling to her lips.

"My lord!"

They both leapt about a foot in the air as Mrs Manning's voice rang out. Turning, they saw they had an audience. She had obviously brought the first swathe of guests to view her astonishing find.

Max surged to his feet, keeping hold of Phoebe's hand but moving to shield her from the gawking eyes about them.

"Forgive me, Mrs Manning," he said, doing his best to look like a man interrupted in a romantic interlude—which he was desperately hoping he had been. "I... I know we ought not be here, but I needed somewhere private to... to ask Miss Barrington if she would be so good as to marry me. Thankfully, she has made me the happiest of men and agreed, but I do apologise for trespassing so."

He heard Phoebe's gasp of shock behind him and squeezed her hand hard, praying she'd keep her mouth shut.

"Ah," Mrs Manning said, her eyes growing misty as she looked upon them, a murmur of interest rippling through the crowd. "How terribly romantic." And then her gaze moved to the empty easel and one hand went to her throat. "The painting!" she cried, rather theatrically in Max's opinion. "Where is my painting?"

She swung back to stare at him, and at Phoebe, who was clutching his hand as tightly as she could.

"Painting?" Max replied, hoping he could be as inscrutable as Phoebe's father. He'd seen Montagu in action and knew how impenetrable a mask he could wear. *Please, God, make it convincing*, he prayed, as he lied through his teeth. "There was no painting when we entered, Mrs Manning, just that empty easel. I assumed you would bring it in when you were ready."

"But the door," she said, as the murmurs and gasps spread, becoming louder. "The door was *locked.*"

"No," Max said again, shaking his head sadly. "No, it was not. I… I did see Baron Alvanly, though. As we came up the stairs, I saw him hurrying down. He'd come from along this corridor. Perhaps he might have seen someone?"

"Oh, the thief!" Mrs Manning cried, and then gave a little moan of despair before she swooned rather deftly into the arms of her latest paramour.

She was swept away as the cries of outrage began in earnest and pandemonium ensued. Max turned back to Phoebe.

"Come quickly," he said.

She nodded, and they made their way back through the crowds and down the stairs, hurrying towards the front door. On the way, they heard the story spread through the crowd ahead of them.

The painting... stolen... a tryst... Ellisborough and Montagu's daughter... Alvanly a thief... In on it together? Surely not!

Max shut his ears against the gossip, all too aware of how a story could spread and grow and morph into something else. He concentrated on Phoebe's hand in his, guiding her through the crowd until they burst outside into the cool evening air. They hurried on, down the road to the waiting carriages until Phoebe spotted her driver. The fellow had always given Max the urge to check his pockets, and he'd never understood why Montagu had kept such an obviously villainous fellow in his employ. He looked more likely to hold a carriage up than drive one, especially with the big ruby glinting in his ear. So, when Phoebe let go of his hand and ran to the man, flinging herself into the old rogue's arms, Max was momentarily bereft of speech.

"Oh, Jack, Jack," she cried, sobbing against the big devil's chest.

"Princess? What is it?" he demanded, his eyes narrowing upon Max. "Did this bastard hurt you? 'Cause if he did, I'll tear his bloody head off!"

Max stilled, quite convinced this was no idle threat.

"Oh, no…. Don't be silly, Jack, Max would never hurt me. It's my fault, as usual. Oh, but this time I've really done the most awful thing and I'm in such a fix!"

Jack gave Max one last suspicious glance before turning his attention to Phoebe.

"Spill it," he commanded. "I can't fix nowt if I dunno what the problem is."

"It's Baron Alvanly. He tricked me into picking a lock for him, and now he's stolen a painting from Mrs Manning and it's worth a fortune. The wretch tied me up, but Max came and found me, but then everyone came in and saw us, and Max lied to save me. He said he'd proposed and now the p-poor man must marry me, and you know I'll make him miserable, Jack, and…. *Oh,* you must help me sort it all out!" she wailed. "We must go after him, at once, and get that wretched painting back, and then I can tell everyone the truth, and it won't be so bad."

Jack sent Max a curious look before getting back to the matter at hand.

"Where does he live, this Alvanly cove?"

"Ryder Street."

Jack nodded. "That's just a few minutes away. Jump in, then," he said, gesturing to the carriage. "Doubt he'll be there, but we might figure out where he's scuttled off to and catch him up."

Phoebe lost no time in doing as he bade her, and Max got in behind them.

"Who is he, exactly?" Max asked, wanting desperately to demand why it was she had said *poor Max,* and why she thought he'd be miserable if she married him, but sensing this was not the time.

"*Who?* Oh, Jack?" she asked, turning to look at him. "Did Papa never tell you?"

Max shook his head and Phoebe smiled. "Flash Jack was sent to murder my father by my Great Uncle Theodore. Jack was a highwayman then and dreadfully wicked, but Papa persuaded Jack he'd be better off working for him instead of Uncle Theodore, and so he switched sides. He's been with us ever since."

Max stared at her. "Your father hired the man who was sent to kill him?"

Good God. He'd known Lucian could be as cold as ice when the situation demanded it, but that… that was….

"Oh, Jack's a sweetheart really," Phoebe said, making Max feel as if his eyes were out on stalks. The huge villain who had threatened to rip his head off was a *sweetheart*? "You know what they say about a poacher turned game keeper? Well, that's Jack. He'd lay down his life for Papa, I know he would. And for me," she added softly.

Max considered this. "And the fact that you can pick a lock?"

Phoebe bit her lip, her hands gripped tightly together in her lap, mortification glinting in her eyes. "Yes, Jack taught me, but you must not blame him. He only did it in case I was ever in trouble, and I was never supposed to use it for such a thing as this. Really, it's not his fault, Max, it's all mine. Oh, well you know that, don't you? It's always me, after all. It's just the sort of reckless, stupid thing I would do," she said, sounding so dejected that he wanted to hold her to him again, and would have done if the carriage hadn't halted.

"We're here!" she said, scrambling for the door before he could say another word.

Max had little choice but to hurry after her.

Chapter 7

Dearest Prue,

I've just heard the wildest rumour. One of our acquaintances was at Mrs Manning's this evening, and we bumped into them on our way home from a neighbour's dinner party. The story is so far-fetched I can hardly credit it, except part of it is about Phoebe. There was some garbled story about a stolen painting which I could not make head nor tail of, but they also said she's to marry Ellisborough?

Is it true? I can hardly believe it.

May I ask Eliza if she would like to go shopping with me this week? I saw the most darling little bonnet that would suit her wonderfully well.

—Excerpt of a letter to Her Grace, Prunella Adolphus, Duchess of Bedwin, from Mrs Minerva de Beauvoir.

7th April 1827. Baron Alvanly's rooms, Ryder Street, London.

Max watched, feeling as if he'd tumbled into some extraordinary dream, as Jack picked the lock to the front door of Alvanly's rooms, sending his equally disreputable looking companion who went by the name of Fred, around the rear to check the devil didn't leave by the alley that ran along the back of the houses. Both men were armed with pistols and cudgels and

Max was disconcerted to discover Phoebe did not bat an eyelid at them breaking and entering.

"Stay here," he commanded her, following in after Jack.

"Not on your life," she retorted, surprising him not a bit.

Max sighed. "Fine, just stay behind me."

He took a tight hold of her hand to make sure she had no choice as they moved quietly into the house. It was soon abundantly clear that Alvanly had been prepared to leave. Max cursed and raised an eyebrow as Phoebe muttered something similar under her breath, but he did not consider remonstrating with her. It would not endear him to her and, in the circumstances, she was entitled to relieve her feelings.

"Princess," Jack barked, waving a crumpled bit of paper he'd taken from an overflowing wastepaper basket. Alvanly might have had time to prepare for his midnight flit, but arranging housekeeping had clearly not played a part in his plans. "Lookie here."

"What is it, Jack?"

"A timetable for the steamboat. Reckon the blighter is off to France."

Max groaned. "Of course. He'll sell the painting in Paris. He'd know his reputation would be shredded here so he's burnt his boats, but he could live well on the proceeds. Damnation, but the devil will evade us."

"That he won't," Jack growled. "I'll go after him. If I 'ave to turn Paris upside down and inside out, I'll get the painting back, Princess. My word on it."

"Oh, no, Jack. At least," Phoebe added. "Indeed *we* will, but you cannot go alone. You don't speak a word of French, and I'm fluent, thanks to all those wretched lessons Papa made me take. And, after all, I made this mess. I think I ought to clear it up."

Jack snorted and shook his head. "You reckon I'd take you along? You're queer in your attic, little lady, that's what you are."

Phoebe crossed her arms, a mutinous expression on her face that Max recognised all too well. "This is all my fault, Jack. I will go, with or without you, but I promised Papa that I'd keep myself safe, so I'd much rather it was with you."

"Your father will string me up by my... never you mind whats! *No.* No. I won't have it, Princess."

Max watched, thoughtful as the argument flew back and forth between them. He stuck his hands in his pockets and discovered the rope that Alvanly had tied Phoebe up with. The bastard. He drew it out, wondering how it had gotten there, and a small slip of paper fluttered to the ground. Max picked it up and stared at it, an odd feeling in his chest.

Do something out of character.

Max would *never* do something as reckless and idiotic as chase a villain halfway across France in search of a stolen painting in company with an unmarried young lady and an ex-highwayman. Never in a million years. He was too sensible for such nonsense. Too level-headed.

Too... dull.

Phoebe thought to set him free from his promise to marry her. She did not want him to marry her. She thought him old and boring and....

"We'll all go."

There was a silence so profound it rang in his ears. Both Phoebe and Jack stared at him, mouths agape. Well, at least he'd surprised them.

"Phoebe, you cannot travel alone, no matter that Jack is there to escort you. You have no maid, no one to accompany you, but if you were in company with your husband—"

"Oh, Max!" Phoebe exclaimed, her eyes bright with excitement, and such a look of admiration that his heart gave the oddest little flutter in his chest. "Do you mean it. Truly? You'll come with us?"

Max quailed as he considered Lucian's wrath when he discovered what he'd done. Well, faint heart and fair maidens and all that....

"I will."

Phoebe squealed and threw her arms about his neck for the second time that night, kissing his cheek. "How marvellous you are, and I do know I don't deserve it, but thank you, Max!"

For just a moment he basked in the glow of her approval, and then he caught sight of Jack's expression. He looked as if he'd returned to the idea of ripping Max's head off.

"Now, wait just a minute, lord," he said, his voice deep and forbidding and enough to make all the fine hairs on the back of Max's neck stand on end. "You ain't married."

"No," Max said, glaring at the man. "But I have told the *ton* I proposed, and Miss Barrington accepted. That is a binding agreement. I am honour bound to marry her now and, I assure you, I am a gentleman. If there were time to marry her before we left, I would, but the day we return I will make her my wife, and you may shoot me dead if I fail to do so."

"Oh, may I?" Jack rumbled, something dark and daunting glittering in his eyes. "Well, that's right nice of you. Reckon I'll take you up on that."

"Reckon we will," his companion, Fred, echoed, earning himself an irritated glance from Jack.

"Oh, Jack, do stop growling at Max and trying to frighten him. The poor man is helping me, and not for the first time. Really, I have been the most unrewarding friend to him, yet he never fails to step in. He hasn't even scolded me yet, and I know I roundly deserve it. You may scold me later, Max," she said kindly, reaching to take his hand. "Only I do feel we ought to hurry."

Max swallowed down the bubble of laughter that was threatening, fearing he might sound a tad bit hysterical.

"Yes. Later," he managed, nodding gravely. "Jack, you best go via my home so I can pack and get funds enough for such a journey. Phoebe can't go home without having to answer a great many questions, so we shall have to buy her what she needs on the way."

Jack returned another dark look, which Max met unwaveringly. After a long moment, Jack grunted and returned to the carriage. Max felt he'd passed a test. He sighed, and turned to discover Phoebe watching him.

"Are you sure you want to do this?" she asked, anxiety glinting in her eyes, which shone silver grey in the moonlight.

Max smiled and nodded. "I'm sure."

"Why?" The word was almost whispered, and he felt the answer was important to her, so considered his words with care.

"I think perhaps I should like to have an adventure."

A smile dawned on her face, bright as sunlight, dazzling him. "Really?"

He nodded, certain now that he was telling the truth. "Really."

She watched as he held his hand out to her, and Max felt a burst of happiness surge through him as she gave him hers. Phoebe looked up and Max laughed, bubbling over with everything he felt. God, this was insanity, utter madness… and he would not miss it for the world.

***

By the time Max had packed, soothed the ruffled feathers of his indignant valet, whom he felt it prudent to leave behind, and arranged funds enough for the journey, the first touches of daylight were staining the night sky.

Phoebe dozed in the carriage, curled up on the seat opposite him, his greatcoat draped over her for warmth. Max wondered at her ability to sleep, for he was alive with anticipation, with excitement, with… his conscience shouting at him, louder and louder with each moment that passed. He was about to take Phoebe on a journey with him which would leave her utterly ruined. That she must marry him now, or she'd be ruined anyway did not seem to quiet the voice that told him he was being a reckless fool. That voice was quite eloquent about the reception he would get from Lucian when they returned home. Both he and Phoebe had written letters to her parents, and Max had made many promises in his, which he prayed might be enough to stop the marquess from slicing him up one tiny sliver at a time.

He looked around as Jack gestured to him from outside the carriage and got out quietly, not wanting to disturb Phoebe.

"Any sign?" he asked.

Jack scowled and shook his head.

"Not a sniff of the shiftless cove," he grumbled. "Reckon he must have changed his mind and arranged passage with smugglers or something of the sort for he's not booked on any of the regular crossings. Stands to reason he'd not want to leave a trail to follow."

Max nodded, disheartened but unsurprised. "Ah well, it was too much to hope for, I suppose."

"You're certain he'll head for Paris?"

"Yes." On this at least he felt confident. "I doubt Alvanly has connections of the sort to get the best price for the painting, but there are dealers enough in Paris with access to the kind of wealthy buyers who won't ask too many awkward questions. He'd not be able to sell it here in time before he was caught, not now."

"Right, then. Paris it is," Jack said. Max went to turn away, but Jack laid a meaty hand on his arm, stilling him. "You'll marry her?"

Max nodded.

"Not just for duty though, eh?"

For a moment Max hesitated, wondering what exactly to say, but it was clear this fellow would walk through fire for Phoebe and it would be wise to discover what it was Lucian saw in the man so, he took a risk.

"I'd have asked her anyway, if I'd thought there was the slightest chance she'd have me."

"You don't care she's illegitimate?"

Max scowled at him, something hot and angry unfurling in his stomach. "I do not."

"Ah," Jack said, nodding thoughtfully, and Max wondered if perhaps that was approval in his eyes. "Does the lord know?"

For a moment Max thought he was asking if God was aware of his feelings, and stared, a little taken aback. Then the penny dropped. "Oh, Montagu. Yes. He knows."

"And he approves?"

Max nodded. "For all the good it does me. Phoebe—Miss Barrington—does not see me as... as a suitor. I believe she considers me too staid and sensible, but—"

"But you're hopin' this little lark might help her change her mind."

Jack stared at him: a piercing, somewhat unnerving scrutiny that made Max's ears feel hot. He cleared his throat.

"Yes," he said, a touch defiantly. "I suppose I am."

The stare continued for a moment longer, and then Jack pursed his lips. "Right ho, then. We'd better get moving. They'll be boarding soon."

Max nodded, once again with the slightly unsteadying feeling of having passed some kind of test. He only hoped he didn't fail one of them, especially whilst they were at sea. Jack looked well capable of pitching him overboard if the mood took him.

He climbed back into the carriage and closed the door quietly, but Phoebe stirred as the carriage moved forward. She blinked owlishly in the dim light, then her gaze settled on Max and her eyes opened very wide.

"Oh, now I remember," she said, sitting up in a rush. His coat slithered from her shoulders and she looked at it in surprise. "You gave me your coat."

"I was afraid you might be cold."

The smile she returned was pleased and a little shy, and quite unlike any he'd ever seen from her before. It struck his heart with the force of a hammer blow.

"That was kind, thank you."

"My pleasure," he said, somewhat winded still.

"What time is it?"

"Close to seven in the morning. We're about to board."

She drew in a shaky breath and it occurred to him that perhaps she was nervous. "Have you ever been on a boat before?"

Phoebe shook her head. "Not at sea."

"It will be fine."

"Yes," she said, brightly, nodding too vigorously to be convincing. "Yes, of course it will, and I'm so looking forward to seeing Paris. I mean, I know we are in pursuit of the painting, and if we catch up with Alvanly quickly, there may be no need to continue, but...."

"We'll see Paris," he promised her, wanting to do anything, give her anything, to make her keep smiling at him. It worked, and her delighted expression left him giddy with pleasure.

"Oh," she said on a breath of delight, and then frowned a little, folding her hands neatly in her lap. "And you mustn't worry, Max. I have learned my lesson, truly I have. I shan't get into any more scrapes or embarrass you. I shall behave properly, I promise."

What? No!

"Oh, there's no need for that," he said at once, but she shook her head, a frown drawing her eyebrows together.

"Yes, there is. You're being too kind, but you've always been kind. I can see that now. I... I was just too headstrong and stupid to see it before, and I'm sorry for that. I think perhaps I need to grow up, and I shall. I give you my word."

Max stared at her, wanting to demand she take it back. He didn't want her to change a bit. He'd fallen in love with her madcap ways and the scandalous things she said, and the fact she was so astonishingly, vibrantly alive. He could say nothing else, though, as Jack came and opened the door.

"Right, we're on. You've got a private cabin, lord. They're arranging for someone to show you to it."

"Thank you," Max said, stepping out of the carriage and helping Phoebe down.

She looked out across a grey sea, the waves topped with little white fringes, and swallowed hard.

"Oh, dear," she said.

Chapter 8

My dearest Papa,

Please don't be cross...

—Excerpt of a letter to The Most Honourable Lucian Barrington, Marquess of Montagu, from Miss Phoebe Barrington.

~~My Lord Marquess,~~

Lucian,

~~I hardly know where to begin.~~

I'll marry her.

—Excerpt of a letter to The Most Honourable Lucian Barrington, Marquess of Montagu, from The Right Hon'ble Maximillian Carmichael, Earl of Ellisborough

8th April 1827. Calais, Pas-de-Calais, France.

"Are you feeling better?"

"Yes, thank you," Phoebe said, lying through her teeth. She was damned if she would be any more of a nuisance to Max, though. As it was, she was burning with mortification and she had never missed Pippin more in her life. Pippin would have known what to do, and would have had some disgusting mixture at hand, which would have made her quite well in no time at all.

Pippin was not there, however, but tucked up comfortably in a neat little cottage at Dern. Phoebe sighed. As someone who rarely succumbed to so much as a sniffle, to have been brought so low by seasickness was incomprehensible and infuriating. Yet, no amount of willpower could rule her ungovernable stomach, and she'd been violently ill for the entire crossing. Worse still, it wasn't even that rough, according to Jack. She could have wept at that information, handed over so cheerfully once they were back on solid ground. Not that it felt solid. It was still swaying and pitching as far as her stomach was concerned, though they'd been disembarked for the best part of two hours. It had taken an age for Max to bribe the necessary officials, as she did not have a passport, and neither did Jack nor Fred… a fact which had not even occurred to her.

In exasperation, he'd finally been forced into telling a whopping lie and had told the *douanier* they had just eloped and were just newly married, so he had not had time to put her on his passport. This, at last, had convinced them—this being France, after all—and they had let him go.

Phoebe glanced up at him, remembering how kind Max had been when she was ill, and how utterly horrified she still was at having had him see her in such a revolting state. To have such a man treat her so gently, holding the basin for her to be sick into…. Oh, she wanted to die. She was still in the dress she had worn last night, which was crumpled and wrinkled beyond saving. Her hair was a mess, as she'd not had the energy to put it to rights, and she was well aware she looked a fright. How was it only now, when he'd seen her at her very worst, when she'd dragged him into this terrible situation, that she saw what she had failed to notice before?

Max was rather wonderful.

He'd not once reproached her for entangling him into this ungodly mess, or for forcing him into a marriage he could surely not look upon with anything but regret. By neither word nor deed had he made her feel the least bit to blame, when she knew it was entirely her fault. Not only was he kind and patient and unfailingly good-humoured, he was also dreadfully handsome.

Phoebe watched him covertly, studying him for perhaps the first time, and discovering herself unsettled by what she saw. She'd always thought the grey hair at his temples made him look rather severe, but it was more that it gave him an air of gravity, of dependability, of a man who would never let you down. Something she now knew was true. His dark eyes—which she'd believed so disapproving—were in fact warm and full of humour, and crinkled at the corners when he smiled... which he did far more often than she might have credited, especially given the circumstances. He also had a square jaw with a little cleft, which was rather adorable, and that she was itching to touch. If she were honest—and Phoebe was always honest—it wasn't the only bit of him she wanted to touch.

She remembered last night, when he'd rescued her from her bindings—rather heroically, now she came to think of it—and she'd thrown herself at his neck. He'd been warm and so solid, and when he'd *eventually* put his arms about her, it had felt...wonderful. So wonderful she'd not wanted to let him go, startled by the rush of feeling she'd experienced in his arms. He had only done what he ought, to comfort her as she'd been overwrought, she knew that. If he'd wanted her in his arms, she supposed he'd have been a bit more enthusiastic about responding to her, but she could hardly blame him. She acted abominably, and now he'd been forced to offer for her. The most terrible part of it all was, she was beginning to see marrying Max in a new light, but he'd only offered because he had to. The idea made her feel sick again.

So, she was turning over a new leaf. She would be a well-behaved, polite, young lady. She would no longer be a hoyden, but behave with decorum and perhaps... *perhaps*, if she tried very hard, Max would decide that marrying her wouldn't be *so* bad.

***

Once Max had dealt with the *bureau* of the customs house, he'd been quite out of temper. Despite being an English lord, or perhaps because of it, he'd been subjected to a rigorous search, from his boots—the polished shine of which was now smeared with fingerprints—and even the band of his hat, for heaven's sake, followed quickly by an interrogation as to his purpose in France that would have satisfied the Spanish Inquisition. What the *douaniers* expected an English earl to be smuggling out of the country he could not fathom, but then he remembered Baron Alvanly had smuggled a priceless artwork and decided he'd best keep his mouth shut. Still, it was not the treatment he was used to, and even the saintliest tempered of men would have found themselves hard pressed to withstand it with equanimity.

That Jack and Fred passed by relatively unmolested did not help matters. Next, they were inundated by *touters,* that breed of fellows who snapped up passengers and all but press-ganged them into staying at the hotel for which they worked. The Hotel de Bourbon at least employed a *commissionaire,* which meant they did not have the further indignity of presenting themselves and their passports at the Mairie. The price of this service was so shocking Max almost protested, but one look at Phoebe's wan face told him she needed to rest, and so he swallowed his ire and demanded they be taken to their room at once.

The moment Phoebe was settled, with a maid in attendance to help her with her toilette, Max sought out the manager once more. The rather inappropriately named Monsieur Joly was a neat, prim little fellow with a small perfectly shaped moustache. The pince nez that perched so precariously on the end of his nose seemed to defy gravity, and Max watched in fascination for the moment they gave into the inevitable and fell off.

"There was a mishap with my wife's luggage on the journey here," Max said, wishing he was better at lying through his teeth and determined to be as inscrutable as Montagu by the time this adventure was over. Practise made perfect, after all, and he had the daunting premonition that he was about to get practice a-plenty. "And she is in urgent need of a new wardrobe. I trust that you can accommodate her needs here in Calais."

The manager's eyes grew very wide behind his ridiculous spectacles, which quivered on his nose. "*Mais, monseigneur*, you tell me you stay only one night and leave in the morning, *c'est impossible!*"

"Nothing is impossible, Monsieur Joly," Max said curtly and placed an outrageous pile of gold coins on the manager's desk. "Not if one is suitably motivated."

Monsieur Joly's eyes lit up and he returned a confident smile. "*Mais, oui, monseigneur,* you ask, and I, Monsieur Joly, will provide."

"I felt sure you would," Max replied dryly. "If you would be so good as to send our dinner to our rooms. A light supper for Lady Ellisborough, if you please. She suffered rather on our journey over."

"Ah, *le mal de mer,* is an 'orrible thing, *monseigneur.* I will have something prepared, light as a feather, *oui?*"

"*Oui,*" Max replied with a distracted nod, feeling somewhat overcome as he realised it was the first time he had referred to Phoebe as Lady Ellisborough.

Lady Ellisborough. Lady Phoebe Ellisborough.

His chest felt tight with hope, and a tentative happiness he had all but given up on. Well, she might not have the title legally yet, but in his heart it was hers and always would be, if only she would take it.

***

Phoebe awoke in the early evening as the pleasant scent of food drifted through the room. Sniffing appreciatively as her stomach gave an audible and hopeful growl, she sat up and then squealed with alarm. Max nearly leapt out of his skin, almost dropping the silver domed cover on the dish he'd been inspecting.

"Oh, I do beg your pardon," she said, once more mortified.

Lud. What a ninny he would think her. They were travelling as man and wife, were they not? Of course they would share a room. Only, this was Max, who was always so conventional, and she had assumed that... that....

Phoebe held the bed covers up to her neck as she realised she was wearing nothing but a thin shift, and Max hurriedly replaced the cover and turned his back.

"Forgive me," he said, sounding a little strained. "They just brought the meal in and... and the bedroom is rather warmer than... and I thought it would look odd... but.... You need not worry. There is a perfectly comfortable day bed in the attached sitting room. I shall sleep there. Don't... Don't be alarmed."

This rather awkward and disjointed statement made her feel even more a fool as she realised that of course, *of course*, Max would not think of her in such a way, let alone take advantage of her. He was far too much the gentleman for that.

"It's quite all right," she said, striving to sound calm and matter of fact, as if she dined with gentlemen in her rooms all the time. "It's only you gave me a start. I did not expect to see you in my room."

"Naturally," he replied and, though his back was turned, she could hear the smile in the word and blushed. How ridiculous. "I believe you will find a dressing gown on the bed. I have made arrangements for gowns and shoes and... and everything else you might need to be brought to you by morning."

"Goodness," Phoebe said, impressed. "So quickly. However did you manage it?"

"Well, I haven't yet, but let us hope the manager has managed it, at least."

Phoebe laughed and reached for the dressing gown, which was a rather lovely deep plum velvet, and very warm and snug, if a little too big. "Did you bribe him or bully him?"

"Oh, bribery, of course. I detest bullies."

Phoebe laughed. "I'm glad to hear it. You may turn around now."

"Are you feeling better?"

"I am," Phoebe said, moving towards the table. "And I'm famished."

"Excellent." Max pulled out a chair for her and she gave him a swift smile and sat down. "It all looks rather good."

It was, and Phoebe practically inhaled two bowls of soup, which Max insisted she must have to ensure her stomach was quite recovered, before attacking the *carbonnade flamande*. A traditional local dish, it was a beef stew with a distinct sweet and sour flavour, and was served with a spiced bread which was quite delicious.

"More?" Max asked politely, viewing her empty plate with an amused eye.

Phoebe blushed, realising she'd barely spoken to him at all, too intent on feeding her face. Good heavens, what a mannerless hoyden he must think her. She cast the dish of stew a regretful look and shook her head.

"No, thank you. I have had sufficient."

"Stuff," Max said with a chuckle. "You're still ravenous, and you've some colour in your cheeks at last. Come, have a little more, to please me."

Phoebe stared at him, wondering if it were possible to fall in love with a man for offering her a second helping instead of looking disapproving when she took it. It seemed to her to be perfectly reasonable to do so.

"Thank you."

Max gave her a generous second helping before serving himself, and they ate in companionable silence for a while.

"That was excellent," he said with approval, pushing away his empty plate. "And this claret is very tolerable. Perhaps we should buy some wine whilst we are here. The cellars at Ellisborough could do with replenishing. I'm afraid I've rather neglected them, not being much of a one for entertaining. At least, I haven't been," he added hurriedly. "I don't particularly care for hunting parties, and one needs a wife for... well. I should enjoy giving parties and balls, if... if you should like to."

Phoebe blushed scarlet, wondering how on earth he managed it. She'd hardly ever blushed in her life before this wretched affair began, and now it was becoming a problem.

"Max...." She knew she sounded utterly miserable but, really, she must tell him he was under no obligation to her. "I think perhaps—"

"Of course, it's late," he said, getting to his feet at once. "And you must be exhausted. Forgive me for keeping you up so late. I shall leave you now to get some rest. I shall see you in the morning. Goodnight, Phoebe. Sleep well."

"G-Goodnight, Max," Phoebe replied, a little dazed by how speedily he'd dismissed himself. Good heavens, had he been so desperate to quit her company? The thought made a wash of regret and sadness fill her chest, which she told herself was stupid. She knew Max did not wish for her company. He only tolerated her because of his esteem for her father, and because he was too much of a gentleman to abandon her in such a fix as she was in.

But then she remembered the way he'd looked when he'd told her he'd wanted an adventure, and hope stirred to life anyway.

"Lud, you are a fool, Phoebe Barrington," she scolded herself, and went to bed.

***

Max closed the adjoining door with a sigh, and leaned back against it. He knew it had been cowardly to make such a speedy exit, but he'd felt certain Phoebe had been about to kindly explain why she could never marry him, not even if the alternative was ruination. That she would prefer that to the horror of being his wife made his chest tight. Yet, she did not seem to dislike him. She even seemed to enjoy his company, but... but he had the lowering suspicion that she could not bear the idea of having him touch her and for that he could have wept. She really did think of him as a kindly uncle, then: one of her father's friends, to whom she would be endlessly grateful, and whom she would rather die a thousand deaths than take to her bed.

With an aching heart and a sense of impending doom, Max knew there was little to look forward to other than a broken heart once this adventure was done. Not to mention Lucian's wrath. If he'd stopped her from haring off on this mad adventure rather than joining her, they could have weathered the gossip well enough and allowed Phoebe to break off their fictitious engagement. There would have been talk, of course, but Montagu could have managed that. Now, though... now she had undertaken a voyage to Paris alone with him. There was no coming back from that if she refused to marry him. Yet having a wife whom he adored to the point of madness, but who merely tolerated him, was enough to make him reach for the brandy decanter. He'd not sleep now, not unless he was foxed, so he may as well get on with it.

***

Phoebe awoke the next morning to find the maid who had helped her undress last night squealing with delight over a great pile of gowns and a tumble of hat boxes.

"Good heavens!" she said, scrambling out of bed to inspect the rather lavish mound of fabrics. "*Good heavens!*" she said again, with rather more force as she saw what Max had provided for her.

"You will look perfectly ravishing, Lady Ellisborough," the young woman said, wide-eyed with awe, as well she might be.

"Good heavens, Max! Whatever have you done?" Phoebe said, biting her lip against the giggle trying to escape, for she had been correct in her estimation that it would be impossible to provide a wardrobe for her overnight.

The manager had clearly done his best, and everything that had been provided was the height of Parisian fashion—for a highflyer. The necklines were nigh on indecent, and the dresses an impossible indulgence of huge gigot sleeves and ribbons and ruffles, and... good heavens.

"Oh, la la!" the maid squeaked, holding up a corset so indecent Phoebe blushed scarlet.

The two of them looked at each other, and fell about laughing.

With some difficulty, Phoebe selected the least shocking of the clothes provided, remembering her new determination to be a proper young lady and not make a spectacle of herself. The effect was spoiled by the scandalous under-things, which—even though no one but her knew they were there—made her feel quite wicked. She fought to ignore them, but it was difficult. Still, the maid, whose name was Yvette, was gazing at her with such wonder she believed that she would not embarrass Max by looking either dowdy or cheap.

The pelisse-robe was a soft sage colour with huge gigot sleeves stiffened at the top with whalebone, and they were the largest Phoebe had ever seen. If there was a strong gust of wind, she saw the daunting possibility of being lifted clear off the floor. The sleeves then narrowed and became tightly fitting with a complicated arrangement of laces. The waist was tightly nipped in and belted, and the full skirts trimmed with several scalloped flounces. Yellow limerick gloves and matching half boots completed the ensemble. It was far more outrageous and frivolous than anything she'd ever worn before and, by the time Yvette had wrestled her hair into some ridiculously fashionable coiffure, and she'd put on the enormous Leghorn hat that came with the dress,

Phoebe felt like a cross between a duchess and a bride cake with too many decorations.

Having swallowed a cup of chocolate and eaten far too many delicate little pastries called *Kipferls* that had been presented alongside it, Phoebe was ready to face Max again. She could not wait to see his face and see if he thought it all as ridiculous as she did.

Momentarily forgetting her vow to act with decorum, she almost ran down the stairs to discover Max waiting in the grand entrance hall for her. His mouth fell open as he saw her. Not only his, however. The entire hotel, which she now saw was quite bustling with patrons, stopped in their tracks to stare.

Phoebe blushed, and wondered if, yet again, she had done nothing but embarrass him.

Chapter 9

My dear Pippin,

We are returning to Dern and I beg you to be waiting to attend Matilda. She is quite out of sorts, increasingly pale and lethargic, and I don't mind telling you I am out of my mind with worry. She has swooned twice in the last week, which she assures me she has never done in her life before. Pippin, I <u>cannot</u> lose her. I shall go mad. I cannot even consider my life without

I beg you to discover what ails her. The vexing creature refuses to see another doctor here and will have no one but you attend her. So, we will be with you midmorning tomorrow, all being well, and I pray you might put my fears to rest.

—Excerpt of a letter to Mrs 'Pippin' Appleton from The Most Honourable Lucian Barrington, Marquess of Montagu.

9th April 1827. Montagu House, St James's, London.

Matilda took a deep breath and forced herself to stand up, fighting past the sudden wave of dizziness. She clutched the back of the chair by the dressing table, willing herself not to swoon again for fear Lucian would cart her off to the nearest doctor by force. Her reflection in the mirror spoke volumes of yet another sleepless night and a lack of energy so profound that all she wanted was to turn around and go straight back to bed. She had never in her life wanted to sleep the day away, but at this moment it seemed an appealing prospect.

In other circumstances, she would have believed herself with child and be delighted, but it was not that. The symptoms were not the same, for she had not had the slightest bit of nausea, and she had not been so dreadfully tired with the boys. Besides which, Thomas' birth had been long and difficult, and her monthly courses had all but disappeared ever since. She had visited several of the most prominent doctors in the country and all had agreed she was no longer fertile. She was too old, and the last birth had taken its toll and damaged her womb. There would be no more children. Even Pippin had agreed it was unlikely, and had nothing to suggest except to prescribe red clover tea, which Matilda drank several times a day, knowing it was hopeless. Although she had been disappointed, having so wished to have given Lucian a little girl, she knew she had nothing at all to be disappointed about. She had given Lucian his heirs and they were her greatest pride and joy, as well as their father's. They had been blessed indeed, and she would not be so ungrateful as to wish for more. Yet if this malaise, which had come on so gradually and worsened so steadily, was not a child, she feared to consider what it might be.

Lucian was terrified.

She could see it in his eyes, and sense it in the way he held her, touching her as though she were fragile, as though she might break. He said nothing to her, of course, only agreed that she was tired, that the boys had run her ragged, the season had been too energetic, etcetera, etcetera. Except they both knew she had never lacked for energy before, and that it was nothing of the sort.

Determined that she would not behave like some swooning heroine in a Gothic novel, she took another deep breath and made her way down the stairs.

"Goodness, what a slugabed you've let me turn into," she said cheerfully as she strode into the breakfast room with a smile for her beautiful husband.

And, Lord, he was handsome still. More so, she thought, though it seemed impossible. But the past twelve years had only made him more imposing than ever. On the rare occasions he omitted to shave, she had noticed a scattering of white against the darker gold of his stubble, but there were no other visible signs of age, and he was as vigorous and vital as he had ever been. Unlike her, sadly.

"Whyever didn't you wake me?" she asked as she closed the door.

Lucian was standing by the window, staring down at a letter. He looked up as she came in. One look at his face and her pretence of jollity fell away.

"Oh, my darling, whatever is the matter?" She rushed to him, putting her hand to his cheek.

He covered it with his own and took a deep breath.

"Phoebe," he said shortly. "She...."

To Matilda's astonishment, he gave a breathless laugh and shook his head.

"Oh, Lord, that girl will kill me. Except that I'm rather afraid she might kill poor Max first."

"Max and Phoebe?" Matilda repeated, bewildered. "Lucian, if you don't explain at once—"

Silently, he handed her the letter. Except, she saw now that there were two letters, one from Phoebe and another from Max. She moved to the breakfast table and sank into a chair to read.

"Alvanly! Oh, the villain!" she cried as she read through as quickly as she could. "Oh, Phoebe, oh, you silly goose."

Matilda looked up, staring at Lucian.

"Thank God for Max. He'll marry her. It will be all right." Lucian did not look away, but said nothing, and Matilda nodded, swallowing. "If she'll have him."

"If she'll have him," he repeated dully, turning back to the window and staring at the square beyond.

"You should go after them, I suppose."

"No." That one word was firm and definite, and Matilda looked up, shocked.

"Lucian!"

He turned around and walked back to her, sinking to his knees before her and taking her hands. "Max is a good man. I trust him, and Phoebe is a reckless hoyden, and I should like to wring her pretty neck, but she's not a fool. They will figure things out between them, and they do not need me poking my nose in and making things worse. If she marries him, as I pray she will, I will rejoice and wish them happy. If not, I shall support her and protect her in any way I can, but if you think I would leave you *now*...."

His voice quavered and he closed his mouth, his jaw rigid.

Matilda's heart ached. If they discovered she was seriously unwell, she feared for him far more than for herself. If anything happened to her, she knew it would break him.

"Lucian, do not worry so. I'm sure once I get to Dern and have some proper rest, I will be quite well again. No doubt Pippin will have some evil concoction to force down my throat that will make me want to vomit, and I'll be right as rain in a matter of days."

He nodded, holding her hands tightly.

"Yes," he said, smiling at her, though terror lurked in his eyes. "Yes. Pippin will put it all to rights."

She returned his smile and he drew her hands to his mouth, kissing each one in turn with such tenderness Matilda blinked back tears.

"I love you," he said. "So much."

"I love you too."

He looked up then, his silver eyes glittering with fear and pain.

"Always," he said fiercely.

Matilda nodded. "Always."

***

9th April 1827. Hôtel du Bourbon, Calais, Pas-de-Calais, France.

Max felt rather than heard the collective intake of breath from those around him, and instinctively looked up towards the stairs, only to acknowledge the sensation of being hit in the head with a heavy blunt object.

Good God.

He was doomed.

All but skipping down the stairs was a vivacious confection in pale green silk. A confection was, indeed, the only description, and Max longed to unwrap her to discover the delights hidden beneath. The hat had clearly been designed by a mad woman as it was enormous and embellished with wide black-and-green striped ribbons and, enough ostrich feathers to allow the wearer to fly to Paris. The illusion was not diminished by the huge sleeves of the pelisse gown, which were trailing laces. Everything moved, from the rustling skirts to the ribbons and feathers on the hat, and the insane profusion of curls that framed Phoebe's lovely face as she hurried towards him. She slowed as she noticed everyone watching her, a pretty flush pinking her cheeks, which made him want to pick her up and carry her back up the stairs so he might ravish her in private. Except that she would be disgusted and hate him for it, so he forced his desires aside with aching regret and moved to greet her.

"Good morning," he said, trying to smile, though the longing in his chest made his expression feel stiff and rigid. He only hoped it looked natural.

"G-Good morning, my lord," she replied, dipping a curtsey.

Good heavens, why was she being so formal?

Max took a breath and tried to dispel the suddenly tense atmosphere. It only worsened as he noticed many of the men gazing at Phoebe with such envy that he felt a burst of irritation.

"You look...." he began, finding his voice inexplicably husky and unable to grasp at words appropriate to describe what he saw.

Edible was the only one that seemed to fit, and he doubted that would charm her. More likely, she'd run back up the stairs and lock herself in her room.

"Ridiculous," she said, laughing, though he thought it an oddly brittle sound. "Yes, I know. Your Monsieur Joly did the best he could, I'm sure, but this was the most respectable outfit I could find in what he sent over. I tried not to cause you embarrassment, I swear, but if you think this outrageous, you should see the under-things. They're all lace and little scarlet silk bows and ribbons, even the garters, and—"

Max felt some thread of sanity inside him snap.

"Phoebe," he said in a harsh whisper. "For the love of God, don't discuss your undergarments."

She blushed then, almost as scarlet as the damned ribbons he'd be thinking about for the rest of this damnable journey.

"I beg your pardon, Max," she said, looking so mortified he wanted to pull her to him and beg her forgiveness.

Oh, God, he'd discuss her undergarments all the way to Paris, and with pleasure, but not if she did not wish him to see them for himself. That way lay madness, and he was already well on the way.

He offered her his arm, unable to rectify the matter when half of Calais seemed to watch them.

"Come along," he said, moderating his voice to something less intense. "The carriage is waiting."

"Oh, but I am sorry… I didn't mean to…."

Max felt a surge of irritation with her apology and waved it aside. She ought to kick him in the shins for being such a brute. She *would* have, he was certain, before he'd told the world he would marry her. Now there was more restraint between them than ever, and he did not know how to fix it.

He guided her outside to where Jack had just fixed the extra trunks containing Phoebe's new wardrobe onto the carriage. He turned, his eyes growing wide as he looked at her. Even Fred snatched off his hat as he saw Phoebe approach, goggling in amazement. Jack whistled, low and approving.

"Blimey, Princess—and you look like one, I tell you. Strike me dead if I tell a lie. The high kick, you are, and that's a fact."

Max smothered his annoyance at not having managed half such a compliment, and only hated himself more for the wan smile Phoebe returned.

"Thank you, Jack," she said quietly as Max handed her into the carriage.

Jack glared at him, as well he might, but Max got in and slammed the door shut before he could be subjected to an interrogation. Phoebe did not look at him, but stared out of the window as the carriage rocked to life. Just moments ago she had been alive with life and happiness and, somehow, he had ruined it all. He wanted to kick himself for his stupidity. He'd never been nervous or clumsy around women before. Though he was not, and had never wished to be considered, a lady's man, he knew how to flirt, how to seduce, and yet he need only get within twenty feet of Phoebe and he turned into a blithering idiot.

"It should be a fine day, I think, once the cloud has lifted," he said, wincing inwardly. The weather. *Really*? That was the best he could do? He deserved to be shot.

"Yes, indeed," Phoebe replied.

This was intolerable.

"Jack was right," he said in a rush, his voice too loud in the confined space.

She lifted her eyes to his, a slight frown between the fine blonde brows that he ached to smooth away with a fingertip.

"About what?"

"You do look like a princess."

"Oh."

There was that pretty blush again, the soft pink one that put him in mind of rose petals, not quite as dark a shade of pink as her lips. Wilfully ignoring his express instructions to behave itself, his libido kicked in, and suddenly he wondered if her nipples were the same delicate shade as her mouth. His body grew taut with desire.

"I-I didn't think you liked it."

"I like it," he managed gruffly, forcing himself to stare out of the window and think about crop rotation and grain yields per acre.

"Thank goodness, for if you think this frivolous, I dare not consider how you might react to the rest of what was sent."

Though he knew it was foolish, Max returned his attention to her.

"Is it dreadfully scandalous?" he asked with interest, unable to exorcise visions of lace-edged corsets and garters trimmed with scarlet ribbons from his wicked mind.

Phoebe bit her lip, which made his gaze fall to her mouth.

She nodded. "It is, rather."

"Then this should be a fascinating trip," he said lightly, somehow sounding amused when he felt as if he was being subjected to torture by a dizzying vision of red satin bows that still danced in his imagination.

"You weren't angry, then?" she asked, staring at him in confusion.

Max shook his head.

"You were when I mentioned the corset," she said flatly.

He could not tell her she was wrong without explaining the real reason.

"Which is quite unfair, Max, really, as you mentioned my corset when you came to my birthday. You told me I had it laced too tightly."

"So I did," he said, aching to move, to sit beside her, to take her into his arms, disarrange those artful curls and send the mad hat tumbling to the floor with a flurry of ribbons and plumes.

"You were right, of course," she added with a sigh, which made him smile. "Max?" she said a moment later, her voice quiet. "Is… is something wrong?"

Max jolted as he realised he'd been staring at her with the intensity of a starving dog outside a butcher's shop. He cleared his throat and shook his head, reminding himself sternly he was a gentleman and he had no business thinking such things unless she agreed to marry him.

"No," he said firmly. "Not a thing."

Chapter 10

Dear Prue,

I am so sorry, but I must refuse your delightful invitation to dine tomorrow night. I would have so liked to have seen you and caught up, but we are returning to Dern tomorrow and to be honest we have been thrown into quite a panic. You will never believe what Phoebe has done this time....

—Excerpt of a letter to Her Grace, Prunella Adolphus, the Duchess of Bedwin, from The Most Honourable Matilda Barrington, Marchioness of Montagu.

9th April 1827. Palais Impérial, Boulogne sur Mer, France.

"Really, Max, do be sensible. It's the only way we will pick up the trail. It's all very well believing Alvanly is going to Paris, but if he gets there before us, we shall have the very devil of a time tracking him down. Asking a few innocent questions will not put me beyond the pale, especially as I am travelling with m-my... my husband."

Phoebe cursed herself for stammering, but the idea of Max as her husband had become something as rare and magical as a unicorn—the kind of thing she'd love to see but had no expectation of, for it was impossible. She did not know how to interpret his behaviour. Half the time he stared at her as if he was trying to read her mind, and the other half he acted as though she did not exist.

She'd been certain he was ashamed of her and the stir she'd caused at the hotel, but then he'd said she looked like a princess. One minute he was kind and affectionate, even a little flirtatious, and the next she felt he was annoyed with her. If only Mama were here, she lamented. She would know what to make of it.

Usually if a man liked her, he would write her poetry, or bring her flowers, or try to kiss her. Max had done none of those things in all the time she'd known him. He *had* bought her some exceptionally fine books, which she'd liked far more than poems, and for her birthday the most exquisite tortoiseshell bird box. It had a small enamelled lid on top, which popped up to display a tiny feathered automaton of a bird which flapped its wings and hopped about, singing the most delightful song. It was one of her most treasured possessions, and it had utterly charmed her. How foolish she had been not to have been charmed by the giver as quickly. She had been blind. Surely, he would not have given her such a beautiful and expensive gift just because of her father's friendship... would he?

Confused, she returned her attention to the ongoing argument. They had stopped to change horses at Boulogne sur Mer, and Max had acceded to her wish to explore the town a little and see if they could discover news of Alvanly. So, they had come to the Palais Impérial—so named as Napoleon had once been a visitor—to eat and do a little discreet investigation. Except that Max's French was excruciating, and he seemed loath to allow Phoebe to exercise hers.

"We ought to keep a low profile," he said, frowning, and she wondered why he would worry about that if he intended to marry her.

Unless he was hoping she would refuse him. The thought plunged her into gloom, but she shook it off. At the very least, she would get that blasted painting back and ring a peal over Alvanly he'd not forget in a hurry. In her current frame of mind, she felt tempted to shoot the blaggard for all the trouble he'd caused.

"Well, it's a bit late for that," she retorted. "You're the one who suggested we travel as man and wife. The Countess of Ellisborough is not a discreet name to carry about." She regretted her lapse in manners at once and turned back to him. "Forgive me, Max, I—"

"Oh, damnation, do stop apologising," he said, sounding exasperated, as he took her by the hand and dragged her inside the hotel. "I'll tie the manager to a chair, and you can interrogate him to your heart's content."

Phoebe hurried in his wake, bewildered once again by Max's sudden changes in temper. She had always believed him to be such a quiet, well-mannered fellow and, yes, *dull* if she was being perfectly honest, but it was clear she hadn't known him at all. He was nothing of the sort. By now she was so uncertain of his feelings or his moods she hardly knew what to think.

They entered the elegant hotel and were quickly recognised as being of *the quality*. They were given a private dining area, where they were feted, and feasted upon *moules marinières*—mussels in a white wine sauce—and a huge dish overflowing with seafood, from lobster claws to langoustines, followed by *sole meunière*— fried sole, served with braised chicory—a dish with potatoes cooked in cream, another of mushrooms and herbs, and several other side dishes Phoebe could not identify. The wine was excellent and plentiful, and they finished with a superb dish of apples cooked in an apple liquor and served with a flavoured cream which Phoebe did not even pretend not to want second helpings of.

All of this seemed to restore Max's good humour, and he did not look the least bit stern when she conversed with the waiter, but only watched her with a strange gleam in his eyes. She liked it when he watched her, Phoebe decided, only it was rather distracting. Trying hard to ignore him, she concentrated on speaking to the waiter. He was a handsome young fellow with curling black hair, and he obviously admired her, which was not an unpleasant situation. She hoped Max had noticed too. Once the man had given her voluble and rather too flattering felicitations upon her marvellous French and her charming accent, he had asked if the meal had been to their satisfaction. Phoebe had been happy to wax lyrical for some time before she concluded.

"Oh, indeed, it was the most wonderful meal, so do send our compliments to your chef, but of course, I knew it would be excellent as an acquaintance of ours recommended it. A Baron Alvanly, do you remember him perhaps? I believe he may be a day or two ahead of us."

The man's face darkened at once.

"Yes," he said, looking very much like he would spit on the floor if a lady wasn't present. "I know him."

"Oh dear," Phoebe said, as it appeared the waiter was not pleased to admit knowing Baron Alvanly. She gave him her most sympathetic expression. "I am aware the baron is a shocking loose screw, though very charming when he wishes to be. Am I to take it he did not act honourably?"

At this question, Phoebe really did think he would spit in response, but the waiter just stood a little taller and replied with disgust that Baron Alvanly had left that very morning and not paid his bill.

***

Max watched the exchange between Phoebe and the young waiter with fascination. How was it that a woman who already held him utterly spellbound only grew more enticing when speaking a foreign language? He had only the vaguest notion of what they were talking about and, once they'd finished discussing the meal, he'd been quite lost. It didn't matter. She could have been discussing the state of the drains for all he knew, and he'd still have been captivated.

Oh, please God, let her agree to marry me. Please. Please.

That the waiter and his entire staff were also halfway in love with her was also obvious. He and a dozen other ingratiating fellows had fallen over themselves to serve *La Comtesse* and ensure she had the best of everything. They had kept her wine glass full, too, and now she looked flushed and excited. Something the fellow had said had clearly pleased her. Max only prayed he hadn't been flirting with her. He didn't think his ego could stand competition from a waiter at this point.

"Oh, Max," she said, turning to him and reaching across the table to clasp his hand.

They had both removed their gloves to eat and, for a moment, he was so distracted by the feel of her skin upon his he did not attend to her words.

"Max, did you hear what I said?"

Max tore his eyes away from her hand and cleared his throat.

"N-No," he stammered. "Wool gathering."

The waiter sent him a glance which was half pitying understanding, and half envy.

"Alvanly was here. He left this morning, but he didn't pay his bill. I hope you don't mind, but I... I said you would. After all, if not for me, he'd never be here and...."

"Of course," Max said easily, happy to do anything she wished if it would soften her opinion of him. "Tell them to add it to our bill."

"Oh, thank you, Max. I will pay you back once we get home."

She beamed at him and turned back to the waiter. He had no intention of letting her pay him back, but her hand was still resting upon his and Max did not dare move or speak for fear she would remember and take it away.

Once the fellow had gone, she returned to look at him.

"We are only hours behind him," she said with excitement glittering in her eyes. "And thank you so much for paying his bill, Max. I shall pay you back, I promise, though I know it was a dreadful imposition of me to offer without asking, and I am sorry—"

"Don't be," he said, aware there was too much unspoken, too much emotion in the words, but he couldn't help it. *"Please.* Don't be sorry."

She stared at him a little uncertainly and gave a hesitant smile. "All right, then."

Max settled their bill and Alvanly's and they walked back to the carriage.

"Do you think he'll stop at Abbeville?"

Max shrugged, feeling a burst of hope as he noticed how happy she sounded.

"I don't know," he said, wanting to say, *I don't care.* He didn't give a damn for Alvanly or the blessed painting, he only wanted Phoebe with him, for her to want to be here with him on this ridiculous adventure. "There's only one way to find out, I suppose."

"Yes," she said as Jack opened the door for them. "Was your meal good, Jack?"

"Not bad," he said, shrugging. "I'd rather an ale pie than mussels to be truthful, but that… what was it called, Fred?"

"Lapin à la moutarde," Fred replied grinning, his accent surprisingly good.

"Ah, yeah. Now, that was tasty," Jack said appreciatively, smacking his lips.

Phoebe laughed and climbed into the carriage and then groaned as she sat down.

"I've eaten too much again," she said with a rueful sigh. "I ought never to have taken that second helping."

In an instant, Max's thoughts returned to her corset and he had to fight the desire to offer to unlace it for her.

"It was worth it," he said, unable to help himself from recalling their conversation at her birthday dinner.

She chuckled, a surprisingly throaty sound which made his heart beat faster.

"Yes, and my corset *is* laced too tightly."

Her face fell as she looked at him and he wondered what she saw in his eyes.

"Are you going to scold me again for speaking of my undergarments?" she asked warily.

Max shook his head. He felt he sat on a precipice. She was so beautiful, and he wanted her so badly, and he'd drunk just enough wine to feel a trifle reckless.

"No," he said, aware that his voice was deeper than usual, breathless. "But if you mention it again, I give you fair warning, I will go in search of those scarlet ribbons."

Her eyes widened in shock and he waited for her to give him a sharp set down, or turn away in disgust and pretend he'd never spoken. She did neither, only stared at him.

"Do you... do you w-want to see them, Max?"

"Of course I want to see them!" he retorted, beyond frustrated. "I've thought of nothing else ever since you mentioned them. I'm going out of my mind thinking about them. My every thought is consumed with the desire to see those blasted ribbons. I've a pulse, Phoebe, not that you seem to realise it. I'm a living man, not yet thirty, not some old fogram as you seem to think. How can you know every waiter in that blasted hotel wanted to throw themselves at your feet, and not... and not know ...?"

"Know what?" she demanded, sounding flustered and truly startled.

No doubt he'd shocked her to her bones. Max shook his head and turned to look out of the window. He was an idiot, and he'd likely just made this entire journey into some hellish enterprise where she'd be uncomfortable to spend another moment alone with him.

"Know what, Max?" she asked again, her voice softer now.

He ignored it. She wasn't that naïve. She'd figure it out.

"Max."

He sighed and forced himself to turn and look at her, and his heart leapt to his throat and jammed there.

Christ.

"I can't reach the ones on my corset without help," she said, blushing furiously as she held up her skirts to reveal one shapely stocking-clad leg, and the red silk ribbon on the garter.

***

Phoebe felt as though she might burst into flames, she was so hot. It was an odd kind of heat, too, a combination of mortification and intense excitement as she saw Max's eyes darken, heard his sharp intake of breath. That was not disgust she saw in his eyes, she knew, though perhaps her behaviour still disgusted him. She was acting like a trollop and she knew it. Suddenly ashamed, she pushed her skirts back down and looked away from him. *Oh, good Lord.* Would she never learn not to be so stupidly rash and impulsive? She was breathing hard, the urge to cry making her throat tight. Had she just ruined everything? Not that there had been anything to ruin, but....

She gasped as Max took her hand and discovered him sitting beside her. She had been so consumed by her own dreadful behaviour that she'd not noticed him move.

"Are you trying to drive me mad, love?" he asked, his voice soft and yet rough at the same time.

Phoebe shook her head and then, being scrupulously honest, she nodded.

"Well, yes. Perhaps a little bit," she admitted, for after all she did want him mad for her. She could hardly deny it.

He laughed, the sound low and rather thrilling. "It's working."

"It is?" she said doubtfully, frowning as she noticed him turn her hand and undo the row of tiny buttons.

"It is," he agreed, his voice brooking no argument.

She watched, still puzzled, as he worked each button in turn. "You'll never manage without a button hook," she said.

He looked up at her, such a fierce expression in his eyes her breath caught. "Do wish to wager upon that, my lady?"

"I'm n-not your lady," she protested weakly, as it appeared he was making short work of the buttons, hook or no.

"I wouldn't wager on that either, if I were you, angel," he murmured, the endearment sending a thrill of astonished pleasure through her.

Angel?

Her?

Was he mad?

Perhaps she *had* addled his brain.

Now the buttons were undone, he had exposed a triangle of skin over the inside of her wrist. Max stared at it for a moment and Phoebe held her breath, wondering what on earth came next. Everything stilled; even the carriage jolting over the dreadful road they were on did not register in her mind. Slowly, he lifted her hand and pressed his lips to the small area. Phoebe gasped, startled by the intensity of sensation that jolted through her. His lips were warm and soft, and she could feel his breath flutter against her wrist. He looked up at her then, and she wondered why he seemed so nervous. Surely it was only her heart jumping around like a landed fish? He was an experienced man, sophisticated and worldly, and... quite obviously anxious.

"Phoebe?"

Her name was spoken like a question, and Phoebe groped about for an appropriate answer.

"Y-Yes?" she stammered.

"Have I shocked you?"

"Y-Yes."

His expression fell, and he set her hand free. "I beg your pardon, Phoebe, I ought not—"

"What? Oh, no, Max, don't...." She grabbed hold of his hand again in both of hers and held on tight. "Don't think... I didn't mean...."

"Didn't mean what?" he whispered, staring at the way she clutched at his hand.

"I didn't mean it wasn't a nice shock," she said, wishing she wasn't so wretchedly clumsy. Perhaps she should have paid more attention when men had tried to romance her. "Only that it *was* a shock. You see, I thought...."

He lifted his gaze to hers and she couldn't think of anything at all, lost in the soft darkness of his eyes, like brown velvet flecked with gold and bronze and copper.

"What did you think?"

Phoebe swallowed and tried to concentrate on the question as the carriage thudded into another pothole.

"I thought you didn't approve of me, t-that you thought I was dreadful and a terrible nuisance."

He gave a choked laugh.

"You *are* dreadful and a terrible nuisance," he said, but with such warmth that it did not sound like an insult. "I never meant to feel this way for you. I knew you thought me too old, too dull, that I would never be your choice, that you would never want me but… but you…."

His voice quavered with emotion and Phoebe felt as if her heart would explode with anticipation if he did not finish the sentence, but then the carriage lurched sharply to one side, throwing them to the right. Max hit the side of the carriage with a thud that made him groan, and Phoebe tumbled against him. He held her tight to her until everything went still.

"Phoebe?" he said, his panic audible. "Phoebe, are you hurt?"

Phoebe blew a tumble of curls out of her face and shoved her bonnet back up. "No. I'm fine," she said, though in truth she was shaken. "What happened?"

"I don't know, a broken axle would be my guess," he said sourly.

"What wretched timing."

He laughed then and she looked down at him and smiled, a little embarrassed to discover she was almost lying on top of him.

"It was wretched," he agreed. "We shall speak of this again, though. Very soon, yes?"

"Yes, please."

He reached out and touched her cheek, and she covered his hand with hers. Max let out a shaky breath and then laughed again, wonder in his eyes. Phoebe marvelled at it, never having thought Max would look at *her* that way. *Max? Good heavens.*

"Princess?" Jack's worried voice came from outside as he wrenched the door open.

"I'm fine, Jack," she said, taking the hand he offered her and clambering out of the carriage with difficulty, hampered by her voluminous skirts. "Are the horses hurt?"

"No, thank heavens. Just the blasted axle. This bloody road is a disgrace."

Phoebe smoothed her rumpled skirts and watched with admiration as Max climbed out, noting—perhaps for the first time—how very athletic he was. How had she been around this man so often and never noticed him, never really seen what was right before her eyes?

"Where are we?" she asked.

"Sign said, Saint Etienne au Mont," Fred said, jerking his head. "And we passed an inn not half-a-mile back. Reckon we'd best see what can be done there, for we ain't going on till that's repaired.

Phoebe stared at the broken axle with dismay. "Oh, drat it, and we were so close behind him."

"Don't worry, love. We'll not let him get away from us."

She looked to Max, feeling a burst of warmth at the endearment he gave her. She nodded.

"Of course not," she said. "Well, Jack, Fred, if you would be so good as to stay with the horses and our belongings, we will walk back and send help at once."

"Right you are, Princess," Jack said affably as he and Fred set about unhitching the horses.

Chapter 11

Dear Aunt Helena,

Thank you so much for the lovely new journal you sent me. I seem to get through them at quite a rate, so it was excellent timing as I have only a few pages left in the one I have.

Please, Auntie, will you speak to Papa when you next come? I have told him I am old enough to learn to drive now, and reminded him he taught you at the same age. He refused and said it was bad enough having to chase his sister all over the countryside and he was in no hurry to pursue his daughter in the same manner. Whatever did he mean by that, do you think?

—Excerpt of a letter to Lady Helena Knight from The Lady Elizabeth Adolphus.

9th April 1827. La Villa Desvaux, St Etienne au Mont, Pas-de-Calais.

It was a pleasant walk through woodland on the way back to the inn, if windy, the scent of the sea, salty and fresh, buffeting them as they walked. Max could not take his eyes from Phoebe and wished he dared recommence their conversation at once. He still could not believe that she had lifted her skirts to show him her garter. There had been nothing calculated in her actions, he knew that, even if she had admitted to wanting to drive him just a little bit mad. *Just a little bit.* He smothered a hysterical laugh. Good

Lord, she could have had him dancing on a string for months by now if she'd only known. Except Phoebe would not do that to him. She was too honest. Honest enough to say he had shocked her, but that it had been a nice shock.

His heart was still beating too fast, invigorated by hope, by her words, her touch, and by that wicked red ribbon. He knew he must not get ahead of himself. If he moved too quickly, he might scare her off, but God knew he'd waited this long just to be noticed, so he'd wait as long as she needed, as long it took for her to come to him as he longed for her to do.

As if she had heard his thoughts, she looked up at him and smiled, and the familiar sensation of having the breath knocked out of him made him feel dazed with happiness.

To his regret, they discovered La Villa Desvaux was before them too quickly for Max to take advantage of that sunny look. They entered the courtyard of the large, busy posting inn, where a huge carriage, called a diligence, was being overloaded to the point of madness. An extremely large lady carrying a bird in a cage was being helped inside, much to the dismay of those already settled, and Max counted no less than sixteen passengers, four of them on the roof, and enough baggage and trunks to make the thing look like a disaster waiting for a place to happen. He only prayed they could repair his own carriage in a timely manner, for that mode of transport did not recommend itself.

The Villa itself had once been an elegant building but was now a little battered about the edges. The painted green shutters were peeling, and the place had an air of shabby gentility that it was holding onto by its fingertips. Chickens scratched about in the courtyard's dirt and two mangy dogs fought over a bone, only to be ushered out of the way by an impatient groom. The clientele seemed to be a mixed bag, and Max guided Phoebe inside with a little trepidation. Cursing himself for not having paid greater attention during French lessons as a boy, he resigned himself to speaking English until the manager's grasp of the language ran out and Phoebe had to step in. Even her beauty and what he expected was a charming accent—it certainly sounded charming to him— could not sway the fellow.

The manager shook his head and shrugged his shoulders.

"He says all his staff are busy and we'll have just to wait until someone can be sent to help," Phoebe said when she turned back to Max, her frustration apparent.

"*Je suis désolé, monsieur*," the man said, not looking the least bit sorry.

"*Monsieur le Comte Ellisborough*," Phoebe corrected, giving his title which, naturally, made all the difference as the fellow bowed low and exploded into a volley of incomprehensible French.

Max sighed, wanting nothing but to be alone with Phoebe and to return to their conversation, and feeling too impatient to endure anything else. He levelled the manager with a hard look before reaching for his coin purse. Setting down a generous sum, he held the man's gaze. "Deal with it."

This was a language the manager understood with no problem at all.

Suddenly everything was not only possible, but not the least trouble in the world and they were shown at once to a private parlour, assured that help would be sent to their servants and refreshments brought at once, whilst their room was made ready. Max's frustration only grew as a seemingly inexhaustible number of servants trotted in and out, cleaning down the tables and bringing wine and ale, bread and cheese, and little dishes of aperitifs.

Just as he thought perhaps they might have five minutes peace, a ruckus began in the yard outside. Phoebe got to her feet and ran to the window.

"Good heavens," she said, kneeling on the padded bench beneath and giving him a rather tantalising view of her shapely ankles.

"What is it?" he asked, distracted by the tussle between his honourable self and the one who was still dreaming of red silk ribbons.

He fought to look away, and lost the battle with a sigh of resignation.

"A fight at any moment, I think," Phoebe said, turning back to look at him.

Max cleared his throat and wrenched his attention to her face. "Then you'd best come away."

Phoebe frowned at him. "Whatever for? Besides, I think I recognise that fellow. Do come and see, Max."

Max did as asked and peered out of the grimy window. "Good heavens. That's Viscount Kline."

"There, see? I knew I recognised him. I met him once or twice in town the year I came out, and I remember Lord Rothborn arguing with Jemima when she insisted they go to his wife's funeral."

"I'm not surprised," Max retorted. "Why on earth would they? She nearly ruined Rothborn's life, not to mention Lady Rothborn's."

Phoebe nodded. "Yes, but Jemima said they should go, for Lord Kline's sake. I felt she had rather a soft spot for him, having been married to such a vile woman for so long. Oh, Max, look, he will get thumped at this rate. We must help."

Before Max could either agree or demur, Phoebe was halfway out the door. Hurrying after her, Max took hold of her hand and towed her to a halt.

"Let me deal with this," he said sternly.

She rolled her eyes at him, but blessedly did not argue and Max carried on, striding over to the impending bout of fisticuffs.

"Kline?"

The man turned, a look of irritation in his eyes, which cleared on seeing Max. "Ellisborough? That you? Good heavens! Well, you're a sight for sore eyes."

"Is there some kind of trouble?" Max enquired politely.

"Yes, there is, dash it. This damned imbecile says I haven't paid my wife's bill, but I don't have a wife anymore, thanks be to God, and yet the villain won't have it."

"How curious."

Max eyed the large fellow—who had been dispatched to face the viscount and deal with the discrepancy—with misgiving. He got the impression this argument had been raging for some time and the chap was a hair's breadth away from losing his temper.

"*Le homme est pas marié,*" Max said in his best French, to which the big man growled something that did not sound encouraging, and spat on the ground.

"Oh, Max, do let me deal with this," Phoebe said, pushing forward and standing between Kline and the Frenchman before he could stop her.

The viscount's eyes grew wide and warmed considerably, an expression of delight on his face as he regarded Phoebe. Even the Frenchman looked rather dazed.

"Phoebe!" Max muttered, trying to drag her back before she started a fight of a different variety.

She glared at him and folded her arms. "Max, you are a man of many talents, but your French is horrible. Leave this to me, if you please."

Kline gave a startled bark of laughter and grinned at Max.

"You lucky devil," he murmured.

Max could only hope he was right.

***

Phoebe eyed the Frenchman and Viscount Kline with a little trepidation. Both were large men, and she did not much want to get between them, but the violent atmosphere had already dissipated somewhat, so perhaps she could sort this out and avoid bloodshed.

"Please, could you describe the viscount's wife?" she asked the fellow.

At this, the man's eyes took on a rather wicked expression and he did as she requested in rather too much detail. Phoebe blushed.

"What the hell did he just say?" Max demanded, pushing forward.

Oh, good Lord.

"Nothing!" Phoebe said in a rush, placing her hands flat on Max's chest and pushing back, which was a rather useless if illuminating endeavour. He didn't budge in the slightest. Goodness, but he was solid. Fighting to keep her mind on the problem at hand, Phoebe looked up at him, pleading in her eyes. "He wasn't speaking of me. I asked him to describe Lady Kline and... and he seems to think she's, er... extremely attractive."

The viscount brightened considerably at this news.

"Really?" he said with interest. "Then I must insist on making her acquaintance."

Phoebe returned her attention to the Frenchman, who growled a response.

"Oh dear, she's taken the diligence and is on her way to Abbeville."

Kline snorted. "It's all a hum if you ask me. The fellow is just trying to extort more money from me."

Phoebe shook her head. "I don't think so, he says she signed the register and you're welcome to see it. She was here two days and left this morning."

She turned back to the indignant Frenchman and gleaned as much extra information as she could manage.

"He says the lady told him her husband had been delayed, but would pay her bills on his arrival. She's going to Paris. He says you can't miss her."

"Indeed, I shan't," Kline said, frowning in puzzlement. "What the devil is going on?"

Phoebe could not explain, having no idea, but she returned once more to speak with the Frenchman. She explained that Lady Kline had died nearly two years ago, and that the viscount did not know who the lady in question was. This produced such a volley of injured feeling from the poor fellow at having been so duped that Phoebe turned pleading eyes on Max. It was not his job to sort out this mess but she did not know who else to turn to as Kline was so obviously angry about the situation.

"Oh, dear, Max."

Max sighed and nodded, and she beamed at him before explaining that Lord Ellisborough would pay the woman's shot for her.

"I say, what's he grinning about?" Kline demanded, suspicious now.

"Oh, I told him Lord Ellisborough would pay, just to keep the peace," Phoebe said in a rush. "The poor man was going to give himself a nervous collapse if he kept on. I understand the manager is his uncle. He's rather a stern fellow and would take it out of his wages."

"Well, that's dashed kind of you," Kline said a little stiffly, "But I can pay my own bills."

Phoebe was extremely pleased to hear this, as Max ought not have to pay and the last she'd heard Kline was in financial difficulties.

"But she's not your wife," Max pointed out.

"No, and she's not yours, by God," Kline retorted, laughing. "But it's my name she's bandying about. Speaking of wives," the viscount added, a glimmer of curiosity in his eyes. "Aren't you going to introduce me?"

Max hesitated, and Phoebe understood his difficulty. It was one thing to go about with *his wife* in France, among people who did not know them, but Viscount Kline was a part of their world.

"I'm Lady Phoebe Ellisborough," Phoebe said, holding out her hand to the viscount before she could think too much about what she was doing. "We have met before, actually, though it was years ago. I was Miss Barrington before we married."

She slipped her arm through Max's, and blushed as she saw the delighted look in his eyes.

"We're on our honeymoon," she added, wondering how she dared.

"So I see," Kline said, looking between them with amusement.

Phoebe ignored his knowing look and carried on. "We were on our way to Abbeville ourselves, as it happens, but our carriage met with an accident and so we're stuck here."

"Well, that's bad luck," Kline said, and she decided she liked the big, bluff fellow. He was ruddy and blond, in his mid to late forties, and looked to be a man who preferred to smile than frown. "But there's plenty of room in my carriage and, as it seems I must away to Abbeville in pursuit of a wife I didn't know I had, you are most welcome to accompany me."

"Oh," Phoebe said, rather delighted by this offer. "Oh, how splendid, thank you. Isn't that splendid, Max?"

She turned to discover that Max looked a little less than enthusiastic about the idea, but he smiled politely.

"Splendid," he agreed, meeting Kline's eyes.

A rueful look passed between the two men, leaving Phoebe a little uncertain, but they seemed amicable at least, and it meant that Alvanly could not get too far ahead of them. Not to mention they had a mystery to solve now.

All in all, Phoebe thought the journey was going marvellously well and was just the adventure that Max had wished for.

Chapter 12

Dear Matilda,

I was so sorry not to see you before you left town. We will be home ourselves next week. I hope you will come and visit. It's an age since we saw you all at the Priory.

And ought I offer felicitations? I hear Phoebe and Lord Ellisborough have married. It was all rather sudden, so I am praying it was a love match and that Phoebe is happy. I believe Ellisborough to be a thoroughly decent and kind-hearted man — so handsome too! He was dreadfully unwise in choosing his first wife, who was a dour and serious creature, but then he was so incredibly young too. I hope they have made a splendid match. Much love to you all.

—Excerpt of a letter to The Most Honourable Matilda Barrington, Marchioness of Montagu, from The Right Hon'ble Lady Jemima Rothborn.

9th April 1827. Montreuil sur Mer, Pas-de-Calais, France.

It was almost dark by the time they reached Montreuil-sur-Mer—some thirty miles from Abbeville—and the charming Hôtel du France, where they would spend the night. Max knew Phoebe was dismayed not to have journeyed to Abbeville itself, but the fictitious Lady Kline had the advantage of an entire morning's travel and they would not catch her so easily.

Max was not in the best of tempers himself, which he fully acknowledged was his own fault. It had been a long and rather tedious journey from his point of view, watching Phoebe and Viscount Kline—or Charlie, as he insisted they address him— getting along like a house on fire.

Which was fine, obviously.

Kline was a likeable fellow and very amusing. Despite his rather dreadful reputation, he was in fact not the libertine he was purported to be. Max knew, and well understood, that an unhappy marriage had driven his behaviour. In the two years since his wife had died, Kline had sobered up, sorted himself out, and was doing his best to be respectable. Max admired him for it. He just wished he'd go off and do it elsewhere. He wanted to be alone with Phoebe so badly that his nerves were jangling and, despite his best efforts, his temper was fraying. The faintly amused, pitying looks Kline sent Max at intervals did not make him feel any better.

Arriving at the hotel, however, did not give Max the respite he'd longed for, and instead produced another frustrating situation, albeit of a different nature. The Hotel de France was ancient and higgledy-piggledy, and surprisingly busy. Which meant, although a lovely room was made available at once for the Earl of Ellisborough, there was only a bedroom, no suite of rooms, and nowhere for Max to escape to. Not that he wanted to escape… which was the reason for his growing frustration.

"Oh, how charming it is."

Phoebe sounded delighted by the pretty room, with its huge bed and thick rugs. The floor pitched violently at one side, and the ceiling was low and thick, with hefty beams under which Max was forced to duck in order not to knock his brains out. In fact, he could not stand up straight in any part of the room. Phoebe turned and looked at Max as he tipped the servants who'd brought their baggage up, and closed the door behind them. She watched them go and let out a nervous breath of laughter.

"Alone at last," she said faintly.

"Phoebe," he said, not wanting her to be afraid of him. "You're safe with me, love. I'd never... never...."

Phoebe smiled at him, an affectionate look of amusement in her eyes. "I know that, Max."

Max frowned, a little indignant at her confident tone. "What do you mean by that?"

Phoebe sat down on the bed and removed the outrageous hat, casting it aside before she eased off her shoes with a sigh of pleasure.

"I mean that you are a gentleman to your bones. You'd never dream of—"

"Of running away to France with a young woman I wasn't married to?" he suggested dryly.

Phoebe looked up, a frown pleating the space between her eyebrows. "Oh, but, Max, that was entirely my fault. You'd never do something so... so reckless if not for me. I know how much trouble I've brought you and I am sorry for it."

"I'm not."

She blinked, looking rather surprised. "You're not?"

Max sat down, having grown tired of standing with his head crooked to one side.

"No," he said, deciding he'd had just about enough of being thought entirely sensible and safe to be alone with. "Come here, please."

Phoebe tensed a little, giving him a doubtful glance, as aware as he of the tension in his voice, of the intensity of the demand.

"Why?"

"Because I wish to continue our conversation."

"Oh." Phoebe gave him a considering look and licked her lips, and his entire body grew taut. "C-Can't you do it from over there?"

"No. You're too far away."

"Oh."

"Unless you prefer to stay all the way over there, but then I can't kiss you."

Colour rose on her skin like a sunrise, and Max ached with longing. He'd meant what he'd said. She was safe with him, but he didn't want her to feel *too* safe. She was safe because he was a gentleman, because he would not take that which was not freely given, not because he didn't want her. Yet he wanted her to feel she was alone in a room with a man who wished to be her lover, whom she *wanted* to be her lover, so no, not safe at all.

She slipped to the floor with a soft rustle of skirts and crossed the room, hesitating close to where he sat. Max held out his hand and she took it, curling her fingers around his.

"You said it was a nice shock," he said, pulling her closer.

Phoebe nodded, her breath coming fast.

"Then I give you fair warning, love."

He reached for her, pulling her down onto his lap with a squeal and a flurry of skirts. They billowed around him as she sat down, her lovely behind nestled neatly in his lap.

"Max!" she exclaimed, looking at him with wide eyes.

"What, love?"

"Well, I… I just didn't expect…."

"Do you want to get up again?"

She stared at him and shook her head and Max grinned.

"You needn't look so smug," she retorted, though laughter glimmered in her eyes.

"Oh, need I not? After I spent the entire afternoon listening to you and Kline babble merrily about everything under the sun, when all I wanted was to have you to myself."

A smile curved over her lush mouth as she regarded him. "Were you jealous, Max?"

"Of course I was jealous," he grumbled. "I've been jealous of every man whose had your attention for bloody months, if you must know. I... I was beginning to despair."

He could not read her expression, but it seemed thoughtful, as though she was only now seeing him for the first time. Perhaps she was, he realised.

"I've been very foolish," she said softly. "And I truly don't understand why... why I didn't.... Oh, Max, please do kiss me."

Max certainly did not need asking a second time and pressed his lips to hers. Oh God, he had waited so long and wanted this so badly, and he was not disappointed. Her lips were soft and sweet and so... so... perfect. He drew back, not wanting to overwhelm her or frighten her and forcefully aware that he was trembling. Her eyes fluttered open, dark with desire, soft and hazy, and Max wanted to whoop with triumph, with joy, with such dizzying relief that he could hardly breathe. She touched her fingers to her lips, staring at him in wonder.

"Oh, Max," she said, his name a breathy sound that made his whole body tingle with anticipation. "Do that again."

And then she threw her arms about his neck and kissed him, hard, wriggling in his lap to get closer.

For a moment, Max was too stunned to react at all, until he noticed her nimble fingers undoing the buttons on his waistcoat. He broke the kiss for long enough to say her name before her lips were on his again.

"Phoe… Phoebe…love…."

It was impossible. She was like quicksilver in his arms. He groaned as she moved and before he knew what had happened she was straddling his lap, tugging at his cravat.

"Phoebe, stop, *stop!*"

She stilled, breathing hard and staring down at him in consternation.

"Stop?" she repeated, looking bewildered. "Whatever for?"

Max gave a slightly hysterical bark of laughter. "Love, we're not married."

"Oh," she said, and then a flush of colour so intense coloured her pale skin he wondered what on earth… but before he could ask, she had scrambled from his lap. "M-Max," she began, looking utterly mortified. "I do beg your pardon. I… I just assumed that… that you wished to marry me. I…."

Her voice quavered and she span around with a sob, giving him her back.

Good God. Did she actually think he didn't *want* to marry her? Was she insane?

"Phoebe!" he said, leaping to his feet. "*Christ!*"

Pain lanced through his head as he cracked it on one of the low beams.

"Max!" Phoebe ran to him, her lovely eyes filled with tears, her face the picture of concern. "Oh, Max, you poor dear. Oh, do sit down again. I'll fetch a cold cloth and—"

Before she could disappear and do anything of the sort, Max sat down again, tugging her with him once again.

"Oh!" she exclaimed as she sat heavily and her skirts billowed up. "I do wish you'd stop doing that."

"Do you?" he growled, cupping her cheek and turning her face to look at him.

"N-No, not really," she admitted sheepishly.

Max laughed. "Phoebe, you silly goose. How could you think for a moment that I don't wish to marry you? It's all I've dreamed of since…. God, since forever, it seems. Don't you know I'm desperately, hopelessly in love with you?"

She smiled at him, such a smile he was certain his heart trembled.

"Truly?"

"Truly, madly, with all my heart."

She blinked at him, and then frowned. "Well, then why did you make me stop kissing you?" she demanded, a little indignantly. "Really, Max. It's no wonder I was confused. Usually if a fellow wants to speak of marriage, kissing is all he can think of."

Max felt a surge of jealousy so fierce it knocked good sense out of the window.

"And what fellows might they be?" he demanded.

Phoebe bit her lip and gave him a sideways glance.

"You really are jealous," she murmured, as though this was a revelation.

Max threw his head back against the chair and closed his eyes with a groan. "I am. I am. God forgive me."

She moved in his lap and he held very still as desire hummed through him. Her soft hands stroked his face, his neck and he opened his eyes again to see Phoebe staring down at him.

"You've not actually asked me, Max. To marry you, I mean."

He smiled at her. "There never seems to be a moment when I can love, and... well, to be honest, I wasn't sure you wanted me to ask you properly. I wasn't sure you wanted me to ask at all."

"I do want you to."

"And when I do, what will your answer be?"

She gave a little snort and pressed a kiss to his forehead and then his nose, and then his mouth, softer, lingering, and he would have held her there if he didn't want to hear the answer so badly.

"Yes," she whispered. "Yes, please."

"Thank God," he said, pulling her closer.

***

Kissing Max was quite a shocking experience. Any kisses she'd had before now had been... well, pleasant enough, but unrewarding. Those kisses had been soft and wet and underwhelming.

Kissing Max was like... like simmering over a low fire, except the fire seemed to burn hotter and hotter with every touch of his lips until she was all aflame, her insides molten and liquid and her flesh ablaze, burning with the need for him to touch her. His tongue sought and gained entry and slid alongside hers, tangling and stroking whilst his big hands stroked too, up and down her spine. She was quivering with need, with the desire for more. Thanks to Mama and Helena, she was far from ignorant of what passed between men and women, but it had never made such perfect sense to her before now. At least, she'd not quite understood how people got themselves tangled into such terrible scandals, when if they'd just stopped....

Except the idea of stopping was impossible, and now it all became blindingly clear.

She wanted Max, wanted to feel his skin upon hers, to feel the weight of his large body pressing her down. An ache had begun inside her, both pleasant and tormenting, a clamouring need for

143

him, a hollow, empty sensation that begged for completion, for him to complete her—to complete *them.*

"Max, oh, Max," she whimpered, tugging her skirts out of the way and climbing over him, straddling his legs.

"Phoebe, darling, wait… don't… Oh, God!"

Phoebe gasped as she sat down and discovered just how perfectly the two of them could fit together as a jolt of pure pleasure lanced through her. Though she'd trapped a layer of petticoats beneath her on top of all his clothes, she could feel quite clearly the evidence of his desire, just where she needed to feel it.

She stared at him with a mixture of delight and shock.

"Good heavens, Max."

"Don't move," he commanded her, his voice sounding odd and rather strangled.

Though her ears heard the words, they did not seem to connect to her brain and Phoebe was running all on instinct now, her instinct being to press closer.

Max groaned, his hands fastening on her hips and holding her still.

"Don't. Move." He sounded rather terse now.

"B-But I want to," Phoebe protested. "Don't you want me to?"

"Holy God, yes!" he exclaimed. "But we're not wed yet and I'm damned if I will face your father with you unmarried and… and debauched!"

"Oh, Max," Phoebe said, smiling at him and sighing. "You are funny."

"Hilarious," he muttered, sliding her from his lap as he stood and cracked his head on the beam for a second time. "Damnation!"

"Oh, good heavens! Max, you really must come and lie down on the bed. I think you will give yourself a concussion if you do that again."

She watched him cautiously as he clutched at his head. He took a deep breath and she had the strong sense he was counting to ten, or possibly a thousand.

"Are you all right?"

"Perfectly."

There was a taut silence.

"I really do think—"

"Phoebe, if you ask me to go to bed with you again, I shan't be responsible for the consequences."

Phoebe pondered this statement.

"Oh, don't you dare," he said, though he was laughing now.

"Well," she said, moving closer to reach for his hand. "You ought not dare me. You know that, don't you?"

Max made an amused sound, and she watched as he reached into his pocket and withdrew a slip of paper. It was old and crumpled and the writing very faded. He handed it to her.

"What's this? *Do something out of character*," she read aloud. "Max?"

"It's a dare from that hat."

"The *hat*? Oh! You took one?" Phoebe had to admit she was shocked that he would do such a thing.

He nodded, a slightly cautious look in his eyes. "You said I'd never do such a thing and… and I was rather hurt you thought me such a hen-hearted fellow."

"So you took a dare," she said softly, her heart aching as she realised just how often she must have hurt him with her indifference. The writing blurred and she tucked it carefully back in his pocket. "That's why you came."

"Only in part," he said. "I… I just wanted you to notice me, Phoebe. I didn't care what I had to do to achieve that."

Phoebe blinked hard. "I'm sorry for… for not.…"

He shook his head and pressed a finger to her lips. "Don't be."

She took his hand away and put it to her cheek, kissing the palm tenderly.

"I've noticed you now," she said, a little mischievously.

"It's a miracle," he replied, grinning. "And I suspect I have a concussion, and it's likely you're going to kill me before this is over, but I don't care. Only, I do care that I treat you right, love. I've waited this long.…"

Phoebe frowned, rather miffed by this attitude. They would be married, after all. Just not today.

He noted her frown and touched his hand to her chin, raising her face to his and brushing a tender kiss over her mouth. Phoebe sighed as he released her.

"You have no idea how my poor ego is soothed by your displeasure, Miss Barrington," he murmured. "Though, we could solve both of our problems, and get married at once."

For a moment, Phoebe's heart leapt at the idea. They could marry in France and.…

She shook her head.

"I can't," she said sadly. "I wish I could, but.… No, Max. I must be married in the Chapel at Dern, if… if you don't mind very much. Papa and Mama would be so disappointed. Oh, and my brothers, and Pippin and—"

"It's all right," he said, laughing. "I'll wait. I'll wait as long as you wish, but I can't pretend I won't be impatient to make you my own."

Warmth suffused her, the pleasure she took from his words making her sigh happily.

"You are rather wonderful, aren't you?"

Max rolled his eyes. "I don't like to say I told you so."

Phoebe laughed and then shrieked as he swept her up into his arms.

"Mind your head!" she cried, and he ducked just in time to avoid another beam.

Placing her carefully on the bed, he leaned down and pressed a soft kiss to her mouth. "I'll have a maid sent up to help ready you for bed."

"Oh, but where are you going?" she protested.

"For a walk," he said ruefully. "A very, very long walk."

Chapter 13

Dear diary,

I do solemnly swear that if my brother and his blasted friend steal my diary again, I shall have no choice but to seek vengeance. They had better understand that my wrath is a terrible thing and best avoided.

Cassius Cadogan – <u>you have been warned!</u>

—Excerpt of an entry by Lady Elizabeth Adolphus, to her diary.

10th April 1827. Montreuil sur Mer, Pas-de-Calais, France.

Despite having prepared himself for the onslaught—well understanding Phoebe's warning that she'd chosen the most respectable of outfits the previous morning—Max still gaped like a fool when she came down to breakfast.

"Holy Mother," Viscount Kline said in a breathless tone of wonder for which Max rather wanted to kick him.

He might have, if he'd been able to tear his eyes from Phoebe. As before, the rest of the hotel seemed similarly afflicted. She was coming down the stairs, this time dressed in a fanciful creation of bright cobalt blue with a green trim that put him in mind of Mediterranean seas and parrots. It was the mad hat and the overabundance of feathers that did it, he was sure. By the time she'd reached the bottom, three young dandies had spied her and were waiting for her to touch her dainty foot to the floor.

Max braced for impact.

The first fool rushed up to her brandishing a lace handkerchief and, though Max could neither understand nor hear what was said, he felt certain the fellow was pretending he'd found it and was asking if it was hers. Phoebe gave the young man a curious look, as aware as Max was that the handkerchief belonged to the young man himself. This ploy, having given the fellow the means by which to speak with her, was quickly taken up by the other two, and now three lace hankies were being brandished in her face.

Max watched with amusement as Phoebe patiently produced her own, smiled, and sashayed past them. The three young men immediately fell to bickering, no doubt about which one messed up their perfectly sound plan and spoiled his chances.

"Does she create this stir wherever she goes?" Kline asked, giving Max a faintly pitying expression.

"Yes."

"That's it," Kline said with a heavy sigh. "The next time, I'm marrying a comfortable, quiet and plain girl. The kind who likes books and staying at home, and can't abide fashion and parties. I've had far too much excitement for one lifetime. Not that I believe Lady Ellisborough to be the least bit like the late, unlamented Lady Kline," he said hastily, looking appalled lest Max should take offence. "It's just that when even the sweetest natured women look like that, they attract trouble through no fault of their own. Men act like imbeciles once they get within a mile of them. It's like… like…."

"Like wondering when and where the next bomb will go off," Max supplied helpfully.

"Quite." Kline regarded him with a thoughtful frown. "You rather like things exploding, though, don't you?"

Max could not help but laugh. "I'm beginning to believe I do."

Kline grinned at him. "You know, you look rather worn out, old man."

Max declined to comment, having spent a restless night in a chair, far too aware of his fiancée tucked up warm in the spacious bed not ten feet away from him.

"I'm sorry I'm so late," Phoebe said, as they got to their feet. "Have I missed breakfast?"

"Of course not," Max said, tucking her arm through his. "As if I would let you go hungry."

Phoebe chuckled.

"It would be a bad idea if we're to share a carriage," she said with a smile before whispering loudly to Viscount Kline. "I'm dreadful when I'm hungry."

"Appalling," Max agreed affably, pulling out a chair for her. "What did you do that took you so long?" he asked in an undertone.

"I shan't tell you," she murmured with a little sniff. "But I can tell you I found more ribbons, and these ones are pink."

Max groaned.

***

10th April 1827. Dern, Sevenoaks, Kent.

Lucian stared out of the window of the library, his stomach tied in knots. Pippin had hurried Matilda away the moment they'd arrived, and he'd been unable to draw a breath ever since. It would be all right, he told himself. He was worrying over nothing. Pippin would see to it, whatever it was. Still, his chest was tight with fear, his heart thudding. Outside, he could see Philip and Thomas walking with their tutor. Mr Evans believed fresh air good for the mind and spirit, and often took them walking while they spoke of that morning's lessons. Philip was listening with a serious frown of concentration, whilst Thomas lagged behind, brandishing a stick like a sword and attacking trees and the occasional rose bush as he went. Lucian felt his heart contract at the idea of having to tell them their adored mama was sick.

No.

No, no, no.

"Please God," he said aloud. "I know I'm unlikely to be one of your favourite people but, please, don't take her from me. I can do better. I *will* do better. Only let her be well. Please."

A knock at the door had him almost leaping from his skin and he ran to yank it open, giving Denton such a start that the poor man took a step back in alarm.

"Mrs Appleton says you may go up now, my lord," Denton said, his eyes full of sympathy and concern, for he must know why they had returned.

Lucian nodded but found he couldn't move, his hand still clutching the doorknob. He drew in a deep breath. "Did... did Pippin say...?"

"No, my lord."

Lucian swallowed.

"Lady Montagu is waiting for you," Denton said softly.

That, if nothing else, got him moving. Whatever it was, Matilda likely knew already, and he would not be such a coward as to allow her to face it alone. Feeling like a man climbing the steps at Tyburn, he forced himself up the stairs and went to Matilda's room, knocking softly.

"Come in," Pippin said.

Lucian hesitated, trying his hardest to bury his fear so that Matilda would know she could rely on him, that whatever they faced, they would face it together. He opened the door and stepped inside. His heart plummeted as he saw Matilda curled up on the bed sobbing. Lucian ran to her, pulling her into his arms.

"My love, my love," he said, desperate to make it right, to fight whatever it was she faced for her. "Whatever it is, we will make it right, we'll find a cure. We can go abroad. I read about a doctor in France who is doing the most wonderful things and—"

"Oh, good Lord, I could knock your heads together!" Pippin cried, interrupting him.

Lucian looked around, confused. How could Pippin speak so callously when Matilda was in such distress? Except now he looked down to find his wife was indeed sobbing, but she was laughing too, her slim frame shaking with mirth.

"Oh, Lucian," she said, reaching out to touch his face. "Oh, my poor darling. I'm so sorry to have frightened you so."

"You're… You're not sick," he whispered, hardly daring to hope.

Matilda shook her head. "No, love. Not sick."

"And you," Pippin tutted at Matilda, shaking her head sadly. "With two babies birthed and not knowing you was carrying again. I do despair."

"But Pippin, even you said I couldn't have another," Matilda objected.

"I said no such thing, my lady," Pippin retorted, folding her arms. "I said your chances were very slim but, if you drank that tea I made for you three times a day and were patient, you might be surprised, and so you are."

Lucian looked between them, still unable to breathe. "A child?"

Matilda looked up at him and gave him a watery smile. "Yes, Lucian, isn't it wonderful?"

He couldn't speak, too many emotions battering his poor heart at once. He could only pull Matilda into his arms and hold on tight, burying his face in her hair and concentrating on breathing in and out. When he had composed himself enough to speak, he turned back to Pippin.

"And everything…?"

"Just as it ought to be, don't you fret," Pippin said kindly.

"But isn't she a little—"

"Lucian Barrington, if the next word out of your mouth is *old*, I shall strike you," Matilda said indignantly.

Lucian snapped his mouth shut and sent Pippin a pleading expression. The woman cleared her throat, her mouth twitching a little. "Your lady is fit and strong, and in excellent health, my lord. It's certainly not unusual, and there is no need to fret unduly. I'll take good care of her, and if she does as she's told and rests, like her body is telling her to, she'll be fine."

"She will," Lucian said forcefully, giving Matilda a warning look.

"Oh, Lord, Pippin. Now I will not be able to lift a finger for months," Matilda said, regarding him with misgiving.

"No," he agreed, fighting the desire to insist she not leave her bedroom again until the child was safely delivered. "You certainly will not, and I shall tell your sons to treat you more gently too."

"Oh, Lucian," she protested, but he only shook his head and she sighed. "Yes, my lord," she said meekly. "If it will stop you worrying so."

"Nothing will stop me worrying," he said tightly, still thrumming with tension that he did not expect to leave him until the child was born, and both the babe and its mother were safe and well.

"Pippin thinks it's a girl," Matilda said, squeezing his hand tightly. "She says that's why I feel different. Not so sick as with the boys. Isn't that wonderful?"

Lucian nodded. He couldn't speak. He had been so fiercely proud of his sons, and his wife for having provided the heirs he'd needed, but though he knew he was asking too much when he had been so blessed with Phoebe, he had longed for a little daughter. A girl with cornflower blue eyes, the image of her beautiful mother.

"Well then, away with you, my lord, and let your wife have a little rest after all the upset," Pippin said, gesturing for him to leave. "She's worn out by it, and if I know anything you've worried yourself to a thread too. You've lost weight, by my reckoning. So, let's leave her in peace for a nice nap, and I'll have Cook bring you tea and biscuits. Not that they're as good as mine, for all I've told her time and again to add more ginger."

"No one makes them like you, Pippin," he said, giving the old woman a fond look before turning back to Matilda. "Rest then, my love, and I shall see you later."

Matilda nodded, smiling at him with such adoration that he could not resist stealing a kiss.

"Not too much later," she whispered as he pulled back, and he chuckled and kissed her nose.

"No. Certainly not."

Reluctantly, he left the bed, pausing to stare at his beautiful wife and thank God for allowing him yet another blessing in his life. *I will do better*, he promised silently, and left the room.

***

"This is excellent," Viscount Kline mused, taking another appreciative sip of the wine.

They had arrived at Abbeville in good time and ordered a light meal to fortify themselves against the challenge ahead. Kline, in pursuit of his wife, who was not a wife, and Phoebe and Max in search of Baron Alvanly.

"It is good," Max agreed, regarding Kline. "Do you know much about wine?"

Kline returned a rather crooked smile. "More than I ought, I fear. The truth is, I'm here on a business trip, though I'd be grateful if you'd keep that to yourselves. Can't have the *ton* know I've been reduced to *working* for a living, can we?"

"What kind of business?" Phoebe asked with interest.

Kline held the glass up to the light, admiring the colour of the wine as he tilted it back and forth. "I'm working for Gabriel Knight. He's making a killing importing wine, but with all his other interests he does not have time enough to spend as long as is required seeking out new suppliers. We got to talking about the subject one evening and he was, er… impressed by the depth of my knowledge."

He gave a self-deprecating chuckle. They all knew he'd had a reputation for hard drinking and gambling, and many other vices. Anything that had kept him away from Lady Kline.

"I needed to refill my coffers quite desperately, though, and this seemed like a pleasant way to do it."

Max looked at him, a considering gaze. "It does, indeed. I have been thinking of restocking the cellars at Ellisborough. May I put you on the case?"

"You certainly may," Kline replied with a pleased smile. "Knight will be thrilled that I've landed him such a customer."

"Excellent," Max said with a satisfied nod. "Well, then, Phoebe. If you are ready?"

Phoebe nodded and Kline rose as she did, holding out his hand to her. He lifted her fingers to his lips and kissed them gently.

"It has been a pleasure to meet you, Lady Ellisborough," he said. "And if your carriage and driver fail to appear, do come and find me. I should be charmed to continue the journey to Paris in your company."

Max made a sound which might have been taken as thanks, but Kline would well know was more like *Not if I can help it.*

"Thank you, Charlie," Phoebe said. "It's been so nice spending time with you. I do hope we see you again soon, and good luck with finding Lady Kline."

The viscount laughed. "Ah, yes, my fictitious wife. I cannot wait to make her acquaintance."

Max guided Phoebe out of the hotel and paused on the steps outside as he noticed her frown.

"What is it?"

"Oh, nothing," Phoebe said, shaking her head. "It's silly, really. Only every time he talks of his fictitious wife, I feel a pang of conscience. That's what I am, after all."

Max covered the hand that rested on his arm. "Not for much longer, love."

"No." She sighed. "Once we have this dratted painting back, we can go home."

"We could go home anyway," Max suggested, too eager to marry her and begin their lives together to care overmuch for someone else's stolen painting. Mrs Manning could well afford to lose a dozen such paintings, after all.

"Max!" Phoebe said, wide-eyed with shock. "And let him get away with it? I think not."

Max frowned, wondering what exactly Phoebe was hoping to accomplish.

"What do you mean? Even if we find him, I can only try to take the painting back, and I doubt he'll give it up willingly. You're not expecting me to haul him back to England in chains, I hope?"

He experienced a tremor of alarm at the flash of annoyance in her eyes.

"Of course not. And I don't want him locked up or anything of the sort. I do understand he's desperate, but it's his own fault for being such a profligate spendthrift, and he can't just go around stealing things. More than that, he duped me, Max, and I'm still vexed to death over it." She gave him a measuring look which made the tremor feel akin to an earthquake. "And what do you mean, *I can only try to take it back*? We are in this together, Max. I will help you get the painting back."

"Oh, no."

A wave of fear rolled over him as he considered Phoebe being in the same room as the villain who had tied her up and left her bound and helpless. His protective instincts rushed to the fore, too forcefully for him to listen to the warning voice that suggested he ought to step with care, ought to consider to whom he was speaking.

"You may help me find the devil, but that is all. Once I know where he is, I shall go and deal with him myself, and you will wait for me to return."

***

Phoebe stared at Max, hurt and dismayed by his words. This was supposed to be a shared adventure, at least she had taken it as such. Though the dare he had taken may have spurred him on, she knew that Max had come on this journey to protect her, and she appreciated his instincts. He was a sincerely good man, but she had also believed that he'd trusted her, that he'd realised she was not a fool, even if she had allowed Alvanly to treat her as one. To discover now that he meant to force her to stay behind whilst he faced the baron and retrieved the painting alone....

Oh, no.

She considered what her life would be like, if Max insisted she must stay at home instead of doing what she thought to be right, and her heart ached. If that was what he expected of her, he was doomed to disappointment. She would be a constant source of irritation, and he would soon regret their marriage. Phoebe knew too well she had been a spoiled and indulged child and given a great deal of freedom. She knew too that she must grow up and take more responsibility for her actions. That she was headstrong and impulsive was something she accepted, and she fully intended to be better, not be so reckless, but she was not so unaware of her own nature to believe it could be curbed entirely. The idea that Max might expect her to behave as most other men seemed to want their wives to act was crushing. She had been quite determined not to embarrass or upset him, but to be put aside… to be told to stay at home like a good girl while *he* sorted things out.…

Oh, Max.

She saw Max brace himself, no doubt awaiting her indignant riposte to his words, but Phoebe could only feel sorrow and said nothing. Last night, when they had kissed, it had felt so right… so perfect and wonderful, and she had been filled with joy to have discovered what it was that her parents had found in each other. She had finally understood all those secretive, longing looks, and the little touches that passed between them when they believed they were unobserved. Yet now, her certainty wavered, and all her doubts returned at once.

"Phoebe, love, please, don't look so disappointed. Surely you did not expect to challenge Alvanly to a duel or steal the painting from him at gunpoint?"

"Of course not! I'm not a silly child, Max," Phoebe retorted, swallowing down the hurt of his words.

"I never said you were," Max returned, sounding somewhat impatient. "But what kind of husband should I be to allow you to confront a man who tricked you into a crime and then left you gagged and bound? Please, love. Let me deal with it and see what can be done, and then I shall take you to Paris and we'll have a splendid time. What do you say?"

Phoebe took a deep breath and forced a smile. She did not want to argue with him, not here in the street, at least.

"That sounds lovely," she said, though there was no enthusiasm in the words.

It did sound lovely, only now she felt that Max would be there—not as her friend, her lover, sharing in the excitement and adventure with her—but as her chaperone, ensuring she did not come to harm. Her Papa had always protected her and made her feel safe, yet he had trusted her, too. He had listened to her and included her in his plans, and had even taken her advice.

"Now, then," Max said, "I think perhaps we should discover where the diligence sets down its passengers. If Alvanly is keeping a low profile, he may well have travelled that way. Maybe someone will remember him."

Phoebe nodded, only half attending. "Yes, though he used his real name back in Boulogne and, if he did use the diligence, he might have remained aboard and gone directly to Paris. It travels through the night, you know."

"True, but we must start somewhere. Unless you have a better suggestion?"

Max looked at her gravely and she knew he was trying to make amends, aware of her having grown quiet, but she was too distracted to think of a better alternative, even if there was one. Her happiness had been diminished, and she could not decide if it was her own fault for having unrealistic expectations of him, or his for having too little faith in her.

Perhaps they were both to blame.

Either way, she was unsurprised when he found the busy coaching inn where the diligence stopped and sat her in a quiet corner whilst he went to make enquiries. Too low in spirits to protest, she sat meekly without a murmur of complaint and wondered what on earth she ought to do.

Phoebe was sunk so deep in her own thoughts she did not at first attend when she heard a vibrant burst of feminine laughter, and only when a flash of vivid pink silk caught her eye did she look up. A stunning woman dressed with as much flamboyant style as Phoebe herself, and with a ravishing tumble of red curls, was walking out of the courtyard with a stream of young men trailing behind her. They carried an assortment of trunks and hat boxes between them, struggling under the bulk and the weight of the contents.

"*Mais,* Vicomtesse Kline," a man protested, waving a piece of paper and running after her. "We kept your luggage until you could come and retrieve it as you asked, but now you must pay your bill, *maintenant, s'il vous plaît!*"

That luxuriant wicked laugh came again, fading as the woman disappeared around the corner.

"Oh, but my husband will deal with it when he arrives," the lady said, as the last flash of pink silk left the courtyard feeling a great deal duller with its absence.

Lady Kline!

Phoebe sprang to her feet and looked around for Max. He was nowhere to be seen and... and... she did not have time to look for him. She had discovered Lady Kline and she would solve this mystery by herself, at least. She would not be made to sit in a corner like a good little girl while Max did everything for her. Phoebe grabbed hold of one of the grooms, who was walking a tired, sweaty horse back to the stables.

"*Monsieur,* please find my husband, Monsieur le Comte Ellisborough, and tell him I have found Lady Kline and that I will meet him back at the hotel later."

She pressed a coin into the fellow's hand and he tipped his hat in acknowledgement. Picking her skirts up out of the dirt, Phoebe hurried out of the courtyard and after Lady Kline.

Chapter 14

Eliza,

*If a knight was on a quest, he would not be so
bottle-headed as to get distracted by a stupid
girl. The story was going along at a cracking
pace until she turned up. Can't you kill her off?
And I can well believe that you would be mad
enough to go hunting a dragon by yourself, but
any sensible girl would know she'd be burnt to
a crisp if she did something so idiotic. At the
very least she ought to have gone with the
Knight, not run away from him to do it all by
herself. She's a silly widgeon, if you ask me.*

I enclose a drawing of the dragon as requested.

**—Excerpt of a letter from The Right Hon'ble
Cassius Cadogan, Viscount Oakley (Aged
11) to The Lady Elizabeth Adolphus (Aged
11).**

10ᵗʰ April 1827. Abbeville, Sommes, France

Though it could only have taken a matter of minutes to have
given her message to the groom, by the time Phoebe left the
courtyard, Lady Kline—for Phoebe had no other name to call her
at the moment—was at the far end of the street and turned a corner,
out of sight.

"Oh, drat it."

With one hand keeping her skirts from the mud and the other holding on to her monstrous hat, Phoebe ran. She finally turned the corner where Lady Kline had disappeared and saw... no one. Gasping—for running in heeled shoes and a tightly laced corset were not to be recommended—she paused to catch her breath. Furious with herself for having lost her quarry, Phoebe hurried down the road, keeping a sharp look out. *Ah ha!* Ahead, she glimpsed one of the poor devils carrying the lady's luggage, and set off again. Further and further into the ancient, winding streets of Abbeville she followed the procession of luggage, slipping on the shiny cobbles in places and hurrying in and out of people going about their business, following the vibrant pink gown as it marched through the ancient streets of the town. Sometimes she got close enough to call after the fellows with the luggage, but they did not turn, too concerned with following their lady and keeping her luggage intact and away from thieves. Finally, after Phoebe had cursed the lady with every wicked word she knew, and begun to believe she meant to lead her all the way to Paris, they turned into a wide street and the men stopped.

At last, Phoebe could catch up with them. She did, just in time to see the lady had entered a theatre.

Phoebe crossed the street, dodging carriages, and hurried towards the building. She blinked a little against the gloom of the interior after the brightness of the day outside as she stepped through the door and heard rather than saw that Lady Kline had headed through a side door. It was marked 'Private' and Phoebe followed, suspecting it led to the dressing rooms. She moved quietly, keeping her distance as she travelled along the narrow corridor, watching as the woman ahead of her turned into a room with a star on the door.

Phoebe moved closer, noting the door was ajar. She held her breath, listening.

"Well, you're here. I admit I did not count on it," she heard the lady say. "So, you had best have the money you owe me after forcing me to leave London when I was doing so splendidly well, and for this… shabby hole in the ground. You cannot possibly expect me to perform in such a place?"

"*Splendidly well,* darling? I think you exaggerate just a tad, but no, dear Nina, I do not expect you to lift a finger, nor to perform. Indeed I have performed so magnificently I believe I shall not only clear my debt to you but come out of it quite nicely too. I think we shall have a deal of fun, my sweet. Just think of all the places we can go now, the things we can see."

Phoebe stilled in horror as she realised she recognised the second speaker: a smug, male voice that made fury rise in her like throwing brandy on burning embers.

Alvanly.

"I don't remember saying I would go anywhere with you, Richard, and why did I have to meet you here? Why did you leave London so suddenly?" Nina demanded—if that was indeed her real name.

"Leaving London was… *prudent*… and as for this place, my friend is an investor in this poor excuse for a theatre, and it is out of the way. My business can be best concluded in Paris, but I thought it safer we meet here first. I did not believe anyone would think to look for me in such a place as this, should there be anyone looking."

"And *is* there anyone looking?"

There was a pause, and Phoebe realised Alvanly might believe her papa would come after him. Papa *would* have come after him, if she had not already left with Max, but he would trust them both to arrange things as they felt best. *He* would trust *her*. She experienced a sudden longing for her papa, the kind she had not experienced since she was a girl. If only he were here. He would know what to do about Max, about Alvanly, about this entirely ridiculous situation in which she seemed to have embroiled them all, even poor Viscount Kline! Though how she could be held accountable for that she did not know.

"I don't know if anyone is looking," Alvanly admitted. "But it is possible."

"Oh, Richard," the woman said, and she sounded tired and exasperated. "What have you done?"

"I have saved myself from the Marshalsea, and you from the drudgery of a second class career as an actress. You have many charms, my dear, but you are past the first flush of youth and the role of ingénue will never be yours. You began too late in life."

There was an amused bark of laughter. "As a romantic declaration that leaves something to be desired, and I assure you, I am well aware of both my charms and their limitations. I'm also aware that men like you are not to be relied upon. I'll have my money back, Richard, and then we'll see about the rest."

"Damn me, but you're a cold bitch."

There was more frustration than malice in the words, and Nina did not seem to take offense for her reply was placid.

"Yes, I suppose so, and it's life that has taught me the lesson well, Richard, dear. You may rely on only yourself in this world or else you will be taken for a fool. If I went with you, we should have a fine time until the money ran out, or you grew bored and abandoned me for a younger, sweeter girl, one who was not so aware that all the pretty words you speak have no substance."

"I would not—"

"Oh, stow it." Her voice was sharper this time. "You're a charming devil, Richard, and I'm fond of you, but don't go pretending you love me any more than I do you. Or are you proposing to marry me?"

There was a telling silence and Nina gave a low, mocking laugh.

"Now, tell me what it is you've done."

Phoebe bit her lip, increasingly irritated by Alvanly as he told Nina of his daring theft, not mentioning her part in it once. She ought perhaps be thankful for that, as she wanted no one else to know, but for some reason it rankled now. She heard paper rustling and assumed he was unwrapping the painting to show it to Nina.

"That grubby little painting is worth a fortune?" Nina said, her tone incredulous. "Good heavens. I wouldn't have it on my wall for anything, but then I never claimed to have any knowledge of art."

"Well, it is our ticket to freedom. It has been valued by an expert. The fellow I told you about that owns a part of this theatre said there's a Monsieur Lemoine, runs a high class pawn shop in the heart of Paris, but he also buys and sells exclusive pieces, artwork, jewellery and the like," Alvanly said, his words interrupted by that rich, vibrant laughter Phoebe had heard earlier.

"And he—and those he sells to—ask no awkward questions about how one acquired such valuables, I take it, hmmm?"

"Quite," the baron replied, testy now. "Well, anyway. I have an appointment to meet with the fellow, so we'd best be on our way. I've booked us into Hôtel Saint Vincent. It's not what I am used to, but it's discreet and clean, according to my friend. I wrote in advance and booked us a room in the name of Mr and Mrs Babbage."

There was a heavy sigh. "Babbage? *Mrs* Babbage, what a come down! And I was so enjoying being a viscountess."

"What?"

"Never mind, Richard. Very well, we had best be on our way, then. The sooner this debacle is over, the better."

Phoebe gasped as she realised they were leaving already. She looked around for somewhere to hide, or another door, but they were all on the far side of the one she stood by. There was no time.

Deciding she must brazen it out, she turned away as the door opened and hurried back down the corridor, hoping Alvanly would just take her for an actress or someone involved in the theatre.

"Miss Barrington?"

Drat.

Phoebe did not turn, just spoke in rapid French. "*J'ai peur que vous ayez fait une erreur. Je suis Mademoiselle Dubarry.*"

"Oh, ho, no you're not, you little cat. I'd know you anywhere."

Phoebe shrieked and picked up her skirts, running for the door she'd come through, but it was heavy and hard to pull open, and Alvanly was already upon her. He put one hand over her mouth to stop the scream she was about to make, the other fastening tight around her, imprisoning her arms. Determined he should not get the better of her this time, Phoebe bit down hard on the fleshy part of his hand and stamped on his foot.

Alvanly bellowed with fury and snatched his hand away, but did not let her go.

"Richard!" Nina shouted. "Leave that poor child alone. What the devil do you think you're doing?"

"This poor child is nothing of the sort," Alvanly returned with a scalding look at Nina. "Don't you see the wretch has followed me here from London?"

"Why? What did you do to her?" Nina's voice was cold and furious, and Phoebe looked at her with interest.

"Nothing!" Alvanly retorted, his tone indignant, almost hurt.

Phoebe gave a snort of disgust.

"Oh, you call tricking me into helping you steal a painting and then leaving me tied up nothing, do you?" she demanded, struggling against his hold. "You're a vile thief and blaggard. You ruined me, you devil!"

"Oh, don't tell me Ellisborough didn't leap at the chance to play knight in shining armour," Alvanly said, unimpressed by her words.

"Of course he did," she retorted, her voice growing thick as she remembered Max, and considered how worried he must be by now. She had caused him nothing but trouble. "Max is a good man and he'd never stand by and let someone suffer if he could do something about it, but I shan't marry him. We... We do not suit," she said, trying to steady the quaver in her voice. "And so I am ruined, and it's all your fault."

"Let her go!"

Phoebe looked around at Nina, her attention taken by the anger in her voice.

"But, Nina...." Alvanly protested.

"Let her go, Richard, or so help me—"

"Fine!" Alvanly said in disgust, giving Phoebe a little push towards Nina. "You deal with her, but she knows what I did, and if she's here, Ellisborough is not far behind, not to mention her darling Papa. Would you like to be on the wrong side of Montagu, darling? For that's who he is, but you can deal with them all, if you wish. I have a painting to sell. I'll see you in Paris, if you figure out whose side it is you're on, but if you want to see your money again, I'd have a care who you choose."

Alvanly stalked off, leaving Phoebe and Nina alone together.

Phoebe stared at the woman before her, wondering what she would do next, and not entirely surprised when she held out her hand out to shake like men did.

"I'm Mrs Abercrombie," she said with a smile. "Though such formality seems ridiculous in the circumstances, so you may call me Nina."

"Not Viscountess Kline?" Phoebe said with the lift of one eyebrow as she took the woman's hand.

Nina clasped her fingers tightly for a moment and then laughed. It was a good sound, that laugh, the confident sound of a woman who knew her own worth and would let no one else diminish her.

"No, sadly," she said with a sigh. "I hear he's a handsome devil."

"He is," Phoebe agreed, seeing the surprise in the woman's eyes. "And he's here, in Abbeville. We travelled down together."

"Oh." Phoebe watched the woman's hand move to her throat. "So soon? I... I believed he was farther behind me than that. You travelled with him?" she added, her gaze considering as she looked Phoebe over.

Phoebe knew where her thoughts would take her. It was one thing for her to be dressed so dashingly when travelling with her husband, the Earl of Ellisborough, but for an unmarried young woman in company with a man....

"I was also with my fiancé," Phoebe said in a rush. "Lord Ellisborough."

Nina tilted her head to one side, the thick pink ribbon that fell from her lavish bonnet resting lightly upon her cheek for a moment. "I thought you said you would not marry him. You are not suited, I believe."

"N-No," Phoebe said, a rush of misery filling her as she remembered. "We are not suited, but... I have not told him so yet."

"Ah," Nina said, her eyes softening as though she understood perfectly, and perhaps she did. "You know, I am tired and dirty and hungry, and Richard is a pain in the... well, you know as well as I. I had no faith in him being here, so I took the precaution of booking rooms across the street. Come with me and we shall rest and decide what ought to be done next."

"The painting ought to be returned to its rightful owner," Phoebe said, not willing to be persuaded on this point, despite the fact she rather liked Mrs Abercrombie.

"Perhaps," the lady said with a wide and dazzling smile. "But let us discuss it over cakes and champagne. Nothing can seem so terribly terrible when one has cake and champagne."

Despite everything, Phoebe laughed and nodded. "Very well then. Cake and champagne, it is."

***

Max stared up at the sky in despair. It would soon be dark, and Phoebe had been missing for hours. He couldn't breathe, terrified as he considered just what trouble a beautiful young woman could get into all alone. Abbeville was not Paris, but it was a large place with plenty of wicked and desperate people, far too many who would not think twice before taking advantage. She was no fool, he assured himself. Phoebe had shown him she was both resourceful and brave, and clever too.

Once again, he remembered the look in her eyes when he'd told her she would play no part in retrieving the painting from Baron Alvanly. It was like someone had snuffed out a candle, all the light and the excitement that had shone there extinguished with a few words. She had not needed to say anything for him to realise how disappointed she'd been. It had not been until it was too late, until he had returned from the booking office for the diligence, that he had realised she had been disappointed in *him*. He had let her down. He had wanted so badly to keep her safe he had done the one thing he had always known would be fatal with Phoebe: he'd tried to hold her back, tried to rein in her fierce spirit.

Now, she had somehow discovered Kline's fraud of a wife, and she did not want him to stop her from what she had planned. Goodness only knew what trouble that discovery would lead her into alone, when he might have gone with her, and might have been at her side.

He had gone back to the hotel they had booked for the night, hoping she might have returned there by now, but there was no sign of her, and no word left for him.

His heart thudded dully as he looked down the street and recognised the carriage emblazoned with Montagu's crest. Jack and Fred had caught up with them, the repairs done in good time, and now… now he had to explain to Flash Jack that his little princess had run away, and was all alone in this place, with the night closing in. He'd be lucky if Jack didn't throttle him on the spot. It wouldn't be so bad if he didn't realise how thoroughly he deserved it.

Jack pulled the carriage to a halt and eyed Max with uncertainty.

"What you lookin' so Friday-faced about, my lord? Is there aught amiss?"

"Yes, Jack, there's something amiss all right. I'm a blithering idiot and I'd not blame you if you want to break my neck, or anything else come to that, but there's no time now. I need your help. Phoebe's run off somewhere and I… I can't find her," he admitted, the words lodging in his throat, a weight in his heart so heavy he wanted to sink to the ground, but he would not.

There would be time enough to regret his actions once he'd found Phoebe, for he had no doubt she would tell him to go to the devil now.

God he was such a fool.

"You can't find her?" Jack replied, frowning at him.

"That's what I said!" Max said, throwing up his hands. Jack seemed far too calm. "We went to the booking office for the diligence, seeking word of Alvanly. I told her to wait for me and—"

"You told her to sit and wait while you sorted things out?" Jack echoed, giving Max a penetrating look that made his ears feel hot.

Fred, who sat at Jack's side, gave a muffled snort.

"Worse than that," Max admitted. "I told her she'd have no part in recovering the painting from Alvanly. That she could help me find him but—"

"But that she had to sit quietly like a good girl while you dealt with the big bad villain?" Jack guessed.

Max nodded.

"And she ran off after that?"

Max nodded again, too wretched to speak.

"You're right," Jack said with a sad shake of his head. "You are a blithering idiot."

"I know it." Max watched him. "I must find her, Jack. She's all alone, and if… if anything happens to her—"

"You stop that!"

The words were hard and angry, and Max snapped his mouth shut as Jack glared at him.

"You might be a blithering idiot, but Phoebe ain't. She's got a brain in her head and she knows a thing or two about the world. More than you realise, I'd wager."

Max swallowed hard. "I have never wanted to be proven wrong more in my life, Jack, but we must find her."

"Aye, reckon we'd best, though likely she'll not thank us for it. We'd best head back to this booking office and go from there."

Max climbed up with Jack and Fred, in no mood to be a passenger. "She left me a note saying she'd found the woman who has been posing as Viscount Kline's wife."

"Right, then," Jack said. "We'll see if we can't find the woman ourselves, and hope our lass is still with her."

Chapter 15

Cassius,

I did <u>not</u> ask you your opinion.

The knight was going to face the dragon alone. So she is no madder than he is and a sight more intelligent. She will use her brains to outwit the dragon, not go in poking at the poor beast with a stupid sword, and she <u>would</u> have gone with the knight if he had asked her, but men never ask women to do things <u>with</u> them! Instead, they tell us we are silly widgeons and ought to stay out of the way. Well, I won't, and neither will my princess.

The dragon is quite magnificent though, Cassius, thank you very much. You really are most terrifically good at drawing. My attempt looked more like a large rat.

—Excerpt of a letter from Lady Elizabeth Adolphus (Aged 11) to The Right Hon'ble Cassius Cadogan, Viscount Oakley (Aged 11).

10th April 1827. Abbeville, Sommes, France.

Max exited the theatre, fuming with frustration.

"Well?" Jack demanded.

"I have no idea. No one speaks a word of English and, as Phoebe so eloquently said, my French is horrible. She could be there this minute and I'd be none the bloody wiser."

"Max?"

Max looked around to see Viscount Kline strolling up the street towards them.

"Charlie? Thank God. You speak French, don't you? I need your help. Now, if you please?"

"Of course," the viscount said, his blond brows drawing together. "But what's all the alarm about, and where is your charming wife?"

Max forced down the panic building in his chest. "Charlie, can I rely on your discretion?"

The viscount stood a little taller and looked Max square in the eyes. "Word of honour, Ellisborough. Whatever it is, none shall hear a word of it from me. I'd be happy to help if I can, especially if it involves the young lady."

"It's Phoebe... Miss Barrington. We're... we're not married... *yet.* Not ever, if I've bungled this as badly as I fear. Oh, God, Charlie, she's disappeared. She was supposed to be waiting for me, and when I returned there was a note saying she'd found the woman who's been masquerading as your wife. That was this morning, and I've not seen her since. She's alone and...."

The viscount reached out and took hold of Max's arm, squeezing it. "Say no more. In fact, I have also been following a trail that led me here, so let us away inside and see what we can discover, yes?"

Max let out a harsh breath. "Yes. Yes, thank you."

Kline smiled and patted him on the back. "Don't worry so, man. We'll find her, both of them come to that, no matter how merry a dance they lead us."

"Come along then. Let's see if you can make yourself understood, for I might as well have been speaking ancient Greek for all the good it did me. Ironically, that's a language I *do* understand moderately well."

Kline laughed and followed him back inside the theatre.

Twenty minutes later, and rather lighter in the pocket, and they were furnished with the disturbing information that no one had any knowledge of a Viscountess Kline, but that Baron Alvanly had been there to meet a Mrs Abercrombie. Max had filled the viscount in on all the ridiculous details of their escapade to date, to which he had listened in incredulous silence.

"Oh, God," Max said, clenching his fists. "If I'd not been such a fool, we might have found him together. If that bastard has got his clutches into her, if he's hurt her—"

"We'll find her, Max," Kline said firmly. "And Alvanly might be a thief and a blackguard, but I have never heard of him ill-treating a woman. All the same, I think we must make haste, and we'll accomplish more if we split up."

Max nodded his agreement. "I'll follow Alvanly to Paris. The fellow said the Hotel St Vincent, so I'll start there. I don't know whether to pray Phoebe is with him or not. You see if you can hunt down this Abercrombie woman. If she's as flamboyant as the chap said, you ought not have too much difficulty."

Kline nodded and reached out to shake Max's hand. "Good luck, I'll catch you up in Paris as soon as possible."

***

Phoebe sighed as Nina refilled her glass. "I wish you would let me send word to Lord Ellisborough. He'll be so worried."

"Perhaps it will do him good," Nina said, selecting a delicate fruit tart and popping it into her mouth.

"Oh, no!" Phoebe said at once, shaking his head. "He thinks me nothing but trouble, and that I need protecting and looking after from the world at large. This will only confirm all his suspicions, I've no doubt."

"Well, go to him, then." Nina gave a shrug and gestured to the door. "I am not holding you captive, dear."

"No, but I'm too curious to leave yet," Phoebe admitted. "I would like to know what is going on. How did you get involved with Alvanly, and why have you been masquerading as Lady Kline?"

"Oh, how dull," Nina lamented. "I would much rather talk about Lord Ellisborough. I can't help but think you are in love with him."

Phoebe blushed. "That's none of your business."

"Neither is mine yours, but I'll share if you will." Nina picked up the tray of cakes and tarts and held it out for Phoebe to take one.

"Oh, very well," she said, huffing and taking a tiny walnut tart. "Max... Lord Ellisborough is... He's the sort of man any woman would wish for in a husband."

"But not you?"

"Yes, sometimes, but—"

"But you have no wish to be protected and cosseted?"

Phoebe glanced up, a little startled by the accuracy of her observation. "Well, sometimes, perhaps. It is nice to be made much of on occasion, but... I am not fragile, I'm not the sort of woman who swoons or has fits of the vapours. I'm pig-headed and too curious for my own good, and not the least bit delicate. I can swear and shoot and fence, and pick a lock and cheat at cards, and I want to make my own decisions and my own mistakes. I'm not stupid enough to think I can do everything by myself, but I would like to be included, and not left at home in case I break a fingernail. If I am to become some man's property, I must know that he will consider my feelings, that he will ask my consent and involve me in decisions that affect our future. If not—"

"If not, you are merely a possession and not a person."

Phoebe nodded, seeing the complete understanding in Nina's eyes. The woman gave a tight smile. "I was married once. It was not a happy experience. Perhaps you are right to stay away, to teach him a lesson. Mayhap he will learn it better than other men."

"Your husband is dead?" Phoebe asked, not liking the implication she was punishing Max. He did not deserve that after all.

"Now," Nina agreed, nodding. "But I ran away from him long before then. Better to be my own mistress and set my own price than be used for free and against my will. I am, as dear Richard observed, a mediocre actress, but I am an entertaining companion, and no man will ever own me again."

"Then you and Alvanly—"

"Not one of my wiser choices," Nina said with a sigh. "I had no idea he was in such debt. His family is extremely wealthy, but they cast him aside two years ago, and I was ever a fool for a pretty face and a fine physique. At least I did not fall in love with him, though I trusted him further than I ought to have. Lending him money was idiotic, though the men he owed were not the kind you renege on, and I feared they really would kill him."

"And now? Now that he has stolen a valuable painting and ruined my future. What now?"

"I don't know."

Well, that was honest at least.

Nina shook her head her expression darkening. "I do not like nor approve what he has done, but that money is all that stands between me and destitution in my old age. My looks will not last forever, no matter how hard I cling to them. I need security, and he'll not pay me unless he sells that painting."

"He might not pay you then," Phoebe observed. "He was quick enough to abandon you here, was he not? You've told him you don't love him, nor believe in his pretty words. I would not trust him to hang around now. Not once he has the money in hand."

Nina sat up a little straighter. "You think he has fallen so low?"

"I think he cast his honour aside the moment he left me tied up and stole that painting. He can't get it back now, so there's nothing holding him back. I would not trust him an inch, let alone all the way to Paris."

Phoebe watched as Nina got to her feet with a swirl of pink skirts. She really was a lovely woman, all voluptuous curves and softness. She could well imagine how sought after Nina would be but, judging from her extravagant outfit, the lady had expensive tastes too.

"You're right," Nina said at length. "I've been foolish to trust him before, I'll not be burned a second time. We'll go after him."

"Excellent," Phoebe said, getting to her feet with a surge of relief. "But I will send word to Max that I am well and will meet him in Paris. I cannot have the poor man tearing Abbeville apart looking for me. He'll be so…."

Her voice quavered and Nina moved towards her and pulled her into a hug.

"You do love him."

"Yes," Phoebe admitted. "But I wish I did not. I can't make him happy, and I couldn't bear to be always disappointing him."

Nina took her face in both hands and stared at her. "I think perhaps you ought to speak honestly to your Max and tell him your fears. At least you must explain to him why you refuse his offer. If he is a good man as you say, you owe him that much."

Phoebe sniffed, blinking hard. "Yes. I do owe him that much."

And a great deal more, she thought sadly.

A sharp knock on the door had them turning and Nina gave a gasp of shock as it swung open without waiting for permission to enter, and a man stepped through.

"Oh, Charlie!" Phoebe said, rushing towards him as she recognised Viscount Kline. "Is Max with you?"

"Phoebe!" Kline held his hands out to her, and she took them as he let out a breath of relief. "Thank God. You know poor Max is out of his mind with worry for you?"

"Oh dear," Phoebe said, guilt settling in her heart.

"Who is this, Phoebe?" Nina demanded, a sharp ring to the question.

Phoebe looked around to see her staring at Viscount Kline, one hand resting on her heart, her breast rising and falling rapidly.

"Why, madam," Kline said, releasing Phoebe's hands and moving quickly towards her. He took her hand in his and raised it to his lips, not looking away from her. "Do you not recognise your own husband?"

"Oh," Nina said faintly. She flushed just a little before rallying and raising her chin. "You're younger than I thought you'd be. Prettier, too."

The viscount grinned. "I might say the same, my lady."

Nina snatched her hand away and huffed. "I'm not your lady, nor a lady at all, as you well know. I'm sorry for using your name so. It was a wretched trick and I know it. I shall repay what I owe you, I give you my word—for what that is worth. I was desperate, or I should never have done such a thing. Only, I had no funds, and I had to come here to meet Alvanly, or I'd never get my money back."

"Alvanly?" Kline repeated, his voice hard and displeased. "You're mixed up with him too?"

Phoebe stared at him in surprise. "Max told you?"

"Everything," Kline said, his face softening as he gave her a sympathetic smile. "And you may trust me, Phoebe."

Phoebe let out a breath and nodded. "Yes, I believe I can, Charlie. Thank you. And yes, Alvanly is a part of this too, though Nina was not involved in the theft, nor in what happened to me. She lent him money to escape some dangerous men and he can't pay her back unless he sells the painting. He's on his way to Paris now."

"Aye, with Max in hot pursuit," Kline observed, watching Nina with interest. "Well, we'd best go after them. If Max discovers Alvanly and no sign of you, Phoebe, there might well be trouble. It's lucky there's a good moon tonight. If you ladies can make ready, we had best not tarry."

"You'll take me too?" Nina asked, regarding Kline cautiously.

The viscount snorted. "My dear, I am not letting you out of my sight. Either of you!"

The next four and twenty hours were excruciating. Phoebe tried her best to sleep as the carriage jolted and bumped through the night, lurching over the dreadful roads, but it was nigh on impossible. Even if she'd had a feather bed and the most luxurious of sleeping quarters, she doubted she'd have closed her eyes. She wished she had not left Max so abruptly, though she was glad to have discovered Nina, whom she was coming to like very much. The woman never complained during the gruelling journey, and did her best to keep everyone's spirits up. Phoebe noticed Kline watching Nina covertly when she was not looking, a curious look in his eyes, and she suspected he was rather charmed himself.

Phoebe sighed as she returned her thoughts to Max. As disappointed as she had been in him, she had behaved badly— recklessly as usual. No doubt he would be all too pleased to release her from their engagement after what she'd done. He must realise by now what a bad bargain he'd struck. She supposed that thought

ought to comfort her for she could not bear to hurt him, but she felt too sorry for herself to find any relief in it.

Well, she would not marry. Nina had chosen not to marry again. Better that than make a disastrous mistake. She would be ruined, and her parents would be disappointed for her, but not surprised, she suspected. There had always been an inevitability about it, and there was freedom in such a state that would not be unwelcome.

Her illegitimacy had always tainted her as far of many of the *ton* were concerned, even if they feared the consequences of treating her with less than respect too much to ever mention it aloud. It was always there, in their eyes. It would not make so much difference, Phoebe supposed. The people she already knew disapproved of her would cut her. That seemed no dreadful loss. She could take lovers, and yet they would have no say in her life, no control over her. Unlike poor Nina, she was financially secure, and need not fear the future.

Her mind drifted back to the night Max had kissed her, the feel of his strong arms around her, the perfection of that moment, and regret filled her heart. She had believed she had found a man she could put her trust in, one she could count on and be proud of, and who would return the same feelings, but Max did not trust her wholly and completely, as she had wished to trust him. That she must leave him, cut him from her life, made her chest feel tight with misery and she wondered if perhaps she could persuade him to be her lover, at least for a little while.

She almost laughed aloud at the idea.

No, Max would never consent to such a thing. He wanted to save her from ruin, not speed her on her way. He was a good, kind, honourable man, but she could not live in a gilded cage, would not be protected from life, from living, and Max wanted to do just that. It would never work. She would only make them both wretched. Her eyes burned and she blinked hard, forcing her thoughts down another avenue, one where the emotion that rose was anger, not sorrow. They must catch up with Alvanly before he sold that blasted painting. How she wished she'd never set eyes on the wretched thing!

"We ought not go to the hotel first."

Kline yawned, smothering it with difficulty and trying to focus bleary eyes upon her. He looked over, somewhat surprised to discover Nina had fallen asleep against his shoulder. Phoebe smiled when he did not disturb her.

"Beg pardon, Phoebe?" he asked, rubbing his face with his hand.

"We ought not go to the hotel. Alvanly will be champing at the bit to get his money. He said he was going to go to a Monsieur Lemoine."

"Lemoine?" Kline repeated in surprise.

"You know him?"

The viscount nodded. "I've... er... had cause to visit him myself before now. My wife—not this one," he added with a rueful nod towards Nina, asleep on his shoulder. "Always had a desire to see Paris. I indulged her and, predictably, it damn near ruined me. I was forced to pawn some valuables to get funds enough to return us home."

Phoebe sat up a little straighter. "Then you know where he is?"

"Aye, the seventh arrondissement, on the edge of where the wealthy and respectable live, close enough to be discreet when they've gambled away the value of their wife's jewels."

"Then we'd best go straight there."

"You do not wish to stop and freshen up?"

Phoebe returned an impatient look. "I wish to get the wretched painting back, and the sooner the better. Alvanly has caused me a great deal of trouble and, whilst I must take responsibility for my part in it, he's the devil who created all this fuss, and I don't intend to let him get away with it."

Kline chuckled, a glint of admiration in his eyes.

"I can see why some believe Montagu is your father," he said, and then held out a hand before Phoebe could give him the sharp side of her tongue. "Oh, don't eat me. I never believed it, and I don't give a damn for your parentage. It was a compliment, I assure you."

Mollified, Phoebe subsided and returned a dignified nod. "In that case, I shall take it as such."

Chapter 16

Gabe,

Yes, the rumours of what happened at Mrs Manning's rout party are true – up to a point.

Baron Alvanly stole the painting, but Phoebe helped him, albeit unwittingly. She picked the lock to let him into the room where it was being displayed. I beg you imagine the scandal if that ever got out. I am trying not to. Alvanly tied her up and left her to the wolves – for which he will pay dearly – but Ellisborough found her first, thank God. He pretended a romantic proposal, hence the news you heard. Whether Phoebe will truly accept him, I do not know.

They have gone to Paris in pursuit of Alvanly. I pity the fellow when she catches up with him. In truth, I believe I pity Max too. I am not entirely certain he understands what he has taken on. Better he discovers it before they marry, though. With luck, she will also discover a thing or two for herself. I believe there is a chance she has met her match.

I dearly hope so.

—Excerpt of a letter to Mr Gabriel Knight from The Most Honourable Lucian Barrington, Marquess of Montagu.

11ᵗʰ April 1827. Hôtel St Vincent, Rue Barbet-de-Jouy, 7ᵗʰ Arrondissement, Paris.

Max exited the hotel, cursing under his breath, and climbed back up to sit with Jack and Fred.

"The devil has still not arrived. I think that painting must be burning a hole in his pocket as he considers its worth. The manager told me there were two pawnbrokers close by: a Monsieur Chappuis, and a Monsieur Lemoine."

"Reckon we'd best seek them out, then," Jack said, with a sharp nod. "D'you get instructions?"

"I did. Lemoine is the closest at hand. Go to the end of the road and turn left, then first right. We're looking for rue de Saint-Simon."

Not more than five minutes later, they pulled up outside a tall, elegant townhouse. Max leapt down and turned as he heard another carriage pulling up behind theirs. It was early morning yet and the street still swathed in shadow as the sun was not yet high enough to light it well. The door of the carriage swung open and Kline jumped out. "Charlie!" Max said in surprise, hurrying forward. "Do you have news? Have you seen—"

Kline grinned at him and held out his hand to someone inside the carriage. Max's heart stuttered to a standstill as gloved fingers took it, and Phoebe stepped down with a flurry of blue skirts.

"Phoebe," he said on a breath of relief so profound his knees trembled.

"Good morning, Max," she said, her smile uncertain.

Max did not think, only acted, his emotions too out of control to consider she might not welcome his embrace as he closed the gap between them and hauled her into his arms, holding her tight against him.

"Thank God," he whispered, his voice unsteady. "Thank God."

He let go slowly, unwillingly, and she moved away from him, out of his arms.

"I'm sorry, Max," she began, but he stopped her, pressing a finger to her lips as he shook his head.

"It was my fault. I know that it was. I ought to know better than to cut you out of proceedings in such a way. Alvanly did this to you, not to me, and it is only right that you face him, if that is what you wish. I was overbearing and domineering, and everything I know you will not stand and for that I beg your pardon, love, only... give me another chance, Phoebe. I promise I shall do better."

She was staring up at him and he was too anxious to believe he could interpret her emotions with any accuracy, but she seemed surprised by his words at least. Hope bloomed in his heart, and he promised himself he would not misstep so catastrophically again.

"Thank you, Max," she said softly. "But I am sorry too, for making you worry so. That was badly done of me and... and I wish I had not left as I did."

Max raised her hand to his lips and kissed her fingers. "I am only glad to have you back with me again, and the chance to make you wish to stay this time."

Phoebe smiled at him, uncertainty still shining in her eyes, but there was warmth there too, and his hopes burned a little brighter.

"Princess?"

"Jack!"

Max watched as Phoebe flew to the old villain and hugged him tightly. What the viscount thought of her hugging her coach driver with such affection, he could not imagine, but the warmth between them was obvious, and Phoebe was as irrepressible as ever. Max looked around to see Viscount Kline was indeed watching with obvious curiosity, and standing with a rather spectacular looking woman, who was dressed from head to toe in vibrant pink.

"Lady Kline?" he guessed, addressing Charlie.

The viscount's lips twitched. "Lord Ellisborough, may I have the pleasure of presenting Mrs Nina Abercrombie? Mrs Abercrombie, Max Carmichael, Earl of Ellisborough."

"My lord," the woman said, giving an elegant curtsey.

Max looked between her and Kline, wondering why the woman was with him.

"Nina went to Abbeville to meet Alvanly, Max," Phoebe said, filling in the gaps for him. "She was not involved in the theft," she added in a rush, correctly interpreting his anger at the idea. "She knew nothing of that. He owes her money, that is all. She came to France to collect it. He intends to sell the painting to repay her and then travel around the continent living off the rest in fine style, no doubt."

"And Lemoine is his pawnbroker," Max said, assuming that was why they were here.

"Yes," Phoebe said, her eyes sparkling with excitement. "So, let us see if he has been here yet."

Max looked down with a surge of pleasure to see Phoebe place her hand on his arm and stare up at him, waiting. He covered her hand with his for a moment, holding her gaze and hoping she could read a little of what he felt for her in his eyes, before he moved forward and led her inside.

***

"*A fake!*"

Phoebe's shocked voice rang out through Monsieur Lemoine's elegant parlour, the place to which he had discreetly taken them once he had ascertained just who he was entertaining.

"I regret, Madame," Monsieur Lemoine said with a shrug of his shoulders, his English good but heavily accented. "But yes. A clever fake, I give you that, but nonetheless...."

He gave another shrug as he spread his hands wide.

"But Mrs Manning had it valued," Phoebe protested.

Monsieur Lemoine's lip curled. "I know not who proclaimed it a masterpiece, but I assure you, I know *un faux*. Whoever it was, 'e was the *idiote*!"

Phoebe huffed with frustration and stalked to the window. She was tired, and her bones ached from hours in a jolting carriage. Her clothes were rumpled, and she had a nasty suspicion she did not smell as fresh as a daisy. They had travelled miles through France in pursuit of the odious baron. And all of it because of *a fake*? Her only satisfaction came from knowing Alvanly would suffer far worse for his idiocy. He had forfeited his honour, could never show his face in England again, and for what? To discover his pot of gold was made of brass.

"Wait, Phoebe," Nina said in an undertone, moving closer. "Did... did you say *Mrs Manning* was the owner of the painting?"

"Yes, she is. What of it?"

"Oh, dear." Nina bit her lip and, although she too would lose money she was sorely relying upon, her eyes twinkled with mirth.

"What is it?" the viscount asked, watching her curiously.

"I'm afraid none of you will be pleased to hear it," she said, looking a little anxious, yet still her lips twitched irrepressibly, whatever humour she found in the situation too much for her to contain. "B-But, I think Mrs Manning has taken her revenge on Richard."

"Her revenge?" Max asked, frowning at her. "You mean she knows Alvanly?"

"Oh, she *knows* Alvanly," Nina said, grinning now, and with such a tone to her voice none of them were in any doubt that she spoke of knowing him in the biblical sense. "I'm afraid to tell you but... Richard threw her over for...."

"For you," Kline finished for her. Rather than looking disgusted or furious, there was amusement in his eyes.

Nina nodded and turned to face Phoebe, reaching out to take her hands.

"I'm so sorry that Richard has caused you such trouble, Phoebe. And you, my lord," she added to Max. "But I fear you have been embroiled in a scheme to teach Richard a lesson. Mrs Manning must know, as I too discovered, that Richard is fine company, but vain and shallow and selfish, and his honour is only a veneer. In truth, I believe he would sell his mother to make a profit, and he would most certainly steal from a lover, as he has done from me, and from Mrs Manning, a fact I believed she counted on." She smiled then, shaking her head with obvious admiration. "What a clever woman. I think I should like her."

Kline laughed a little. "So she need only drop a word in the ear of someone she knew would pass it on to him that she had a priceless painting, and that it would be on display, and count on the fact he would crawl out of the woodwork like the vermin he is."

"I believe so," Nina agreed.

There was a long silence as everyone digested that fact.

"Very well," Phoebe said, folding her arms. "So, the painting is a fake, and we need not have troubled ourselves to retrieve it, but the fact remains that I have a bone to pick with the baron and pick it I shall. The question is, what will he do now?"

She glanced at Max and braced herself, waiting for him to tell her that their adventure was at an end, that they must return home at once and be married, to save her reputation. She thought perhaps she saw the desire to speak such thoughts aloud glimmer in his eyes, but then he took a breath and his words were not what she'd expected.

"Alvanly was fooled by the painting, and even Monsieur Lemoine here said it was a clever fake."

"Indeed it is," Lemoine added, nodding at Max. "To one with less experience than myself, it would look like what it purported to be."

Max nodded. "So why would he not try to pass it off as the real thing?"

"But how?" Phoebe asked, still a little startled and wondering if Max was merely humouring her.

"What kind of man is Alvanly, and what kind of entertainments does he favour?" Max asked, raising one eyebrow.

"He'll wager it," Nina said, a tinge of excitement creeping into her voice. "That's what got him into this mess in the first place, gambling money that was not his to lose."

"Yes!" Phoebe said, clapping her hands together. "Oh, well done, Max!"

Phoebe almost blushed at the burst of pleasure she saw warm Max's expression at her praise, and at the knowledge that her words had meant so much to him.

"Oh, and I know where he'll go! He told me of a club," Nina said, almost bouncing with excitement now. "He was eager to go there, to try his luck. It is run by two young men. One is the Comte de Villen, the other his illegitimate brother. It has become *the* place to be seen in Paris. It's quite a sensation, from what he told me."

"Ah," Lemoine said, nodding sagely. "Casino Rouge et Noir. *Oui,* it is exclusive, *très chic.*" He looked them over and gave a delicate cough. "You will wish to… ah, see to your—" He waved a hand at their rumpled clothes with a little moue of distaste. "Only a select few may enter. Le Comte 'as nothing to do with the club, though, his brother is lord and master there. Nicolas Alexandre

Demarteau. If you say at the door that Lemoine sent you, you will gain entry, but 'ave a care with both Le Comte and Demarteau. Do not underestimate them for their youth; they are ruthless."

"Thank you, Monsieur Lemoine, you have been most gracious to help us," Max said, at which Lemoine preened a little. "If you could furnish us with the address, and perhaps recommend a hotel where we might make ourselves fit to be seen, we will leave you to your day."

"*Bien sûr, bien sûr*," Lemoine said smoothly. "You leave everything with me, *monseigneur,* I will see to it."

As good as his word, and generously recompensed by Max for it, Monsieur Lemoine had them installed in the elegant if surprisingly named Hotel Westminster, just on the other side of the Seine, and only a quarter of an hour from the exclusive destination of Rouge et Noir.

Phoebe looked at the selection of clothes she had to choose from and decided that, if there had ever been an occasion for something a little scandalous, this was the moment.

The hotel had supplied Phoebe with a maid to help her dress, and the young woman's eyes grew round and wide as Phoebe selected the scarlet silk gown. The bodice was tightly fitted and low cut to display a generous amount of bosom, and the sleeves were set off the shoulder before billowing into large puffs of scalloped silk edged with black silk trim. From elbow to wrist, the material was fitted to her arm and secured with a parade of tiny black silk buttons. The waist was cinched in tight by a belt of black silk with a gold buckle, and the wide skirts were trimmed with the same scallop design as the sleeves, in a wide band of three tiers above the hem. Black silk gloves and red silk slippers completed her outfit. To Phoebe's astonishment, the French had even more extraordinary fashions for hair than at home, and she winced and bit her lip as her blonde locks were wrangled into a complicated arrangement of curls and plaits, which were then adorned with three red roses.

"*Magnifique!*" the maid breathed with a happy sigh, as she stood back and inspected her handiwork.

Phoebe had to admit it was an impressive arrangement, if designed with the intention of giving her a migraine before this adventure was very much older. Still, it was nice to be dressed at the height of fashion, even if she did look more like a Cyprian than an earl's wife. With a jolt, she wondered if she *would* be an earl's wife.

Max had acted so very well when they had met at Monsieur Lemoine's. He had been gracious, and he had apologised for his behaviour, and she believed he had meant it. After all, he had not once reproached her for worrying him so, and she had seen the relief in his eyes for herself. The poor man had been beside himself. Yet a tinge of doubt remained that he had only acted so to avoid a scene. Would not his instinct always be to keep her in the dark if there was something that might worry or disturb her? She still feared that he would not share his troubles with her and allow her to be a part of his world, a true partner in their lives together.

Well, tonight would likely be a good test for them both. Max would see what manner of woman he wished to tie himself to for life, and Phoebe would discover if he had really understood what that meant. She admitted to herself that she wanted more than anything for Max to want to marry her still, but she would not pretend to be something she was not. Growing up and doing her best not to create a scandal every time she set foot out of the door was one thing, but acting the part of dutiful, well behaved wife who sat at home doing needlepoint was a role she had no desire to play, and was not one she could even contemplate.

It was all or nothing and, tonight, Alvanly would not be the only one playing for high stakes.

Chapter 17

Brother,

*I will be with you again by late this evening,
but I have just received word from Lemoine that
a certain Baron Alvanly will try to gamble
upon the value of a painting, which is, in fact, a
fake. The Earl of Ellisborough and Viscount
Kline are in pursuit of this man, and I am
assured that they will deal with him. Although I
know you would prefer such an affront dealt
with swiftly and by your own hand, remember
that we have no wish to involve ourselves in an
affair of honour with the English. It is more
than likely we may have need of their good
opinions in the future, and I would rather
cultivate their friendship than interfere in
something that does not concern us. A warm
welcome across the Channel would not go amiss
for either of us. After all, we have enough on
our plates at present.*

*I beg you to stay out of it and do your utmost to
further relations with our guests. Lemoine has
ascertained that the Lady Ellisborough is the
adopted daughter of the Marquess of Montagu
and that is an association we would be foolish
not to nurture.*

*Make friends for once in your life, Nicolas, not
enemies.*

*—Excerpt of a letter to Nicolas Alexandre
Demarteau from his brother, Louis César
de Montluc, Comte de Villen.*

Translated from French.

11ᵗʰ April 1827. Hôtel Westminster, 2ⁿᵈ Arrondissement, Paris.

Max repressed the desire to sneeze and moved away from the
lavish display of hothouse flowers in the centre of Hôtel
Westminster's sumptuous marble entrance hall. Viscount Kline
shifted beside him, looking as though he was anticipating Mrs
Abercrombie's appearance as much as Max was Phoebe's. Max
knew well that she would test him tonight, that any decision
Phoebe made about their future would be based in some measure at
least, upon how he treated her and he was not going to mess it up
again.

Any musings or decisions about exactly how he would behave
came to an abrupt halt as his eyes lifted to the staircase, and his
vision filled with an image that would be seared upon his brain for
all time.

"Holy God," he murmured under his breath.

"Courage, man," Kline said in his ear, his voice full of
amusement.

Max dragged his eyes from Phoebe for a bare moment, to see
Kline watching Mrs Abercrombie make her way down the stairs,
dressed all in glittering black and silver.

"Once more into the breach," Kline said softly before meeting
Max's eye and winking. "I was ever a fool for a beautiful woman.
Pray I make a wiser choice this time, my friend."

Max let out a huff of laughter and turned back to Phoebe.
Choose me, he willed her silently as she moved towards him,
vibrant and smiling, her eyes more blue than grey this time, a

summer sky bright with the promise of endless days and passionate, warm nights. Longing swelled his chest, his heart aching with wanting her, with wanting to be worthy of her. He would not fail this time, for if he did, he did not deserve such a prize.

"Good evening, Max," Phoebe said, her gaze moving over him, studying the black and white of his evening attire. She returned her scrutiny to his face, her blue eyes darker now and he felt a surge of heat, of pride, as he realised she wanted him too. Badly. "You look terribly handsome."

He laughed and shook his head. "I believe it is I who is supposed to bring compliments, my lady, but you have chased the words, and any ability to wield them, clean away. You astonish me, as always, Phoebe."

She returned a mischievous look, her eyes glimmering now. "Well, I shall take that as a compliment, though I suspect it could go either way."

Max grinned and took her hand, lifting it to his lips and kissing her gloved fingers. "No, only one way. I am besotted, beguiled, yours to command. Only name your desire and I shall obey."

For just a moment something hot and dark flickered in her expression, and his entire body grew taut. Then she gave a regretful sigh.

"This night has a purpose and I wish to achieve it, but...." She blushed a little but held his gaze, lowering her voice. "I shall not forget you said that, Max."

"Phoebe, darling," Mrs Abercrombie said as she and the viscount drew closer. "You look ravishing. My word, that gown is quite...."

"Scandalous," Phoebe said, with a delighted grin. "Yes, I know. My poor father would have conniptions if he saw it."

"Somehow I cannot imagine Montagu having conniptions," Kline said, shaking his head. "I could believe his jaw might grow tight and his eyes get that icy look of displeasure that freezes one to the marrow."

Phoebe laughed.

"Oh, but that *is* a conniption for Papa," she said gravely.

Max smiled and let out an uneven breath as he considered just how the marquess would greet them if he returned his daughter ruined and still unwilling to marry him. One problem at a time, he counselled himself. After all, if Phoebe refused him, he wasn't entirely sure he cared what happened to him next. Lucian could do his worst, and it would be nothing compared to the regret of having lost Phoebe through his own idiocy.

They escorted the ladies out to the waiting carriage, and Phoebe bade Max wait a moment before he helped her in. She moved towards the horses to where Jack waited at their heads.

Jack scowled as he glimpsed the scarlet gown beneath her cloak, but Phoebe just laughed, drawing the old villain to one side. The two spoke in low, hushed tones that Max could not decipher and so he turned away, lest the desire to eavesdrop became too fierce. A light touch on his arm drew his attention, and Phoebe smiled up at him.

"Ready when you are, Max."

***

From the outside, the façade of Rouge et Noir was entirely forgettable, a building like so many others on the street, rising to six storeys and with every window shuttered against the night… and against prying eyes. There was no theatre in its presentation, no opulent entrance, only a small sign—one side black, the other red—that swung gently as the breeze buffeted it back and forth on well-oiled hinges. It bore no writing, no instruction, and the black door before them bore no number.

Max knocked and it opened at once to reveal two large men, the kind one would not wish to meet unexpectedly on an unlit street.

"Monsieur Lemoine said we might be welcome here." Max handed his card to one of the men, who gave it a cursory glance, nodded, and stepped back.

They were in.

At first, Phoebe was disappointed, having expected greater things than the dim corridor they moved through.

"The red door," one of the men said in heavily accented English, nodding at one of two doors, one black, one red.

Phoebe glanced at the black door, intrigued, but the burly fellow just grinned and shook his head, wagging a finger at her.

"Red door," he insisted.

Phoebe resisted the urge to laugh and stick out her tongue, and gave a regal nod of her head, sweeping on to the red door which Max held open for her.

"Curiosity killed the cat," he murmured, his eyes alight with amusement as Phoebe realised he knew exactly what she'd been thinking.

"That's why they have nine lives," she countered, raising her chin though she could not resist the smile that tugged at her lips. "*Oh!*"

All thought of what lay behind the black door vanished at the scene laid out before her. The wealthy, the famous, and the scandalous of Paris must all be here, the women in lavish silks and satins, jewels glittering beneath the light of five massive chandeliers. Men in their harsh black and white attire smoked and flirted with companions—not all of them respectable—and the concentration in some quarters of the room, as people gathered around card tables and roulette wheels, was tense and absolute. The room was enormous, far larger than anything she had considered possible from outside, and she realised the brothers must own far more than the one house that appeared to belong to Rouge et Noir from the outside.

Now she could see the houses had been altered to make one vast building. Serving staff moved through the crowds seamlessly, dressed all in black except for the scarlet red of their waistcoats. The walls were adorned with frescoes—lush, erotic scenes on a red background—and the windows covered with heavy swathes of red velvet. Gold-framed mirrors glinted, reflecting light and the scene before them, adding to the sense of space and grandeur. Here was the theatre that had been absent on the outside, the scene set as a playground for the rich and the reckless.

Phoebe felt Max's arm stiffen beneath her hand, and looked up to see a man approach them. He was tall and dark, hair glinting blue-black like a raven's wing as he moved beneath the glare of the chandeliers. Whoever he was, people stopped to watch him pass, the women's gazes admiring his broad shoulders and lithe form, the men stepping out of his way as he brought with him an air of menace that came as a surprise when he stepped closer, for he was a young man, certainly no older than Phoebe, and dreadfully handsome. Eyes as black as a sloe berry regarded her solemnly for a moment before he bowed to them.

"My Lord and Lady Ellisborough, you and your guests are most welcome at Rouge et Noir this evening. I am Nicolas Alexandre Demarteau, proprietor of this humble house." There was a glimmer of something dark and amused in his eyes as he spoke, the arrogant devil, for he knew well enough there was nothing the least bit humble about Rouge et Noir. "I 'ope you will have someone inform me if there is anything you need," he proceeded smoothly, "but for now, I believe you might be interested in one of the private games." He gestured to a shadowed archway, cloaked with a heavy black velvet curtain, and then held out a bag of gaming chips. "I understand you to be a man of integrity and honour, my lord."

Max nodded his thanks and accepted the bag. "All and any debts shall be paid in full, you have my word, and now I believe we will take a look behind that curtain. Thank you, Monsieur Demarteau."

"My pleasure, my lord, lady. I hope you have a... *successful* evening."

Phoebe watched the man walk away before lifting her gaze to Max again.

"He knows," she said, a little shocked.

"I suspect that a man who runs a business such as this makes it his business to know everything," Max said, his tone dry.

The viscount laughed softly and nodded. "I made a few discreet enquiries about the brothers who own Rouge et Noir, but there was no one willing to breathe a word about them. Not so much as a murmur. I think that speaks volumes."

"Well, then, shall we go and see what Richard is about?" Nina asked, turning her attention from Charlie to Phoebe.

She spoke lightly, but there was a thread of tension in the words that revealed her true feelings. The viscount frowned down at her and covered the hand that rested lightly on his arm.

"There is no need for you to involve yourself in this. No need to provoke the baron's anger. He need not know you led us here, nor that you had a part to play in it."

Nina shook her head. "I have always been honest with Richard. I despise falsehoods, trickery... though I would not blame you for disbelieving that, having posed as your wife these past days. Nonetheless, I prefer to face him. There was no great love affair between us, but there was affection, on my part, at least. I do not like to believe my faith in him was so ill-placed, but I shall face him and look into his eyes. I believe I shall know if he thought to cheat on me and leave."

Kline regarded her with such obvious admiration that Nina laughed, that good, hearty sound that Phoebe had liked so well.

"I may be a whore, Lord Kline, but I flatter myself I am an honest one."

Kline's face darkened and he took her hand, raising it to his lips. "I see only a lady, and one that has faced adversity and survived. Come, let us face this young dandy and see what manner of man he truly is."

Phoebe read a startled look on Nina's face, followed by a flush of pink that she suspected surprised the lady even more. Nina did not strike her as a woman who blushed easily, if at all, but she followed Kline as he led them towards the curtained alcove. The viscount held the curtain back and Nina stepped through, followed by Phoebe and Max, with Kline lowering the curtain behind him as he joined them.

There were four good-sized round tables set up in the large room, lit only by oil lamps, one suspended above each table. Three of the tables were occupied, the players so intent on their game that not one looked up. The tension here was palpable, the stakes high. On the far side of the room, Phoebe saw Alvanly. His face was relaxed, his posture likewise, but she saw the fist that rested on his thigh beneath the tabletop was clenched. As they moved towards him, his opponent laid out his cards, and Alvanly let out a long, slow breath and then smiled. He leaned in and swept the pile of gaming counters in the centre of the table towards him.

"*Tant pis,*" he said to the man before him, who got up with a muttered curse and stalked from the room.

The baron chuckled, the sound dying in his throat as he saw who was watching him. He stood then and smiled broadly, though the expression did not meet his eyes.

"Why, good evening, my lords! *Miss* Barrington, oh, and the lovely Nina. Have a care, Kline, she's expensive. Can you afford her?"

Phoebe saw Lord Kline stiffen at the insult, but Nina just laughed, and Phoebe's heart ached for her, knowing she had surmised the truth just as they all had: Alvanly would have cheated her.

"Darling Richard, how like you to say such a thing, when it is *you* who have cost *me* money. It's you who are expensive goods, for I cannot afford to keep you, nor do I find any lingering desire to make the effort."

She moved towards the table and held out the voluminous skirts of her lavish gown, sweeping the counters he had just won into the lush fabric as he glared daggers at her. "I believe this will pay the debt, give or take a few pounds," she said, holding the baron's furious gaze for a long moment before turning to Phoebe. "My debt, at least. I believe you have another to settle yet."

She smiled as Lord Kline moved to her and offered his arm once more.

"Shall we go and change those into something more useful, Mrs Abercrombie?"

"Yes, please. I have a debt to pay of my own," she said, her gaze softening as Kline looked upon her and did not look away. Her breath caught, and she gave a surprised little laugh before turning to Phoebe. "Happy hunting, dear," she said, before allowing Kline to guide her away.

"Well, Miss Barrington, Lord Ellisborough, what can I do for you?"

"A game," Phoebe said brightly before Max could speak. She ignored the way Alvanly kept referring to her unmarried status. He was only trying to ruffle her, and it would take a good deal more than that to do so. She took the purse of counters Max held from his hand and dropped it on the table with a muffled clatter. "I shall play you."

Phoebe felt rather than saw Max react to her words, felt his desire to warn her, to tell her not to play such a man. She turned to look at him. Max held her gaze for a moment, and then smiled, pulling out the chair for her to sit down.

Alvanly laughed and held out his hands to display the empty table before him. "But what with? They have denied me credit here and I have nothing left to wager."

Phoebe tsked at him like she was scolding a small boy. "Now, now, my lord. Do not be obtuse, not when we know you are still in possession of that valuable painting, and Max will lend you... shall we say fifty pounds on my behalf? I shall pay you back of course, Max"

Max stared at her and she could see his desire to speak, to ask what she was playing at, but he said nothing and nodded his agreement.

Greed flickered in Alvanly's eyes, and Phoebe knew she had him. Her ability to pick locks aside, he had no reason to believe her anything less than a nice young lady who thought she had a fair hand with the cards because she won against her friends and family. She smiled at him, allowing him his illusion. Alvanly chuckled and looked up at Max, his gaze considering.

"You'll allow this?" he asked. "It's foolishness."

Max returned an icy glare that her father would have been proud of. "You did the lady a great wrong, Alvanly. If she chooses to exact revenge in this manner, that is her affair, her choice. I will only see to it that you do not renege on any deal she strikes."

"Oh, *I* won't renege," he said, so smug that Phoebe's hand itched with the desire to smack him about the head. "But who will ensure the lady pays up when I relieve her of her fortune?"

Phoebe returned a disgusted glare. "Any bills will be paid in full. I am hardly penniless, and some of us have a shred of honour to our names."

Alvanly's gaze darkened, all evidence of the charming young man he purported to be dissolving like smoke and leaving all who saw in no doubt as to how thin the veneer had been. Max had been right to warn her about this man, to feel concern for her interest in him. She looked up at Max now, standing beside her, solid as an English oak, protecting her but allowing her this, her choice, her decision.

"Max."

He looked to her at once, his dark eyes searching hers.

"Yes," she said softly.

For a moment he frowned, not understanding, and then his breath caught. There was such joy in his eyes, she knew she had chosen right. He would never crush her, never bully or impose his will upon her, and when he was wrong he would apologise, and make amends. Wryly, she was forced to acknowledge that she was the one most likely to spend her time apologising, but she would learn too, learn how to be the wife he deserved.

"If you still want—" she added in a rush, realising too late her hubris in believing he might still wish to marry her.

Before she could finish the sentence, he had bent and stolen a swift kiss.

"More than you can possibly know," he whispered, for her ears only.

"If you two love birds have quite finished…?" Alvanly drawled.

"No," Max replied coolly, looking at the baron with deep distaste. "But I can wait. Phoebe has a matter of honour to settle."

Alvanly snorted and shuffled the cards, but Phoebe wagged a finger at him.

"Oh, no," she said, smiling and gesturing to one of the serving staff who stood unmoving in the shadows, awaiting orders. "A new deck, *s'il vous plaît*."

The baron smirked and poured himself a glass of wine from the half empty bottle at his elbow. "And what are we playing, Phoebe, dear? Whist?"

"No, Ecarté," she said simply, and smiled.

Chapter 18

My dear Gabriel,

I have made the most interesting friends since I have been in France and have also the great delight of informing you, we have a new customer in the person of Lord Ellisborough, who wishes to both invest and to restock his own cellars.

I admit I never dreamed that life in your employ would lead me into such extraordinary circumstances. You have given me a new lease of life along with the chance to redeem myself and my fortunes.

I am ever in your debt. Especially now as I believe perhaps my luck has changed. Life can sometimes take such a surprising turn...

—Excerpt of a letter to Mr Gabriel Knight from The Right Hon'ble Viscount Charles Kline.

11th April 1827. Rouge et Noir, 7th Arrondissement, Paris.

Phoebe allowed Alvanly to win the first three hands, playing recklessly and *apparently* with little regard to her cards. In truth, the baron had the devil's own luck tonight and she knew she'd only have won two of the three *if* she had played to the best of her ability. This was another kind of game altogether, though, luring the baron onto the path she wished him to take, and she wasn't about to play fair.

Alvanly would play wagering a painting he knew well to be worthless. He had used her, stolen from Mrs Manning, and would have cheated Nina out of her money too. Phoebe felt no compunction about using the skills Jack had taught her as a girl to even the score. The only problem was, Max did not know of her skill with the cards, or just how well she could cheat. She wondered briefly if he would be disgusted by her having done so, but pushed that thought aside. It was time to trust in Max, to believe that he would know she had done it for the best, as he was trusting her to carry through her mad scheme, even though he did not understand what she was doing.

She made a great show of concentrating on the next hand, and grinned with delight at Max when she won. He smiled down at her, though concern lingered in his gaze and she wished she could tell him what she was about. She had considered it, but there had been so little time, and in truth, it suited her for him to appear on edge, for it added verisimilitude to the picture of innocence she wished to present to Lord Alvanly. That edgy anxiety rolled off poor Max in waves as Phoebe lost the next three hands, and her debt to Alvanly racked up to two hundred pounds.

"Dearest Phoebe, do you think you are perhaps in over your head?" Alvanly taunted as he poured himself another glass of wine.

"Oh, no, my luck is sure to turn," she said brightly, shuffling the card so ineptly that two fell free of the deck. "Oopsie."

Alvanly rolled his eyes as Phoebe reached for the fallen cards, unaware of the fact she had just palmed the king of hearts. She dealt the cards in batches of two and three, five each, and then turned the next one up to reveal the trump, the king of hearts.

"Oh, I get a point for that, don't I?" she said disingenuously.

Alvanly scowled. "I propose."

"Oh, how sweet," Phoebe said, batting her eyelashes at him, well aware that meant he wished for another card. "I refuse."

Alvanly's scowl deepened. But it was the dealer's right to accept or refuse, and Phoebe wanted to play immediately, having arranged a perfect array of cards through some judicious sleight of hand.

"That's two extra points to me if I win," Alvanly muttered.

"But you aren't going to win," Phoebe said, smiling sweetly, and proceeded to take the trick, and the next, and the one after. "Oh!" she crowed, having won back fifty pounds. "I told you my luck would turn."

Naturally, she then lost disastrously, losing three hundred pounds, much to her opponent's amusement, but it was all a part of the deeper game she played, reeling him in.

"I think we should make things more interesting," she said, having dealt the next hand and made out as if she were trying to hide the fact she had excellent cards. "A thousand pounds," she declared.

Max jolted beside her and she looked up at him. There was a pleading expression in his eyes, and she reached out and took his hand, pressing a kiss to his gloved fingers as she held his gaze. He let out a ragged breath and smiled, saying nothing, though she knew he must be biting his tongue. He squeezed her fingers in a silent show of support, and Phoebe turned back to Alvanly to see avarice and excitement glittering in his eyes.

"But I don't have a thousand pounds, as you well know."

"But you do have the painting," Phoebe pointed out.

Alvanly laughed and wagged a finger at her. "Oh ho. No, my dear. That painting is worth far more than a thousand pounds. Ten thousand, at least."

"I'm not playing you for ten thousand pounds," Phoebe said in disgust, though her heart was hammering with excitement.

"Then I shall not play." Alvanly sat back and folded his arms.

Phoebe bit her lip, as if considering his proposal.

"Two thousand."

Alvanly snorted.

Phoebe looked up as a dark figure drifted towards the table and Monsieur Demarteau appeared. He stood watching, his sloe black gaze drifting to Phoebe, and she smothered a curse. Even Jack could not tell when she was cheating. Her fingers were so nimble, too quick for most eyes, even if they knew what to look for, but a man like that…. His dark eyes focused on her, making her heart thud and her stomach churn so hard she felt sick. She felt as if he could *see* everything. The last thing she needed was to be caught cheating. Well, there was no help for it. She was committed to this course; she had to take the chance.

"Five thousand pounds," she said, putting her chin up and ignoring Max, whose fists were clenched now. He put them behind his back and paced away from her for a moment before returning to stand at her side, his jaw rigid with tension.

"That's half its value. Less, even," Alvanly said in disgust.

"Yes, but it's cash, and it's yours if you win, *and* you keep the painting. All that money without the bother of finding a buyer. Heaven knows how long that would take. And then there is that little matter of provenance," she added, lifting one eyebrow.

The baron's gaze drifted to Demarteau and back to Phoebe, his lips compressing into a thin line of displeasure.

"Fine."

Phoebe fought to suppress a grin of triumph as Alvanly reached beneath the table and retrieved a small, paper-wrapped parcel. He tugged at the string holding it closed to reveal the grubby little picture that had caused all this bother.

"I wager the painting."

"And the three hundred pounds you have there," Phoebe added with a glittering smile. "And I shall wager five thousand, three hundred. I believe that is fair."

"As you like," Alvanly replied sullenly. His gaze flickered back to Demarteau, who lingered in the shadows, silent and still, and a little unnerving.

Phoebe took a breath, and a moment to calm her jittery heart, before she shuffled the cards, expertly this time, allowing Alvanly to see her skill as the cards flew between her hands. His eyes grew wide and he looked sharply at her. Phoebe looked back, unsmiling.

She dealt, her fingers moving quickly, floating the cards she wanted to the top of the deck and once again turning up the king as trumps, spades this time.

"Oh, would you look at that," she said, badly feigning surprise as Alvanly's jaw set rigid.

She dared a glance up at Demarteau to find him watching her intently, his dark eyes fierce and considering. He did not know, but he suspected. Phoebe waited, wondering what he would do, if anything. One corner of his mouth kicked up just a little. Phoebe let out a breath of relief.

She could feel Max's gaze upon her, and sensed his astonishment as she played card after perfect card. Alvanly was sweating now. Not that he had anything of real value to lose. He knew as well as she did that the painting was a fake, but to have had the money so nearly in his hands—as he believed, at least— and to have it snatched away, by her of all people. He was sick with it.

Phoebe held his gaze as she laid the card that sealed his fate and won the game.

"You lose."

***

Max was coiled so tight he felt ready to burst. His hands were fists behind his back, palms sweaty, his lungs locked down hard, and he could not draw a breath.

When Phoebe finally laid the winning card, it was all he could do not to shout in triumph. The little beauty, she'd done it! Good God. She'd beaten Alvanly to flinders. He did not understand how, could not fathom how she had played so terribly to begin with and then....

Except, of course, she had been playing a deeper game than he had realised. Her eyes had begged him to trust her, and even though he had been desperate to save her from folly, from losing a fortune to this loathsome man, he had allowed her to continue. He had not interfered, not counselled her to stop, not *insisted* she stop, and thank God for that. She would never have forgiven him for not trusting her. And now he saw... saw the brilliance of it, the sheer daring. He hadn't the slightest doubt that Jack had taught her such skills, and she had been toying with the baron from the start, utterly in control.

God, she was magnificent.

"You lose."

Alvanly surged to his feet.

"You cheated!" he raged, pointing a finger at her. "I'm not giving you anything, you tricky little bitch."

Max erupted in fury, but Demarteau was there before he could lay his hands on the baron for saying such a thing.

"*Arrêtez!*" he said sharply, holding Max back with surprising force for such a young man. "Stop. Your lady does not need your assistance."

Max turned his head and froze, seeing the truth of the Frenchman's words with a gasp of shock. Phoebe was sitting quite calmly in her seat, holding a small pearl-handled gun on the baron.

He had seen that gun before.

"The painting and my three hundred pounds, if you please," she said, her hand perfectly steady.

"You wouldn't dare," Alvanly sneered.

Max choked, torn between shock and laughter. She really would get the bloody painting back at gunpoint.

"Honestly, I wouldn't bet on that," he said, meaning it. "You ought never dare, Phoebe. It's a dreadfully bad idea."

"Lord Alvanly," Demarteau said smoothly, as he moved towards the baron. "I watched the game. You lost, the lady won. We 'ave no room for bad losers at Rouge et Noir. I would like you to leave now. I counsel you... do not come back 'ere again. I think you would not like the welcome you receive."

Alvanly looked at Demarteau, who exuded menace though he did not move so much as an eyelid. He just watched the baron placidly. Alvanly turned his gaze looked to Phoebe, who had not lowered her gun, and let out a soft laugh as the tension fell away from him. He shook his head.

"I really could have fallen for you, Phoebe, dear," he said, staring at her with something like hunger in his eyes, before turning to Max. "I wish you joy of her, Ellisborough. She'll lead you a merry dance, by God. I admit, I envy you that."

And then he turned his back on them all and walked away.

Max let out a breath and turned back to Phoebe, wanting to congratulate her and apologise for ever having doubted her, but before he had the chance, she had launched herself into his arms and was holding on tight.

"Oh, Max! Max, thank goodness you were here. I was so afraid I would mess it up."

She clung to him, trembling in every limb, and Max held her to him, beyond words that she had turned to him, his heart so full he almost trembled himself with the enormity of everything he felt.

"Afraid?" said he asked incredulously. He tipped her head up, his fingers gentle on her chin as he looked down at her. "I don't believe it. You were ice cold the entire way through. I've never seen such a steady hand, and the way you drew him in, losing those first hands... my God, Phoebe. You were incredible. I've seen nothing like it before in my life."

"Nor I," murmured a soft voice beside them.

They turned to see Demarteau watching them with interest.

"I should like to try my hand against you, Lady Ellisborough, should you 'ave cause to return to Rouge et Noir. I believe it would be an—'ow do you say, *une expérience éclairante*?"

"An enlightening experience," Phoebe translated for him with a nervous smile.

"Quite so," Demarteau said, the glimmer of a smile tugging at the corners of his mouth. "Though I would prefer it if you did not use those quick fingers of yours with quite such skill when we meet. A fair fight, *alors*? I shall have the counters changed up for you. The money will be waiting at the door, with the painting when you leave. If you wish to celebrate there is dancing in the ballroom. One of my men will show you the way. Good evening to you both."

He gave a deep and respectful bow and left them alone.

Max looked back to Phoebe with a frown. "He knew."

"Yes," Phoebe said, her expression sheepish. "I don't usually cheat, I promise, though I admit it's tempting, but I had to win against Alvanly. I *had* to. You do see?"

There was fear in her eyes, and he realised she was afraid he might not see, might not understand why she had done what she had. He had no words to tell her what he felt, all he had experienced and learned and understood from the moment they had set foot in Rouge et Noir, and so he simply leaned down and pressed his mouth to hers.

"I love you," he said.

She sighed, her anxiety melting away as she leaned into him. "I should like to dance with you, Max."

"Your wish is my command, my Lady Ellisborough."

Phoebe looked up and beamed at him. "I am your lady."

"Yes," he said, unable to keep the emotion from his voice. "Yes, you are."

***

Though it was closer to morning than evening, the ballroom was alive still. Music swelled and Cyprians and scandalous women, the fashionable and the richest in the city, came together to dance. It was not dancing of the kind Phoebe was used to. A waltz was still shocking enough, even after so many years of acceptance in the *ton*'s ballrooms, but always there was a proper distance kept between partners. Not so here. The waltz here was a different creature, passionate and indiscreet as men held their ladies far too close, their hands too low on their backs. Phoebe saw one man kiss his partner's neck as she closed her eyes with a sigh of pleasure. She hurried Max to the dance floor, wanting that now. At once.

He swept her into the melee and Phoebe laughed with the joy of it. His eyes reflected her laughter, and it shone in the warmth of his smile, happiness radiating from him. She had done that. She had made him happy.

"I want to dance until the sun comes up," she said, gasping as Max pulled her close against him, delighted that her proper, polite Lord Ellisborough should act so outrageously.

"Then we shall," he said, leaning in to nip at her ear.

Phoebe gasped as desire lanced through her, and wondered if she might rather go back to the hotel at once.

Max shook his head.

"Not until dawn," he murmured, amusement lurking in his dark eyes.

Oh, well, she had said she wanted to dance until the sun came up, and all good things came to those who waited, she supposed. She grinned at him and he swept her into a quick turn, spinning her so fast she almost stumbled. His arms tightened about her, keeping her steady, and on they went, with Max guiding her effortlessly through the crowd. He would not act so in life though, she realised. He would always steady her when she stumbled, but he would not choose her path for her.

Phoebe closed her eyes and let the music spin her away.

***

Max stared down at the glittering look Phoebe gave him and felt his breath catch. The night was over, the sun touching the sky and lighting the darkness, but Phoebe did not look the least bit sleepy.

"Take me back to the hotel," she said, and Max became aware of a new challenge. How the devil to get Phoebe back to her parents and marry her, without debauching her at every opportunity between here and Dern?

Judging by the stormy darkening of her eyes, it was an endeavour Phoebe had no intention of helping with.

He took her hand and placed it firmly upon his sleeve, guiding her out of the lavish ballroom.

"Should we find Charlie and Nina before we go?" she asked as he steered her through the crowds.

"No," he said, smiling a little. "I suspect they left hours ago."

Phoebe grinned, and he chuckled at the pleasure in her eyes. "Do you think they'll marry?"

Max shrugged, less certain of that than the fact that Charlie had every intention of getting to know Nina a good deal better. "I think it would take a great incentive to get Kline to walk the aisle again, after his last experience."

"Oh, but Nina is nothing like his last wife, I'm certain of it, and I'm an excellent judge of character."

Max sent her a bland look and Phoebe huffed.

"I *knew* Alvanly was a rogue, Max, so don't look at me like that. I admit I was immensely stupid to fall in with his plans, but I thought he only meant to seduce me, and I'm very capable of foiling *those* sorts of plans."

Max stilled, something hot and angry unfurling in his belly. "What do you mean by that? If some devil has tried to—"

Phoebe sighed and reached up a hand to touch his cheek, such a tender caress he shivered with longing, wishing they were already at the hotel and away from prying eyes.

"No, Max. There are no more villains for you to protect me from. I only meant that I am not so innocent as that. I know how to defend myself if the need arises, and if that had been Alvanly's plan he would have failed, but I think perhaps you are coming to see that for yourself."

He let out a soft breath of laughter. "Indeed," he murmured.

It seemed an eternity before they had collected their cloaks and hats, but finally the black painted door of Rouge et Noir closed behind them and Max handed Phoebe up into the carriage. He had barely closed the door and sat down when Phoebe landed herself in his lap with a soft rustle of silk skirts and petticoats.

Desire lanced through him, all the restraint he had meant to hold himself back with snapping in an instant as her soft behind nestled against his groin. With a groan he reached for her, sinking his fingers in the insanity of her latest hairdo and pulling her mouth to his. He was neither tender nor sweet, his mouth urgent upon hers, seeking, taking, demanding more, but he sensed his passion only inflamed her. This was his Phoebe after all, bold and brave and unlike anyone he'd ever met in his life before. She tugged at his cravat and he stilled her hand.

"We have to walk through the hotel yet," he said, laughing a little at the frustration in her eyes.

"But I want to touch you," she said, her impatience sending a jolt of lust directly to his groin.

"You must wait," he commanded, astonished he got the words out and not the least bit surprised his voice was deep and harsh.

Phoebe shivered in his arms and he realised she had rather liked that tone, a revelation he tucked away to be considered later.

"But I can touch you," he added with a wicked smirk.

He tugged at his gloves, biting into the finger ends to pull them off and casting them down on the seat beside them before reaching for the hem of her skirts. Phoebe gasped as he found his way beneath the yards of silk and the petticoats that frothed beneath until his hand closed around one dainty, stocking-clad ankle.

"Got you," he murmured, leaning in to nuzzle the sweet spot beneath her ear and nipping at the soft lobe as his hand moved up, slowly but inexorably, following the curve of her calf and then caressing the sensitive skin at the back of her knee. He kissed the line of her jaw, aware of the way her breathing quickened, the rapid rise and fall of her breasts pushing against the indecent neckline of her gown. His questing hand moved on, lingering on the garter just above her knee. "Show me."

Her breath caught at the dark command, but she lost no time in reaching for her skirts, hiking them up until he could glimpse the ribbon and the neat little bow.

"Black," she whispered.

Max groaned and sought her mouth, revelling in the sweet taste of her, the enthusiastic slide of her tongue against his. He almost laughed with joy as he considered her enthusiasm, compared to the disaster of his first marriage. His poor first wife had been raised with such a fear of physical intimacy she would not even look upon her own nakedness, let alone his. He had been filled with regret and pity for her, and he had tried his best to be kind, even when she was not.

Never again, though. Never again would he suffer years of loneliness because of vows that tied him to a woman who could not bear to have him touch her, who found the act of lovemaking not only distasteful but abhorrent. Phoebe moved closer to him, seeking more, pressing herself against him, hiding nothing of her desire for him, wanting him so blatantly that he wondered how to keep a hold on the situation when he was mad with wanting her too. He did not, however, wish for an interruption from Jack, which would likely see him dead in a ditch if the old rogue believed he had laid hands on his princess.

"Max," she whimpered against his mouth. "Max, please...."

He hushed her, kissing her deeper, crooning love words as his hand slid over the warm silk of her thigh and brushed the curls that marked the sweet centre of her.

She gasped and he chuckled. "This is what you want, darling."

"Yes," she agreed, clinging to his neck, her eyes drifting shut as he slid his fingers through the curls to the delicate skin beneath.

It was his turn to gasp, to hold his breath against the tortured moan that built in his chest as he found what he sought, hot and slick with desire.

"Oh, God," he whispered, the words ragged with need. "I want to kiss you here, to put my mouth upon you and taste you."

For a moment, he wondered if he had gone too far, if even Phoebe had her limits. She was innocent, after all. She might believe herself otherwise, but he knew Montagu had guarded her as well as anyone could guard Phoebe...

"Yes. Yes, please."

She was staring at him, her eyes dark, cheeks flushed, and Max laughed at his own foolishness, imagining he could shock Phoebe of all people.

"Please, Max," she whispered.

Max swallowed, his mouth watering with the desire to do as she wished, but he could not, not here.

"No," he rasped. "Not enough time. We'll be at the hotel in ten minutes, and I'm damned if I'll rush such a thing."

"Oh, but...."

"Hush," he soothed her. "Let me touch you."

He shifted her across his lap to lean into the corner of the carriage, kissing her slow and deep while his fingers caressed the soft place between her thighs. His heart thudded too hard, too fast, his body aching with need, but he was focused on nothing but her pleasure. Max slid a finger inside her, his breath catching as hers hitched too.

"Oh," she said, her hands clutched in his hair, tugging his mouth back to hers as his questing finger slid deeper into her tight heat.

For, a moment he imagined himself there, imagined the pleasure of it, slick and warm and welcoming, and the tide of desire almost drowned him. He fought against it, fought for control as he coaxed and tempted Phoebe into losing hers. Finally she gasped, her head tipping back, exposing the elegant line of her neck. Max leaned in, nipping at her tender throat gently, and she fractured in his arms. She trembled and gave a soft, shuddering cry that made his heart soar with happiness as she took the pleasure he gave her, without shame or apology. When she came back to herself, she stared at him with quiet delight, without a trace of regret.

"How beautiful you are," he said. "And how I love you."

"I love you too, Max."

Max stared at her, hardly daring to breathe, to believe she had said the words he had ached for. He knew Phoebe desired him, knew that she liked him—most of the time—and that had been more than he'd dared dream of. He'd hoped love would come, in time, but he had not expected....

"Did you not know, Max?" she asked, a little shy now as he shook his head, too overwhelmed to speak. She chuckled and snuggled into him and he heard her smother a yawn. "Well, I do. I love you, very much. Lord, I'm sleepy."

She let out a soft sigh and closed her eyes, asleep within moments.

Max stared at her, beguiled and amused that she should fall asleep at such a moment.

"Oh, my love," he said, unable to hold back his laughter, his joy. "Thank you. Thank you for reminding me what it is to be alive."

Max carried her into the hotel as the sun rose over Paris, uncaring of the scandalous glances they received. He would not have woken her for the world. She stirred as he laid her gently on the bed and tried to unwind her arms from his neck.

"No," she said, shaking her head. "Stay. Stay with me."

He knew he ought not. Though they had signed in as man and wife, they were not, and he ought not court disaster, but he did not wish to leave her alone.

It was not impossible to sleep chastely by her side. Difficult, but not impossible. If he rose before she woke, all would be well. So he went with her, down to the bed, holding her to him, her head on his chest as she sighed and fell back to sleep.

Chapter 19

My dear friend,

I have the greatest joy in telling you that Phoebe has agreed to marry me. Although it seems still to be some extraordinary dream, she does not do so only to protect her reputation. Indeed, if that were the only consideration, I know she would refuse me. By some miracle she returns my feelings, and I believe I need not explain to you how happy I am. I flatter myself that this news will not be unwelcome, but I give you my word of honour that I shall do all in my power to be everything she needs, to give her everything she desires, and never to cage her free spirit.

She wishes to marry at Dern, upon our return to England. To my dismay, she is also holding me to my promise to allow her to enjoy Paris. We will return as soon as I can persuade her to leave such delights behind. I beg you will make the necessary arrangements so we might be married at once.

—Excerpt of a letter to The Most Honourable Lucian Barrington, Marquess of Montagu, from The Right Hon'ble Maximillian Carmichael, Earl of Ellisborough.

12th April 1827. Hôtel Westminster, 2nd Arrondissement, Paris.

Phoebe sighed, blinking a little as sunlight slanted through a crack in the curtains. Little by little, the events of last night returned to her: besting Alvanly at cards, and Max standing at her side, trusting her to do as she wished. Dancing until dawn, and then the wicked pleasure Max had given her on the journey back to the hotel. A smile curved her mouth as she remembered him in the carriage, the way he had kissed her, touched her, the sinful thing he'd said he wanted to do. She had never realised he had such a side to him. How had she always thought him so very proper, such a perfect gentleman—which he was, without a doubt—but he was also....

"What are you thinking about, you dreadful girl?"

She jolted and turned, the smile growing wider as she discovered him lying beside her, his head propped on one hand as he stared down with a lazy, somewhat predatory glint in his eyes.

"About what you said to me last night," she replied, aware that her heart was racing.

Lord, but he was big. Broad shoulders and strong arms, the scent of him wrapping about her, something clean and citrusy, and another scent beneath that, musky and male. It made her want to snatch at his shirt and lick his skin, as if he was strawberry ice. The thought made her blush.

"That I loved you?" he suggested, smiling.

"No," she admitted, biting her lip as he raised an eyebrow at her. "Not that. Though that was lovely, too, but I knew already."

He gave a bark of laughter and lay back on the bed, chuckling to himself. "Oh, Lord. I ought to have left before you woke, but I couldn't make myself do it."

"Why should you leave?" she demanded, sitting up with a rustle of her scarlet skirts, gazing down at him. He was rumpled, his immaculate evening clothes all creased and his hair mussed, one thick dark lock tumbling over his forehead. She reached out and pushed it back, delighted that she could, that she had the right to touch him so.

"You know why," he said letting out a heavy sigh. "I have to look your father in the eye when we go home, and I'd rather he not feel the need to slice me into tiny pieces."

"Pffft," she said, shaking her head. "He's not such a hypocrite as that, and we shall write and tell him we are going home to be married, though not yet. You promised to show me Paris, remember?"

Max groaned. "Let's go home and get married, and then come back to Paris for our honeymoon."

Phoebe rolled her eyes. "We're here now, Max, and I have no desire to repeat that awful sea crossing again so soon. Going home will be horrid enough."

He flung an arm over his eyes and muttered a curse. "Phoebe, love. I'm not sure I can wait that long for you."

"Then don't." Phoebe hitched up her skirts and climbed over him, catching hold of his wrists as he moved to shift her away. "Be still," she said firmly.

Max subsided, something wary and hot shifting in his eyes that made her stomach tighten.

"You ought to be innocent when you walk down the aisle." The protestation was almost sulky, and Phoebe gave a hoot of laughter.

"Oh, Max, you are adorable."

He scowled at her and she leaned down and pressed a kiss to his mouth.

"Your wedding night…." he persisted, and she kissed him again, cutting off his indignant words.

"Max," she said softly as she moved her lips away. "When I say my vows I ought to be committed to them, to believe them with my whole heart, and mean them to the depths of my soul, and I will. That is what is important, that we love each other and mean the promises we make. Whether or not we have... *anticipated* our vows by a few days is neither here nor there. Papa cares only for my happiness, and you make me happy. I am safe with you, safe to be myself, as dreadful as that may be, and I want this. I want you. All of you, with no holding back, no politeness, no distance."

"Phoebe," he whispered, reaching out and touching her face.

She turned into his caress, kissing his palm.

"You know how horribly spoilt I am, Max. If I want something, I must have it. I *will* have it."

To her dismay, Max shook his head. "No. Not now," he said, his voice low and rough with desire. "But... soon. If you're certain."

Phoebe grinned at him, delighted by his capitulation. *Soon* did not mean after they were wed. "I am. I am certain of you."

"Then we shall take things slowly and, when you are ready, you shall have all that you desire, but for now...."

The shimmer of something wicked shifted behind his eyes again and Phoebe shivered with anticipation.

"You never told me." His words were low and caressing now and her breath caught. "You never explained what it was you were thinking about."

Despite everything, she blushed a little. His words had scandalised her, but only because she had not known he would *want* such a thing. Mama had told her much of what to expect, but that detail she had left out. His words had caught her skin aflame, though, and the desire in his expression only made her burn hotter.

He moved suddenly and Phoebe squealed as she landed flat on her back, with Max pinning her wrists to the mattress.

"Tell me," he said urgently.

She stared up at this new vision of Max, one she had only glimpsed before. There was something wild in his eyes. The quiet calm she had always associated with him burned away to leave something far more primitive in its place, something that made her shiver with pleasure and anticipation. He was so strong, strong enough to overpower her, yet strong enough that he would never try to.

Phoebe gathered her courage, determined not to be missish and coy when he clearly wanted her to say the words. "You said you wanted to k-kiss me."

"I did." He stared at her, hunger in his expression. "And you want that? You want my mouth on you?"

"Yes," she could hardly get the words out now. Her breathing was shallow, coming too fast. "Very much."

"Where? Where do you want my mouth?"

He released her wrists and, with hands that were not entirely steady, Phoebe reached for the silken hem of her skirts and the lace of her petticoats, all of them crumpled and in disarray. Max moved back, sitting on his heels as she drew them up over her legs, over her knees.

Impossibly, his eyes darkened further as she revealed her garters and the little black ribbons, and then the first glimmer of her skin at her stocking tops.

Max swallowed, his gaze following the fabric as it rose. She thought perhaps he was holding his breath.

"More," he said, sounding as though his throat was parched, as if he had been wandering a desert for days and she was his oasis.

She did as he asked, until he could glimpse the dark gold curls at the apex of her thighs. He let out a shaky breath, his chest rising and falling as though he'd been running. Suddenly he moved, stripping off his coat and flinging it away from him before prowling up the mattress towards her.

"M-Max?" she said, a little uncertain now at the predatory glint in his eyes.

"Your wish is my command, Phoebe," he murmured, sliding his hands up the backs of her ankles, her calves, and then tugging so she fell back against the pillows with a gasp.

He rubbed his cheek against the soft skin of her inner thigh, his breath fluttering against her so intimately she couldn't speak. Perhaps sensing her tension, he looked up, and the pure lust in his expression made her quiver, made a hot liquid rush fill her as though that look had melted her from the inside out.

"You can say no. You can tell me to stop."

Phoebe licked her lips, hesitating for a moment. "Don't stop."

He smiled then, a purely masculine smile of triumph that made her want to laugh, except that at that moment he did just as he'd promised and covered her with his mouth. The laughter died in her throat as a combination of shock and wonder rippled through her. Good heavens, that was... that... that was....

"Oh, Max. Oh, that's... *wicked.*"

He chuckled against her skin. "You like it?"

"It's utterly sinful," she breathed the words, gasping as his tongue slid over her in one, long, sinuous lick. "Of course I like it."

"Good, because I like you. I like you very much, especially the way you taste, sweet and tart and delicious."

Phoebe blushed, astonished that Max would say such things to her, that he would be so... so different from how he had always seemed. To think, she had once believed him staid and boring and... dull. What a little simpleton she'd been.

She could not think at all after that, as he returned to his sensual attack on her person, leaving her giddy and dazed as he made her cry out, louder and with greater abandon, seeming to revel in the wanton sounds she made. Finally, she shattered, the sensation one of flying, of being flung into some high, bright place that sparkled through her as pleasure rippled through her body. Through all of it Max stayed with her, easing every last shudder of bliss from her sensitive flesh until she was wrung out and boneless in the afterglow. Then he lay down beside her and praised her, told her she was beautiful, wonderful, utterly perfect... which made her giggle and turn in to his chest, laughing uncontrollably.

"P-Perfect," she stammered helplessly, clutching at his shirt.

"You are," he insisted. "Perfect for me. I had forgotten what living felt like, what joy felt like. It has been so long since I felt it I believed I had outgrown it, that it was for children and fools, those who had not seen the truth of life." He cupped her face within his hands, his eyes so full of adoration that her throat grew tight. "I thought I might marry someone who would be a friend, who would keep me company as the years passed, but I never expected... I never thought for a moment.... You made me remember who I once was, Phoebe. Who I want to be again."

"I love who you are right now, Max," she said and kissed him.

***

The rest of their time in Paris was perfect. To begin with, Max took her shopping, insisting she buy an entire new wardrobe for their return to England.

"I do not propose to marry a prettily behaved little wallflower, love," he said, his eyes alight with mischief. "I want my wife to turn heads, and make all the old tabbies gasp and murmur behind their fans. So we had best buy you everything that is the height of fashion, had we not?"

"Oh, well, if you insist, Max," Phoebe said demurely, struggling to keep her countenance. "For I *do* want to be a good wife to you, and if that is what you wish...."

"It is," he insisted, and was endlessly patient and good-humoured as she was measured and pinned, and chose a wardrobe of outrageously vivid colours and styles, precisely calculated to do just as he had asked.

It was marvellous.

They visited Place Louis XVI—where that monarch and his Queen, Marie Antoinette, had lost their heads to Madame La Guillotine—the Louvre, the gardens of the Tuileries, Place Vendome, and the Pont Neuf. The cemetery of Père Lachaise was perhaps a morbid destination, but Max indulged her, happy to take her anywhere, apparently delighted by her delight in everything they saw, every memory they made together. They met up with Nina and Charlie, who looked to be enjoying Paris—and each other—very thoroughly, and most days they went out together. They shopped and danced, and visited the theatre and the opera house, and at night Max took her to bed and taught her a little more of all that they could have together—all they could be together—but always he stopped short of making her his, of taking his own pleasure.

Phoebe did not insist or complain, sensing that this slow seduction was the only way he felt at peace with not waiting for the night of their marriage. She sensed too that he was eager to return home, to begin their lives together, but not once did he voice his wishes. Never did he do anything to diminish the pleasure she took in discovering all that Paris had to offer them.

They were returning from a trip to Place de Vosges, having left Nina and Charlie to find their own entertainment, when she decided they had both been patient enough.

"Max," she said, turning to look at him. "I have one last thing I wish to do before we leave Paris."

He frowned a little. "Leave? I thought you were having fun."

She laughed at that and leaned in to kiss his cheek. "Of course I'm having fun. It's been marvellous, every second of it, but… but

I think I should like to go home, Max. Tomorrow, if you don't mind. I wish to see my family and for us to be married, with all of them around us. And then, I should like to go home—to your home—so you might show it all to me."

His eyes warmed and she knew she had pleased him which made happiness bloom in her own chest. "*Our* home, love. It will be our home."

"Yes."

He leaned in and kissed her, and she sighed, feeling the now familiar tug of arousal. He had been careful to limit their bedtime adventures, and she admitted to feeling a gnawing sense of impatience, a desire to have everything he had promised her.

"And what is it you want, on your last night in Paris?" he asked, his tone such that she knew he would not deny her anything she wished.

"I wish to go back to Rouge et Noir and play Monsieur Demarteau at cards, and...." She hesitated.

"And?"

"And I want you to make love to me, Max."

He smiled, a wicked smile even though a sheepish glimmer sparkled in his eyes. "Do you want the truth, love?"

"Always," she said, wondering what he would say.

"I was going to anyway," he whispered, nuzzling the tender skin beneath her ear. "I cannot wait another night. I shall run mad."

Phoebe chuckled, delighted by the admission.

"Oh, I am so glad," she said with a sigh of relief. "But may we go to Rouge et Noir too?"

Max snorted and pulled her close. "Yes, love. Anything. Whatever you desire. Though I beg you, do not cheat the owner. I suspect he would not take it well."

Phoebe tutted at him. "Of course not."

And then she gave a little shiver, remembering the look in Demarteau's eyes. No, she did not think he would take it well, either.

***

18th April 1827. Rouge et Noir, 7th Arrondissement, Paris.

Max smiled at the delight in Phoebe's eyes as he guided her back into the maelstrom and the explosion of decadent pleasure that was Rouge et Noir. Glasses chinked and champagne corks popped, the chatter of voices punctuated at intervals by shouts of triumph or dismay as large sums were wagered on cards, dice, or roulette. Ladies who were less than respectable, and occasionally daring wives, hung off the arms of noblemen, self-made men, and politicians alike, and the air simmered with expectation.

In truth, Max was impatient for this part of the evening to be done, aching with desire for the beautiful woman at his side, but he knew the value of patience. There was spice in anticipation, though the past days had taxed his fortitude to its limits. Yet he did not wish to cut the evening short either, not when he could see the fascination in Phoebe's expression as she looked about. He was glad to give her this, to share this evening with her and bring her to a place that ought to be forbidden to her, but was safe enough whilst he was at her side. He wanted nothing to be denied her and knew his greatest pleasure in life would always be granting the most outrageous of her wishes and enjoying them with her.

The rich, the titled, and the scandalous all gravitated to this, the most fashionable gambling den in all of Paris. How two incredibly young men had created a business of such obvious wealth and success so quickly was a mystery, but everything about Nicolas Alexandre Demarteau and his brother, Louis César de Montluc, the Comte de Villen, was a mystery. Nicolas was only three and twenty, his brother younger still, yet they ruled this elegant and sophisticated venue with an iron fist, and no one dared speak against them. From what little gossip there was to be had, their parents had escaped *Le Terreur,* when the nobility of France were losing their heads to the guillotine, and they had lost everything of value. They had made the choice between their lives and their fortunes and chosen to live, escaping with little more than the clothes on their backs. What happened next, no one seemed to know, except that their older siblings had died, and that Louis César, the Comte de Villen, had been born into poverty with his illegitimate half-brother standing guard over him.

Two years ago no one knew their names, and in that short space of time they had proven themselves to be clever and resourceful, and dangerous enough that no one would speak a word about them, which only added to the air of mystery that lingered around them.

Max looked up as Demarteau moved to greet them.

"Lord and Lady Ellisborough," he said bowing deeply. "It is a great pleasure to see you here again."

"My wife has ambitions to play you at cards," Max said, sliding his arm about Phoebe's waist. "And she won't leave Paris until that ambition has been fulfilled. Might I ask if you would indulge her, so we can return home at some point soon?"

Demarteau grinned, his even white teeth flashing in the light cast by the massive chandelier overhead.

"It would be a great honour to play you, Lady Ellisborough," he said, holding out his arm to Phoebe.

Phoebe glanced back at him and Max smiled.

"Do you play also, my lord?" Demarteau asked politely.

"No, not tonight, but I should enjoy watching, if you please."

With a nod, Demarteau guided them through the crush of people to a red door, flanked by two impressively intimidating guards. They moved aside as Demarteau approached, opening the door for them. The sounds of revelry muted at once as the door closed and they were led down a long, dimly lit corridor to another door, also guarded. Phoebe met Max's eyes as they both wondered where they were being led.

"Our private quarters," Demarteau said, his dark eyes amused, having read their curious expressions quite correctly.

"We're honoured," Phoebe said, as Demarteau opened a door for them.

Once again, they were surprised, for—having seen the opulence and excess of the décor that was Rouge et Noir—Max had expected more of the same. What they discovered was warmth and luxury and understated elegance, with a surprisingly homely feel to it. Thick rugs muffled their footsteps and the walls were covered with artwork. Everywhere there were haphazard piles of books and magazines, some left open as though the reader had just stepped away for a moment and would return with a drink in hand.

Demarteau led them to a comfortable sitting room painted in shades of blue and green, where a fire blazed in the grand marble hearth and a man sprawled in a large wing-back chair. Long legs extended out before him, his booted feet set up on a footstool. In one hand he held a book, obscuring his face, and in the other he dangled a glass of wine negligently by its rim, his hold so precarious Max feared it would fall.

"Brother, we have guests," Demarteau said.

The figure in the chair stiffened for a second and then relaxed, the book lowering to reveal thickly lashed eyes of such a startling blue that Max was a little taken aback. He was a very young man, little more than a boy, perhaps sixteen or seventeen, eighteen at most. It was hard to tell his age. Though his face was astonishingly beautiful, his eyes held the weight of an older soul, one who had survived. His hair was very dark, close to black like his brother's but not quite, the candlelight burnishing it bronze. He stood in one fluid movement, almost catlike.

"I am honoured," he said, his voice soft as he moved towards them and bowed. "I am Louis César, and it is a pleasure to meet you."

***

Phoebe looked around the table, a little disconcerted to find herself playing cards with both brothers. She had lost two games so far and Demarteau was watching her, an amused glint in his eyes. It was the look a cat gave a mouse when it was cornered, she decided. He was wondering if she would cheat or not. She bristled a little, glaring back at him. It was one thing to cheat a wretch like Alvanly, but quite another in a game of this sort.

"Ignore my brother, Lady Ellisborough. He likes to try to… *unnerve* his opponents."

Phoebe looked to Louis César, who had addressed her and who had won both hands, though he scarcely seemed to be attending the game, his attention riveted to his book which he'd set on the table.

"Is that what he's doing?" Phoebe said, quirking one eyebrow. Demarteau grinned at her. "Is it a good book?" she asked, a little peeved that Louis César should win so effortlessly whilst his attention was elsewhere. She had been concentrating furiously and had still lost.

He looked up and turned wide blue eyes to his brother.

"Yes, Louis, you are being rude," Demarteau said dryly.

To her surprise, the Comte closed the book and set it aside.

"My apologies," he said, sounding sincere.

Phoebe looked at him with interest. In truth, it was hard to look anywhere else. She had never seen such a beautiful young man. Pretty, even. She wondered if he could pass for a girl and suspected it was possible, for now. There was the promise of broad shoulders and a strong build in his lean body. He would make an impressive figure in a few years when age had filled out his frame.

His brother was ahead of him in that respect, a solid, masculine figure even now, despite his youth.

"What were you reading?" she asked, interested.

"*The Eve of St Agnes*," he replied, playing his next card.

"Oh, Keats," Phoebe said in surprise. "You like English poetry?"

Mischief danced in his blue eyes for a moment. "I like English ladies who like English poetry."

Max chuckled beside her. "So you seek to improve your chances with our womenfolk?"

The comte's lips pursed.

"*Mais non*," he replied, wide-eyed with faux innocence, which made him appear boyish indeed. "I seek only to improve my skills with the language, but... if by chance that 'elps also...."

He shrugged, making them laugh, and Phoebe wondered at him being so flirtatious and confident already. Louis César would grow to be a dreadfully wicked man, she decided.

"Helps," Phoebe corrected him. "You must sound the 'h.'"

Louis César gave a heavy sigh and nodded. "*Oui, oui,* I know, but it is difficult, an ugly sound... *h*elps."

Phoebe grinned at him. "Very good. You know, your English is excellent."

"Yes, it is," he said nonchalantly. "Though I'm better at cards."

A flicker of humour in his eyes made her smile at the arrogant words as he took the next two games. When he also won the third, Demarteau threw down his hand in disgust.

"I knew I ought not have asked you to join us."

"Then why did you?" Louis César asked, his expression genuinely curious.

Demarteau scowled. "I was being polite."

"Ah, always so polite, Nicolas," he said softly, his lips twitching.

They played three more games, Demarteau winning the next—and Phoebe suspected Louis César had allowed him to—before Louis César won the next two. Phoebe set down her cards with a huff.

"Well, I am only glad Alvanly doesn't have your skill. You have the luck of the devil."

Something shifted in Louis César's eyes.

"Yes, *le diable*," he murmured. "Well, I shall bid you a goodnight. I hope you enjoy all that Rouge et Noir has to offer. You are most welcome here. It has been a pleasure to meet you both."

He glanced at his brother, who gave an approving nod, before leaving them alone.

"That was unfair of me," Demarteau said, grinning at Phoebe. "But I felt you might enjoy the experience."

Phoebe snorted. "You think I enjoy losing?"

"No, but I think you enjoyed meeting him and he you. He has little patience for most people, but tonight he was pleased."

She nodded. "I did enjoy meeting him. I've never met someone as lethal with cards, though. I shall remember if we ever cross paths again."

"If I may say so, Lady Ellisborough, you were most unlucky this evening, but I 'ave met no one who can... er... *play* the cards as you do. You 'ave an exceptional skill. Who taught you?"

Phoebe knew he was not speaking of the game they'd just played, but the way she had floated the cards she wanted to the top to deal to herself when playing Alvanly.

"A highwayman," she said, knowing instinctively that this was a man who kept secrets such as those.

He frowned, the word obviously unfamiliar.

"*Un bandit*," she corrected, amused as he gave a delighted bark of laughter.

"*Un bandit*," he repeated, shaking his head. He wagged a finger at her. "The next time, I shall let you cheat Louis César. I think it is possible even he would not catch such skilled fingers, and the experience would do him good."

"I should be delighted to," she replied, meaning it. "But we return to England in the morning. However, if you are ever visiting the other side of the Channel, I should be pleased to accept the challenge. Thank you so much for this evening. It's been fascinating."

Demarteau bowed and took her hand, kissing her fingers before turning to Max. "Lord Ellisborough, your wife is quite remarkable. You are a lucky man."

"Yes," Max said, putting her hand firmly on his arm with a smile. "I am."

Chapter 20

Dear Helena,

Phoebe will soon be home! I am so excited to see her again.

—Excerpt of a letter to Lady Helena Knight from The Most Honourable Matilda Barrington, Marchioness of Montagu.

Still the night of the 18th April 1827. Hôtel Westminster, 2nd Arrondissement, Paris.

"Well," Max said, as he opened the door to their rooms. "What did you make of the enigmatic brothers?"

"I hardly know what to think," Phoebe said with a laugh, setting her cloak aside, though her thoughts had long since drifted from the brothers, as fascinating as they were. "The comte was a strange young man. So beautiful and so skilled with the cards, but...."

"Yes, *but*...." Max agreed. "I should not want to be on the wrong side of that one, I think. For all his brother, Nicolas, looks the part of a devil. Those angelic blue eyes hide the mind of a rapier if you ask me."

"Hmmm," Phoebe said, not wishing to discuss them any longer. "And what do you suppose this dress hides, Max?"

She turned to look at him, tugging at the fingers of her gloves until she could draw one from her arm, the white silk dropping to the floor. She began on the other glove as Max stilled, watching her carefully.

"I hardly dare presume," he replied, his voice having lowered to that deep, wicked rumble that made her stomach flutter with excitement. "But I am hoping for... red ribbons."

Phoebe grinned and cast the second glove aside before reaching for the hem of her gown. It was a deep blue silk tonight, and the cool fabric slid between her fingers as she raised her skirts. Max's eyes darkened, and he let out a little sigh of appreciation as he saw the red ribbons on her garters.

"I knew they were your favourites," she said, laughter in her voice.

"They are," he agreed, taking a step towards her. "So much that I think I shall have a closer look."

Phoebe dropped her skirts and returned a coquettish expression. "Oh, will you? I do not remember giving you permission."

A glint of appreciation lit Max's eyes. He knew full well what she wanted of him tonight, and knew that she was playing with him, teasing him for the sheer delight of it, knowing what would come of it.

"But you are my wife, my property, *mine* to do with as I please," he countered, a devilish look on his face that made Phoebe catch her breath, even though she knew he was only playing along.

"Indeed, I am not," she retorted, enjoying this immensely. She put up her chin and tried to look prim and innocent, which was something of a challenge. "We are not married *yet*, my lord. Nor shall we be if that is your attitude."

"As you wish," he said, stalking closer as Phoebe backed up. "But here you are alone with me, so I think I shall take what I want whether or not you wish to marry me."

"Oh, you villain!" Phoebe cried, running from him so that the love seat was between them, pressing the back of her hand to her forehead in a dramatic gesture. "I shall die before I give myself to such a wicked man."

"Is that right?" he demanded, clearly struggling to keep a straight face.

Phoebe lunged away from him, rushing towards the bedroom door with Max in pursuit. He caught her—as she had intended him to—sweeping her up into his arms and throwing her over his shoulder.

"Oh! Put me down you horrid man. I shall never be yours, *never*, I say!"

"We'll see about that," Max retorted, giving her backside an enthusiastic smack.

"*Ow*! Max that hurt!"

"Good," he replied, sounding as if he was enjoying the role of villain rather too thoroughly as he flung her down upon the bed.

Phoebe scrambled backwards, but he was on her before she could get far, pinning her hands to the mattress.

"Now I have you."

Phoebe gasped as he pushed her knees apart, settling between them, the weight and warmth of his solid body making her shiver.

"I shall never submit!" she retorted, loving the way his eyes flashed.

"Oh, I think you will, wench."

"*Wench*?" Phoebe repeated in outrage. "You said you'd marry me."

Max shrugged. "Why buy the cow when I can have the milk for free?"

Phoebe gasped at the vulgar phrase, even knowing he didn't mean it in the least. "Oh, you…."

"Villain," Max supplied helpfully. "You said that already."

Phoebe smothered a laugh at the idea of Max saying such a dreadful thing at all. He rolled off her then, much to her disappointment, and settled back against the pillows, his arms crooked behind his head.

"Well, wench. If you want to have a chance of me keeping my word to marry you, I suggest you please me."

Phoebe watched him for a long moment.

"Please you how?" she demanded, trying her best to glower as heat pooled low in her belly.

"Firstly, you may disrobe." He waved a negligent hand at her and she stifled a laugh and clambered off the bed.

She made quite a production of it, taking her time, enjoying the heavy-lidded gaze that settled upon her, weighty as a caress. By the time she stood before him in nothing but her stockings and garters, he was breathing hard.

"Come here," he said, his voice low and dark.

Phoebe moved towards him, kneeling on the bed and Max pushed her down, climbing over her. His hand cupped her breasts, squeezing and kneading, pinching her nipples until she gasped.

"Mine."

The word was fierce, possessive, the look in his eyes precisely matching the sentiment, and she was no longer certain they played a game. He lowered his body to hers and circled the hard nub of one nipple with his tongue, making her shiver, before taking it in his mouth and suckling hard. Phoebe cried out, clutching at his hair, uncertain if she had meant to drag his head away, but holding him to her as pleasure with a hint of pain lanced through her and made her whimper beneath him. One hand slid down her body, finding the place between her legs that ached for him, that had longed for him every time they had been together this way. He had always left her sated and replete, but never yet had he filled the hollow yearning that wanted him so badly.

"Max," she whispered as he caressed her, making her arch into his body. "You're wearing too many clothes."

A rumble of laughter vibrated through him. "I rather like it this way. I like you naked like this while I am dressed. I think it should be this way as often as possible."

Phoebe huffed.

"That is unfair," she grumbled, though in truth, there was something delicious about being naked when he was fully clothed. Nonetheless, she wanted her hands on his skin, wanted to feel the heat of his body against hers. "Max," she protested, tugging at his shirt.

"Whatever you want, love," he said, sitting back and stripping off his coat and waistcoat.

Phoebe watched with avid interest as he tugged his cravat aside and then pulled his shirt over his head. Her breath caught, and she found herself delighted with the play of muscle beneath his skin, and with the dark trail of hair that led beneath the waistband of his trousers.

"Enough?" he queried, all innocence.

Phoebe scowled at him and he chuckled, shaking his head. "And you said I was wicked."

Max swung his legs to the side of the bed and stripped off shoes and stockings before getting to his feet. He shucked everything else in one smooth movement, giving her a wonderful view of a taut backside and powerful thighs, and then he turned to face her.

Whatever it was he saw in her face as she looked at him—hungry to touch everything she saw—galvanised him into action and a moment later he was pushing her down again, his mouth on hers, hungry and demanding. Whatever had held him back before, whatever had made him cautious, it was gone now.

Phoebe sighed, overwhelmed by the feel of his body against hers, hot and hard and heavy. The weight of his arousal burned against her intimate skin and she pressed closer, sliding her own aching flesh against his, encouraging him not to wait any longer. He made a low sound of pleasure as his large hands kneaded the softness of her behind, tilting her hips just so. She gasped as the blunt head of his erection pressed against her and he stilled.

"No! No, don't stop, don't stop," she pleaded.

There was a muffled laugh.

"Couldn't if I wanted to," he managed, pressing against her again.

Phoebe shifted beneath him, helping him and her breath snagged in her throat as he slid inside her. She made a soft sound, surprise more than pain as he filled her, the sensation foreign and a little uncomfortable.

"Phoebe."

Max's voice was strained, his body taut as he held himself still.

"It's all right," she said, knowing he was giving her time, allowing her to accept the intimate invasion. "I'm all right."

He moved again, deeper and then deeper still in one firm thrust and she held her breath at the slight pinch of discomfort, there and gone as Max took her attention. He bent and kissed her, slow and lingering, and then he was moving again. Phoebe ran her hands over his shoulders, down his back, revelling in the shift of muscle beneath her fingers, the silk of his skin. It was all new, all astonishing, the tenderness and the comfort of his embrace, the trust and the knowledge that she was loved so deeply. Even though they had been intimate before, it had not been like this, this sense of completion, connection. The sounds he made, of effort, of carnal delight, made her own body react with heat and desire, wanting more of him. She slid her hands to his buttocks, enjoying the powerful thrust of his body beneath her palms and clutched at his backside, squeezing, urging him deeper, harder. He made a sound that rumbled low in his chest, that made pleasure ripple through her.

Phoebe stared up at him, the strong line of his throat, his handsome face, eyes closed as he gave himself over to this, to loving her.

"I love you," she said, and his eyes opened, dark and warm and filled with adoration as he gazed down at her.

"And I...." he began, the words lost as pleasure overtook him.

He reached between them, his fingers seeking the place that would hurry her to join him, caressing her as Phoebe moaned under his touch. He watched, his breathing erratic, the sinuous slide of his body into hers becoming fractured and urgent.

"Phoebe," he said, before closing his eyes, turning his face into her hair. "Oh, love...."

Phoebe held tightly to him as his big body shuddered, her own desire peaking as she watched him give himself over to pleasure, to her, spilling himself inside her with a helpless cry. It was too much, enough to overwhelm her and send her tumbling in his wake, holding tight until at last they subsided. She clung to him, still breathing hard, and quite unable to keep the delighted smile from her lips.

Max let out a long, slow sigh before he raised his head to look at her.

"Are you all...?" The question died on his lips as he regarded her smug expression and he gave a rueful bark of laughter. "You're happy now I've ruined you, then?"

Phoebe pulled his head down and kissed him. "I am blissfully happy. Thank you, Max."

He snorted and turned on his back, taking her with him.

"Anytime, love," he said dryly. "It was my pleasure, I assure you."

"Mmmm," Phoebe sighed, snuggling into his warmth. "Mine too," she murmured, and drifted happily to sleep.

Chapter 21

Dear Florence,

Phoebe is coming home on Friday and the place is in uproar. It's supposed to be a secret wedding to avoid a dreadful scandal, but that's not stopping Mama from preparing like the King himself is coming to stay. I'm glad you're coming too, but do try to keep Evie from following us. I'm not getting into trouble if she gets lost again.

—Excerpt of a letter to Miss Florence Knight from The Right Hon'ble Philip Barrington, The Earl of Blakeney.

24ᵗʰ April 1827. Dern Palace, Sevenoaks, Kent.

Max handed Phoebe down from the carriage, uncomfortably aware of her father's cool gaze upon him. The back of his neck prickled and he had the awful suspicion that he might blush, but then Phoebe gave a shriek of delight and threw herself into her papa's arms, kissing his cheek and hugging him tightly.

"Oh, Papa! We've had such an adventure. I can't wait to tell you all about it," she said, before kissing him again and running to embrace her mother.

"Phoebe, darling," Matilda said, laughing and crying at once. "Oh, we are so glad to have you home again. We've been so worried."

"Whatever for?" Phoebe asked, looking a little put out. "Surely you knew Max would look after me, and I'm not such a ninny as all that. Well… mostly I'm not," she added, sending Max such a joyful smile his heart skipped.

Good Lord, but he was smitten, so helplessly in love with her that it was a good thing she had agreed to marry him. He wasn't certain he could have survived losing her. He straightened abruptly, suddenly aware he'd been gazing at her like some lovesick mooncalf, and discovered Lucian watching him again.

Max stiffened as the marquess approached him and, to his great relief, held out his hand. Almost daring to breathe again, Max took it.

"Welcome home," Lucian said, smiling now. "And thank you for keeping her out of trouble."

Max cleared his throat and rubbed the back of his neck awkwardly, uncertain he could accept thanks for that in the circumstances.

"No," Lucian said, silencing him before he could speak. "There's no need. I know better than anyone that it is impossible to keep her entirely out of trouble, but she's here in one piece and she's happy, that much is obvious."

"She is," Max said, able to agree with that with no problem. "We both are."

Lucian nodded. "I'm glad. More than I can say. I have always worried that she would fall for the wrong sort of man, someone who would not deserve her."

Max gave a rueful smile. "I'm not certain I deserve her, but I love her, Lucian. With all my heart. I'll be good to her."

"I believe you. After all," Lucian added lightly, "we are both members of Angelo's."

A wicked glint of amusement shone in his eyes and Max cleared his throat, aware it was a joke, but… still.

"So we are," he replied.

"Papa, don't frighten Max," Phoebe scolded her father, running back to thread her arm through his.

Lucian looked down at her, his adoration quite obvious as he covered her hand with his own.

"As if I would, Bee," he said, reproach in his expression. "Besides, I believe Max is not so easily intimidated. He would never have won your heart if he was, I think."

"That's true." Phoebe beamed at him and then turned to smile at Max. "And I do love him, very much."

Max's throat tightened and he took a breath as he looked at her father, surprised to see the intimidating Marquess of Montagu blinking back tears.

"I'm glad, dearest Bee," he said softly. "For you know, I could not have parted with you for anything less."

"I could not bear to be without him, Papa," Phoebe said, something in her tone that made Max believe this was something her father had needed to hear. "Just as you promised."

Lucian nodded and pulled her into his arms, resting his head on hers. "Then I shall let you go, sweetheart, but you must promise to come back and visit us very often, for I shall miss you dreadfully. We all shall."

"Oh!"

Max turned to see Matilda sobbing into a handkerchief and Lucian held out an arm to her, holding both his wife and daughter close.

Phoebe hugged her mother tightly and then looked down with a frown.

"Mama...?" she said, a quizzical note ringing out.

Max frowned as Matilda blushed a little.

"Oh, Phoebe, yes, there is something we were going to tell you too—"

Before either of them could say a word, Phoebe gave a squeal of delight and embraced her mother again before turning back to Lucian.

"*Papa!*" she said, her expression one of feigned outrage.

"Bee, you are dreadful," Lucian said, shaking his head, though his eyes were alight with laughter.

Phoebe laughed with delight.

"If I am it's entirely your fault," she pointed out. "But this is marvellous. You shall have another little girl so you won't miss me so dreadfully, though I hope she won't take my place in your affections," she added with a coquettish smile.

"As if anyone could," Lucian replied, laughing now and holding his Matilda close to him. "And we cannot be certain it will be a girl, love."

"Oh, but it must be, for that will be perfect, and everything today is perfect. Isn't it, Max?"

Max nodded, too overwhelmed to speak as he realised what he had at last. The family he had always dreamed of having about him would not only comprise his beloved Phoebe and any children they were blessed with, it would also mean being a part of this. Her brothers, Philip and Thomas, ran up to him, taking an arm each and tugging him through the house and out to the gardens, determined he should see the new model sailing boats they had. He went with them, glancing over his shoulder to see Phoebe smiling happily. She blew him a kiss as the boys chattered beside him. He grinned at her and went along with her brothers, happy to be a part of it all.

***

They were married at the private chapel in the grounds of Dern Palace. Helena and Gabriel came with their daughters, Florence and little Evie, who was not yet five years old.

Phoebe had cried when she'd seen what Mama had arranged for her, the doorway to the chapel smothered with an archway of white roses and peonies, gypsophila and honeysuckle, the sweet scent delicious as she waited outside on her father's arm.

"Thank you, Papa," she said, leaning into him as he smiled down at her.

"For what?"

"For taking me in when you might so easily have left me where I was. For protecting me and giving me a home, and for being so very kind. I love you more than I can say, you know that?"

Her father leaned in and kissed her forehead and was quiet for a long moment before he spoke. "Thomas would have been so immensely proud of you, my darling, Bee. I know I am."

Phoebe blinked back tears, only to see her father do likewise. They both laughed and she hugged him, careful not to spoil her flowers or the beautiful yellow gown her mother had prepared for her to be married in.

"It's time," he said, holding out his arm to her.

Phoebe took a deep breath and nodded and turned towards the church. "Then take me on to my next adventure, Papa."

Lucian covered her hand with his and stepped forward, leading her into the church. To marry the man she loved.

Epilogue

My dear friend,

I am coming home. It seems forever since we were all together last. Is little Lottie still getting into mischief? I imagine everyone has changed a great deal in the two years I have been away. I had a letter from Leo yesterday. Have you seen him of late? My word, Eliza, I have so much to tell you. Such things I have seen and done. You must come to France as soon as you have the opportunity. Perhaps next summer we can persuade the duke to take the whole family. Your mother would love it too, I know.

—Excerpt of a letter to The Lady Elizabeth Adolphus from The Right Hon'ble Cassius Cadogan, Viscount Oakley

Eleven years later…

5th June 1838. Dern Palace, Sevenoaks, Kent.

Lucian sighed and set down the letter he'd been trying to read. Matilda's house parties were something he always enjoyed, but it never failed to astonish him how a vast place like Dern seemed to shrink when all the family and their friends were in residence.

"Bee, when did I gain so very many children?" he asked, giving his daughter the benefit of a pained expression.

She laughed and reached over, patting his hand. "They're not *all* yours, Papa."

"They're not, but I am!"

Lucian looked beside him to where his youngest child was sitting, having stolen her mother's place. Matilda was having a well-earned lie-in after an extremely late night last night. Lucian's lips twitched as he remembered why that was.

Lucian peered at his daughter, eleven years old and the image of her mother, except for her eyes. Her eyes were his, silver-grey. They *were* silver. He had to admit to that now, having insisted for many years his own were a light grey. Catherine, his darling little Cat, proved he'd been wrong.

"Are you quite sure?" he said dubiously, narrowing his eyes at her.

"That wicked girl could belong to no one else," her big sister replied tartly.

Cat stuck her tongue out at Phoebe and they both laughed.

Lucian retreated behind his newspaper.

"When does everyone go home?" he grumbled, knowing they were all aware he didn't really mean it, though a bit of peace at breakfast would not go amiss in his opinion.

"Not until the end of the week," Phoebe said cheerfully.

Max walked into the room with Jacob—Lucian's first grandson, who was just a year younger than Cat—and holding the hand of his granddaughter, Rose, who was seven.

"There, see, here is Mama," Max said soothingly to the little girl, who ran to Phoebe and threw her arms about her neck.

"Oh, darling, whatever is the matter?" Phoebe asked the child, looking to her husband.

"Jake was rude to her," Max said, giving his son a stern look. "But he has apologised and promised not to do it again."

Jake glowered, his arms folded, and privately Lucian thought that promise would not hold past teatime.

"Oh!"

A shriek came from the other end of the table to where Lady Elizabeth and Lady Charlotte Adolphus were breakfasting with his sons, Philip and Thomas.

"Cassius is coming home!" Eliza cried with excitement, only to mutter a curse a moment later as her sister, Lottie, snatched the letter from her hand.

"When? What does he say?" Lottie demanded, getting up and running from her sister's reach when Eliza tried to take the letter back.

"Give that back, Lottie!" Eliza demanded as Pip and Thomas laughed and shook their heads.

"Oh, he's bringing friends," Lottie exclaimed, dancing out of her sister's reach. "Goodness, the Comte de Villen and his brother. A real life French Comte! That's like an earl, isn't it, Lord Montagu?"

Lucian smothered a sigh and nodded, lowering his newspaper. "It is."

"Oh, Max, it's Louis César and Demarteau!" Phoebe exclaimed with delight.

Max grinned at her. "You might get that game you wanted after all, love."

Lucian laughed at her obvious excitement, remembering the story she had told him about playing cards with the enigmatic brothers.

"Oh, how exciting!" Bella cried as her mother, Alice, exchanged an anxious glance with Matilda's brother, Nate.

"Give me my letter, Charlotte," Eliza demanded again, trying to snatch it back.

Lottie ran from the room with Eliza in pursuit, closely followed by Bonnie's twins, Elspeth and Greer.

"When's he coming back, Lottie?" they cried in unison, their voices echoing as they disappeared.

Lucian sighed and looked to his grandson, Jake. "Come along, let us find somewhere quiet, away from all these noisy girls."

"Will you teach me to fire a pistol?" Jake asked, his dark eyes alight with hope. "Mama says you're the best one to teach me, and she's better than Papa."

Lucian's lips twitched. "Is that so? Well, I might, if you promise not to be rude to your sister again."

Jake gave this the consideration the question clearly merited, before sighing and giving a nod of agreement. "I promise."

"Very well, then." Lucian got to his feet to discover Cat leaping up to follow them.

"Can I come too, Papa?"

"We're keeping away from girls, Cat," Jake said, folding his arms and looking mutinous.

"But I'm not like the rest of them," Cat protested, mirroring his stance and glaring at him. "I like all the same things you do."

"Well, Jake, you must admit there is truth in that."

Jake sighed a long-suffering sigh and rolled his eyes. "Oh, all right then, but you're not to be better than me."

Catherine cut him a look. "But Papa started teaching me last year. I'm bound to be better than you."

"Ugh. Girls," Jake grumbled, and stalked out of the breakfast room.

Lucian exchanged an amused glance with Phoebe, took his daughter's hand, and followed him out.

***

Phoebe watched her father pause as her mother entered the room. Her papa lingered to kiss his wife, whispering something to her that made Mama blush and smack him lightly on the arm before she came and sat down at the breakfast table. Eliza followed her in, holding a rather crumpled letter triumphantly in her hand before flopping down at the table again.

"Am I the last?" Mama asked Max.

"No, we've not seen Helena, nor any of her brood yet, though Gabriel is out with Jasper and Jerome."

"Good morning, Mama."

Phoebe watched as her brother Philip, or Pip as everyone knew him, leant down and kissed Mama. "We're going to take a picnic out to Mast Head. Can you tell Florence and Evie where to find us if they ever deign to wake up?"

Phoebe looked her brother over. He had grown into a fine looking man, as handsome as their father, with his pale golden hair but eyes that were more blue than grey. Thomas, the younger, had darker gold hair, but the two of them made an exceptional picture together, and they had become used to the way women gazed upon them and sighed.

A little too used to it, in Phoebe's opinion.

She hoped some forthright girls were out there waiting for them, and would have the gumption to take them down a peg or two. Not that they were unkind or uncaring, far from it, and she loved them dearly, but they were spoiled and accustomed to having everything their own way.

"Come along, Rose," Pip said kindly, holding his hand out to her daughter, who was still sulking. "Come to your Uncle Pip and

I'll take you for a ride on my horse while everyone gets ready for the picnic."

"Oh!" Rose said, instantly mollified as she ran to her uncle and took his hand. "Thank you, Uncle."

She gazed up with adoration at Pip, and Phoebe smiled.

"Have you finished, love?"

Phoebe looked around to find Max watching her, his dark eyes warm upon her.

"I have, why?"

Max winked at her and got up. Phoebe followed him out, intrigued as he moved towards the stairs.

"Where are you taking me?" she asked suspiciously.

"Somewhere quiet."

"For example?" she probed, trying to smother a grin as she knew full well what he was about. Max chuckled, grabbed her hand and towed her up the stairs, making her shriek and snatch at her skirts before she tripped over them.

"Both our children are occupied," he said, his voice urgent. "It's too good an opportunity to miss in this madhouse."

Phoebe laughed and ran after him as he tugged her along until they got to their room and kicked the door shut behind him. She hadn't the time to speak before she was in his arms and decided she didn't need to say anything after all. Phoebe sighed, tangling her fingers in his thick hair, greying now, far more than her father's. She liked it, for it made him look quite serious and distinguished when, in truth, he was funny and irreverent and just a bit wicked, a point he proved as his hand yanked up her skirts and burrowed beneath.

"I prefer the good old days when there were no drawers to get in the way," he grumbled, seeking the slit at the crotch as Phoebe snorted with laughter.

"Yes," she said. "I remember our return journey from Paris. You made good use of that fact in the carriage, as I remember."

Max huffed. "You have a different memory of events than me then, love. I was attacked, as *I* remember, and debauched at every opportunity. There I was, terrified that Jack would murder me, and you were set on having your wicked way whenever you could."

Phoebe laughed, delighted and unable to deny it. "Oh, let us visit Jack and Pippin after lunch today. I'm so happy those two married at last. I thought Pippin would keep him dancing to her tune to the end of their days."

"No, love," Max said gently. "She loved him too much for that. She just wanted him to know she was worth waiting for, so he'd appreciate what he had."

Phoebe smiled and took his face between her hands, staring into his dark eyes. "I appreciate what I have, Max. I love you more than ever. You know that, don't you?"

"I do," he said, his adoration quite visible. "As I love you, and I think it's about time I reminded you how much."

Phoebe sighed as his mouth sought hers again and she wrapped herself around him. As his lips drifted from her mouth to her neck and his clever fingers undid her buttons, Phoebe smiled to herself.

"Let's go back to Paris soon, Max, and to Italy. I should love to see Italy."

"An adventure, darling?" he murmured against her skin.

"Yes, an adventure," she whispered, closing her eyes as he got to his knees before her. "Though life is never exactly dull, is it?" she added with a soft laugh.

"With you?" Max replied, looking up at her with wide eyes. "No, love. Life is certainly never dull with you."

"Nor with you, Max."

Phoebe sighed as he pushed up her skirts, tangling her fingers in his hair and smiling, as he reminded her how very far from dull her husband really was.

***

If you would like to know more about the enigmatic Comte de Villen and his brother, and all about the next generation of Peculiar Ladies, don't miss my new series following their scandalous adventures.

The Daring Daughters!
Dare to be Wicked... on pre-order now.

From the author of the bestselling Girls Who Dare Series – An exciting new series featuring the children of the Girls Who Dare...

The stories of the **Peculiar Ladies Book Club** and their hatful of dares has become legend among their children. When the hat is rediscovered, dusty and forlorn, the remaining dares spark a series of events that will echo through all the families... and their

Daring Daughters

Dare to be Wicked
Daring Daughters Book One

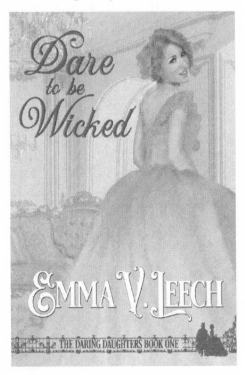

Two daring daughters ...

Lady Elizabeth and Lady Charlotte are the daughters of the Duke and Duchess of Bedwin. Raised by an unconventional mother and an indulgent, if overprotective father, they both strain against the rigid morality of the era.

The fashionable image of a meek, weak young lady, prone to swooning at the least provocation, is one that makes them seethe with frustration.

Their handsome childhood friend ...

Cassius Cadogen, Viscount Oakley, is the only child of the Earl and Countess St Clair. Beloved and indulged, he is popular, gloriously handsome, and a talented artist.

Returning from two years of study in France, his friendship with both sisters becomes strained as jealousy raises its head. A situation not helped by the two mysterious Frenchmen who have accompanied him home.

And simmering sibling rivalry ...

Passion, art, and secrets prove to be a combustible combination, and someone will undoubtedly get burned.

Pre Order your copy here: Dare to be Wicked

Want more Emma?

If you enjoyed this book, please support this indie author and take a moment to leave a few words in a review. *Thank you!*

To be kept informed of special offers and free deals (which I do regularly) follow me on *https://www.bookbub.com/authors/emma-v-leech*

To find out more and to get news and sneak peeks of the first chapter of upcoming works, go to my website and sign up for the newsletter.

http://www.emmavleech.com/

Come and join the fans in my Facebook group for news, info and exciting discussion...

Emmas Book Club

Or Follow me here......

http://viewauthor.at/EmmaVLeechAmazon

Emma's Twitter page

About Me!

I started this incredible journey way back in 2010 with The Key to Erebus but didn't summon the courage to hit publish until October 2012. For anyone who's done it, you'll know publishing your first title is a terribly scary thing! I still get butterflies on the morning a new title releases but the terror has subsided at least. Now I just live in dread of the day my daughters are old enough to read them.

The horror! (On both sides I suspect.)

2017 marked the year that I made my first foray into Historical Romance and the world of the Regency Romance, and my word what a year! I was delighted by the response to this series and can't wait to add more titles. Paranormal Romance readers need not despair however as there is much more to come there too. Writing has become an addiction and as soon as one book is over I'm hugely excited to start the next so you can expect plenty more in the future.

As many of my works reflect I am greatly influenced by the beautiful French countryside in which I live. I've been here in the South West for the past twenty years though I was born and raised in England. My three gorgeous girls are all bilingual and the youngest who is only six, is showing signs of following in my footsteps after producing *The Lonely Princess* all by herself.

I'm told book two is coming soon ...

She's keeping me on my toes, so I'd better get cracking!

KEEP READING TO DISCOVER MY OTHER BOOKS!

Other Works by Emma V. Leech

(For those of you who have read The French Fae Legend series, please remember that chronologically The Heart of Arima precedes The Dark Prince)

Girls Who Dare

To Dare a Duke

To Steal A Kiss

To Break the Rules

To Follow her Heart

To Wager with Love

To Dance with a Devil

To Winter at Wildsyde

To Experiment with Desire

To Bed the Baron

To Ride with the Knight

To Hunt the Hunter

To Dance until Dawn (August 14, 2020)

Daring Daughters

Dare to be Wicked (February 19, 2021)

Rogues & Gentlemen

The Rogue

The Earl's Temptation

Scandal's Daughter

The Devil May Care

Nearly Ruining Mr. Russell

One Wicked Winter

To Tame a Savage Heart

Persuading Patience

The Last Man in London

Flaming June

Charity and the Devil

A Slight Indiscretion

The Corinthian Duke

The Blackest of Hearts

Duke and Duplicity

The Scent of Scandal

The Rogue and The Earl's Temptation Box set

Melting Miss Wynter

The Winter Bride (A R&G Novella)

The Regency Romance Mysteries

Dying for a Duke

A Dog in a Doublet

The Rum and the Fox

The French Vampire Legend

The Key to Erebus

The Heart of Arima

The Fires of Tartarus

The Boxset (The Key to Erebus, The Heart of Arima)

The Son of Darkness (October 31, 2020)

The French Fae Legend

The Dark Prince

The Dark Heart

The Dark Deceit

The Darkest Night

Short Stories: A Dark Collection.

Stand Alone

The Book Lover (a paranormal novella)

Audio Books!

Don't have time to read but still need your romance fix? The wait is over...

By popular demand, get your favourite Emma V Leech Regency Romance books on audio at Audible as performed by the incomparable Philip Battley and Gerard Marzilli. Several titles available and more added each month!

Click the links to choose your favourite and start listening now.

Rogues & Gentlemen

The Rogue ***

The Earl's Tempation

Scandal's Daughter

The Devil May Care

Nearly Ruining Mr Russell

One Wicked Winter ***

To Tame a Savage Heart ***

Persuading Patience

The Last Man in London

Flaming June ***

The Winter Bride, a novella ***

Girls Who Dare

To Dare a Duke

To Steal A Kiss ***

To Break the Rules ***

To Follow her Heart

The Regency Romance Mysteries

Dying for a Duke ***

A Dog in a Doublet **

The Rum and the Fox **

The French Vampire Legend

The Key to Erebus (coming soon)

** Available on Chirp

*** Available on Chirp and Audible/Amazon

Also check out Emma's regency romance series, Rogues & Gentlemen. Available now!

The Rogue
Rogues & Gentlemen Book 1

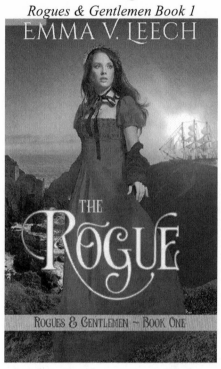

1815

Along the wild and untamed coast of Cornwall, smuggling is not only a way of life, but a means of survival.

Henrietta Morton knows well to look the other way when the free trading 'gentlemen' are at work. Yet when a notorious pirate, known as The Rogue, bursts in on her in the village shop, she takes things one step further.

Bewitched by a pair of wicked blue eyes, in a moment of insanity she hides the handsome fugitive from the local Militia. Her reward is a kiss that she just cannot forget. But in his haste to escape with his life, her pirate drops a letter, inadvertently giving

Henri incriminating information about the man she just helped free.

When her father gives her hand in marriage to a wealthy and villainous nobleman in return for the payment of his debts, Henri becomes desperate.

Blackmailing a pirate may be her only hope for freedom.

Read for free on Kindle Unlimited

The   Rogue

Interested in a Regency Romance with a twist?

Dying for a Duke

The Regency Romance Mysteries Book 1

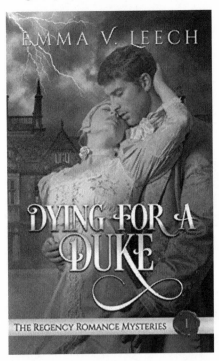

Straight-laced, imperious and morally rigid, Benedict Rutland - the darkly handsome Earl of Rothay - gained his title too young. Responsible for a large family of younger siblings that his frivolous parents have brought to bankruptcy, his youth was spent clawing back the family fortunes.

Now a man in his prime and financially secure he is betrothed to a strict, sensible and cool-headed woman who will never upset the balance of his life or disturb his emotions ...

But then Miss Skeffington-Fox arrives.

Brought up solely by her rake of a step-father, Benedict is scandalised by everything about the dashing Miss.

But as family members in line for the dukedom begin to die at an alarming rate, all fingers point at Benedict, and Miss Skeffington-Fox may be the only one who can save him.

FREE to read on Amazon Kindle Unlimited.. Dying for a Duke

Lose yourself in Emma's paranormal world with The French Vampire Legend series.....

The Key to Erebus
The French Vampire Legend Book 1

The truth can kill you.

Taken away as a small child, from a life where vampires, the Fae, and other mythical creatures are real and treacherous, the beautiful young witch, Jéhenne Corbeaux is totally unprepared when she returns to rural France to live with her eccentric Grandmother.

Thrown headlong into a world she knows nothing about she seeks to learn the truth about herself, uncovering secrets more shocking than anything she could ever have imagined and finding that she is by no means powerless to protect the ones she loves.

Despite her Gran's dire warnings, she is inexorably drawn to the dark and terrifying figure of Corvus, an ancient vampire and master of the vast Albinus family.

Jéhenne is about to find her answers and discover that, not only is Corvus far more dangerous than she could ever imagine, but that he holds much more than the key to her heart …

FREE to read on Kindle Unlimited The Key to Erebus

Check out Emma's exciting fantasy series with hailed by Kirkus Reviews as "An enchanting fantasy with a likable heroine, romantic intrigue, and clever narrative flourishes."

The Dark Prince
The French Fae Legend Book 1

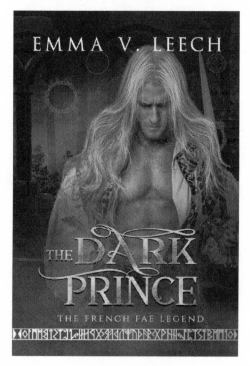

Two Fae Princes

One Human Woman

And a world ready to tear them all apart

Laen Braed is Prince of the Dark fae, with a temper and reputation to match his black eyes, and a heart that despises the human race. When he is sent back through the forbidden gates between realms to retrieve an ancient fae artefact, he returns home with far more than he bargained for.

Corin Albrecht, the most powerful Elven Prince ever born. His golden eyes are rumoured to be a gift from the gods, and destiny is calling him. With a love for the human world that runs deep, his friendship with Laen is being torn apart by his prejudices.

Océane DeBeauvoir is an artist and bookbinder who has always relied on her lively imagination to get her through an unhappy and uneventful life. A jewelled dagger put on display at a nearby museum hits the headlines with speculation of another race, the Fae. But the discovery also inspires Océane to create an extraordinary piece of art that cannot be confined to the pages of a book.

With two powerful men vying for her attention and their friendship stretched to the breaking point, the only question that remains...who is truly The Dark Prince.

The man of your dreams is coming...or is it your nightmares he visits? Find out in Book One of The French Fae Legend.

Available now to read for FREE on Kindle Unlimited.

The Dark Prince

Acknowledgements

Thanks, of course, to my wonderful editor Kezia Cole.

To Victoria Cooper for all your hard work, amazing artwork and above all your unending patience!!! Thank you so much. You are amazing!

To my BFF, PA, personal cheerleader and bringer of chocolate, Varsi Appel, for moral support, confidence boosting and for reading my work more times than I have. I love you loads!

A huge thank you to all of Emma's Book Club members! You guys are the best!

I'm always so happy to hear from you so do email or message me :)

emmavleech@orange.fr

To my husband Pat and my family ... For always being proud of me.

Made in the USA
Columbia, SC
10 October 2023